"Those New York folks bought the house right and proper and they've got a right to know what they've got themselves in for."

"So does the house have ghosts, then?" Maggie asked.

"Some say it does. Some say there's a woman who walks the halls. A woman with a baby. Haven't heard the story in years, though."

Maggie shivered slightly. Maybe Amy wasn't crazy.

Maggie Summer, owner of Shadows Antiques, visits an old New England home—and solves a very modern murder—in Agatha Award–nominated author Lea Wait's

SHADOWS ON THE COAST OF MAINE

"Wait knows her old Maine houses . . . [and] the rippling tremors former inhabitants seem to leave within the walls of such homes. *SHADOWS ON THE COAST OF MAINE* is a breezy page-turner. . . . [A] fun and compelling summer mystery."

—*Portland* (ME) *Sunday Telegram*

"Tremendous charm. . . . A fast and engaging read."

—*Booklist*

"Wait charmingly attends to the delightful business of going to au~~~~~ ~~~~ ~~~~~ among other entertaining things. . . . [M~~~~~~~~~~~~~~~~~~~~~~~~~~~~ ~~~~ ntique documents to ~~~~~~~~~~~~~~~~~~~~~~~~~~~~ f local legend."

DO583431

Review

"The fairground setting beckons like a weekend in the country. . . . "

—*The New York Times Book Review*

"Wait renders the print business, the fair, and the mystery intriguingly and with a sense of style."

—*The Boston Globe*

"Wait seamlessly weaves information about antiques fairs [and] prints into the narrative. . . . [T]he premise is intriguing and the mystery credible."

—*Booklist*

"Homicide and antiques combine smoothly in this well-crafted mystery. . . . Full of fascinating information about antiques and antiques fairs. . . . This solid debut will appeal to cozy fans who appreciate a realistic background."

—*Publishers Weekly*

"This new series hits the spot. . . . You'll learn a bundle about antique prints and 'the business'. . . . Highly recommended. More please!"

—*Mystery Loves Company*

"Thoroughly enjoyable!"

—*Northeast Magazine*

"*Shadows at the Fair* crackles with suspense, intrigue, and authenticity."

—Maine Antiques Dealers Association

Shadows
on the
Coast of Maine
An Antique Print Mystery

LEA WAIT

POCKET BOOKS
New York   London   Toronto   Sydney

This book is a work of fiction. Names, characters, places and incidents are products of the author's imagination or are used fictitiously. Any resemblance to actual events or locales or persons, living or dead, is entirely coincidental.

 POCKET BOOKS, a division of Simon & Schuster, Inc.
1230 Avenue of the Americas, New York, NY 10020

Copyright © 2003 by Eleanor S. Wait

Originally published in hardcover in 2003 by Scribner

ISBN: 0-7434-5621-1

First Pocket Books printing July 2004

10 9 8 7 6 5 4 3 2 1

POCKET and colophon are registered trademarks of Simon & Schuster, Inc.

Cover illustration by Joyce Patti

Manufactured in the United States of America

For information regarding special discounts for bulk purchases, please contact Simon & Schuster Special Sales at 1-800-456-6798 or business@simonandschuster.com

For Bob, who brought joy back into my life.

And for Susanne Kirk, caring and exacting editor, who believed in me and in Maggie.

The summer I was five I woke in the night and saw a great white owl perched in the moonlight on the post of the bed I shared with Sally and Eliza. The house was new then, in 1774, and Grandma Brewer had opened our shutters for the river breezes. Even in Maine there are stifling July days.

I can still see that owl looking down at me as I lay naked under my shift. Just looking. I stared at it until it raised its wings and flew out and over the Madoc River.

I told no one, because I knew it was a sign meant only for me.

Now changes are coming to this house, which has been mine for so long. Mine by right of pride and heritage, and because no one else wanted it and I kept the roof in repair and the bats from the chimney. Despite those years, soon the house will be moved to the mainland, and although my cousin says I am welcome to stay, I know I am not.

But parts of me will go with this house, and one part will be these words. I pray they will bring rest to me, and to the house, and to everything within it. Now, and in years too distant to see, there must be an end to the evil I have brought to this place.

The dark is coming on. The cows need tending. The living must always be tended before the dead. There will be time for words later.

Chapter 1

―――∽―――

The District of Maine, *map of pre-1820 Maine
(when it was still a part of Massachusetts) by
Philadelphia engraver John G. Warnicke,
c. 1812. Hand-colored lines marking county
boundaries of that time. Horizontal fold mark.
11 x 15.25 inches. Price: $260.*

"Please, Maggie, you have to come to Maine a day
early. I need you. Drew has to fly back to New York
overnight and I don't want to be alone. Not in this
house."

Maggie Summer kept hearing Amy's words as she
gave her excuses to Gussie White. She'd been staying
on Cape Cod with her friend Gussie while she displayed her nineteenth-century prints at an antiques
show. She'd been looking forward to an extra day of
relaxing on the beach, but Amy's call was too strange
to ignore.

"Amy is the most realistic, straightforward, organized person I have ever known," she explained to
Gussie as she tightened the tops on her shampoo
and conditioner bottles before packing them. "In

high school, before she got her driver's license she took an auto mechanics course. In college her term papers were always done early, her dorm bed was made, and when she said she wanted to go to homecoming with Joe Smith, that's what happened. She's the last person in the world to be nervous about staying alone. That's why I have to go."

Gussie had given her a hug and nodded. "If you're worried, then I am too, Maggie. You go. Let me know how everything is once you're settled in."

That had been five hours ago. Maggie took another swig of diet cola. She'd forgotten just how far midcoast Maine was from the Cape. Thank goodness she was finally off the Maine Turnpike and heading up Route 1. She glanced at the directions she'd taped on the van dashboard. Madoc shouldn't be far now.

She hadn't seen Amy in a couple of years, not since Amy's wedding to Drew Douglas. It had been an elegant affair at the Short Hills Country Club in New Jersey, with Amy's mother and stepfather looking stylish and proud. And rich, Maggie thought to herself. Maggie had gotten by with scholarships and loans at the state college, but Amy had never explained why, with her family's money and her top grades, she hadn't gone to a private college or university. Maybe even Ivy League. "Montclair State is close to home" was all she'd say, as she crossed off the next item on her day's "to do" list. Amy's daily list started with "healthy breakfast" and went on from there.

Rooming together had sometimes been frustrating for both of them, Maggie remembered. But she had always known whom she could borrow deodorant from, and who would have an extra box of typing paper the night before a report was due. Amy was reliable. And she put up with Maggie's bed not always being made, and Maggie's casual social life. Amy would never go out for pizza without scheduling it ahead of time. Never.

When Amy had called in May, Maggie had been glad to chat, as always. She had sat down in amazement when she learned Amy was not calling from her condo in New York City near the ad agency where she worked and uptown from Drew's office on Wall Street, but from a small town in Maine.

"You have to come and visit. It's a wonderful house, Maggie. Built in 1774, on a hill with a great view of the river. You'll love it. And you can give me advice on historic preservation. You know about these things. And, of course, I'll be needing a lot of antique prints for these old walls, so be sure to bring some from your inventory."

Maggie's time was her own. She wasn't teaching summer courses at the college this year; all she had planned was doing several antiques shows. Since her husband Michael's death last winter, she had been restless. Besides, Maine was a great place to find new inventory to add to her business, Shadows. Shadows of past worlds; shadows to share with the present. Maggie loved her print business's name. She loved her life, even if it was a lonely one just now.

Amy was right; she couldn't say no to a trip to Maine to see an old friend.

So here she was, driving her faded blue van up the coast through postcard-pretty towns full of two-story, white houses, art galleries, gift shops, and BEST LOBSTER ROLLS HERE signs. Many of the antiques shops looked inviting. But not today. She would stay a week or two; there would be time later.

Amy's house stood on a hill, rising above the road and a line of pines close to the Madoc River. Maggie drove around the curve in the road that made up two borders to the property, then made a sharp left turn into the driveway. She parked near the ell that joined the barn and the house in true New England fashion. She didn't need to see the pickup truck already parked next to Amy's Volvo wagon or the ladders leading up to the roof to know that the old house needed work. A lot of work. The roof was probably only the beginning.

"Maggie!" Amy came running from what must be the kitchen door. "I'm so glad you're here!"

"What's happening? Why the emergency?" Amy looked as always—short blonde hair in place, fitted designer jeans, and a NEW YORK CITY navy T-shirt. The only unusual part of her attire was a wide, white bandage circling her left arm. "Are you hurt?"

"I'm fine, now that you're here. I'll tell you all the gory details and you can tell me I am absolutely crazy after you get settled in and I open a bottle of wine."

"Speaking of wine . . ." Maggie reached behind the faded red Metropolitan Museum canvas bag that served as her travel pocketbook and pulled out two bottles of a good Australian chardonnay. "I can never resist those New Hampshire wine prices." Despite her bandaged arm Amy managed to balance the bottles while Maggie picked up her duffel bag. "It's a beautiful site, Amy. No wonder you love it. I can hardly wait to see the house."

"Tour coming right up." Amy seemed more relaxed than she had sounded on the phone that morning. But Maggie noticed that Amy didn't look directly at her and was chattering more than normal. As they started toward the house, several old wooden shingles tumbled from the roof and fell directly in front of them. "Giles! There are people down here!"

Maggie could now see a big man and a teenaged boy balancing on the roof of the ell, holding hammers. "Sorry, Mrs. Douglas. They slipped again."

Amy shuddered. "Well, be more careful." She turned to Maggie as they entered the house. "Giles and his son Brian are doing the roof, and I hope they'll have time to help with some other work. Depends on how many calls Johnny Brent's construction company gets this summer."

Maggie looked around in delight. The kitchen was large, full of light, and lined with high cabinets. Storage space! The appliances were 1930s vintage, and the walls could use paint, but the possibilities were limitless.

"Crystal, this is my college roommate, Maggie." The attractive blonde teenager who was washing dishes smiled at them. "I'm hoping she will be staying with us a couple of weeks."

"Nice to meet you." The girl wore tight jeans and a short, bright pink tank top.

"And since I'll have company, you can go for the day after you finish the dishes. I'll be fine."

Crystal nodded. "If it's okay, I'll stay till Brian is finished. He said he'd give me a ride home."

"No problem." Amy turned back to Maggie. "Just wait until you see the rest of the house! After apartment living for fifteen years, I'm loving the space. There's a small room just off the kitchen; I'm turning it into my study. I'm not sure yet what I'll do there—maybe take up oil painting—or learn to quilt—but it will be all mine!" The small room was indeed cozy. It was almost filled by an executive-office-sized wooden desk covered with piles of papers and a floor-to-ceiling bookcase half-filled with books.

"Looks as though you've already got at least one project going."

"I've been checking the town archives for information on this house. I'm curious about who lived here before us."

"This must have been the birth and death room," said Maggie. "They were usually small rooms, easily heated, and close to the kitchen for warmth and accessibility."

"I knew you'd be able to figure this place out. Just wait until you see the view from the living room!"

The house was just as Maggie had imagined it: a

classic New England home with a central hall, fireplaces in most of the rooms, and four bedrooms on the second floor. A space that might have been for storage at some time had been made into a bathroom, and there was electricity, but otherwise the house looked as it must have a hundred or more years ago. The faded wallpaper still hanging on the cracked clamshell-plaster walls was definitely late nineteenth century. Possibly earlier.

"Drew is using one of the bedrooms as his study," Amy explained as Maggie touched the crumbling black-and-white-speckled plaster and wondered how complicated it would be to repair. "And this is our guest room, all yours for as long as you can stay." Maggie hoped the cracks in the buckling ceiling didn't indicate problems of immediate concern. Amy had found a bright modern brass bed and covered it with a quilt. The quilt was no doubt made in China, but it was patchwork. The room was bright and cheerful despite the crumbling plaster.

Amy and Drew's bedroom was the most finished of the rooms Maggie had seen, with new yellow paint and small-sprigged floral wallpaper that made it cozy and welcoming. And the four twelve-paneled windows had the same wonderful view of the Madoc River as the living room below.

"And this"—Amy smiled, opening the door to the fourth bedroom—"is for the future." The room was a perfect Saks Fifth Avenue display nursery. A white crib topped by a lace canopy stood in the center of the room. In one corner an upholstered, navy blue rocking chair waited, next to a bookcase filled with picture books. Floor-to-ceiling shelves held an assortment of stuffed animals and toys near a newly built closet. Of course. A house of this age would not have been built with closets.

"You didn't tell me! Congratulations!" Maggie grabbed Amy and gave her a hug. "Oh, how wonderful! I have to tell you, I'm a little envious!"

"Not yet," Amy said, as she closed the door and walked into the hall. "No congratulations yet. But we have plans. You unpack your clothes and then let's break out some of that wine."

Plans? Amy would not be drinking wine if there was a chance she was pregnant. Maybe they were adopting. But why hadn't she said so?

By the time Maggie had unpacked her clothes and hung them in a pine wardrobe, she found Amy sitting on the front porch overlooking the river. Amy poured the wine into red bohemian glasses and offered a plate of wheat crackers and Brie.

"Mmmm." Maggie settled into the green-and-white-striped cushions on the Adirondack chair and looked around. "I'm set. You may have to move me after a while, this is so comfortable." She sipped her wine and then turned toward Amy. "So what is happening? Why did you call this morning?"

Amy hesitated. "I don't know, Maggie. That's the problem. Or one of them. Nothing seems to be turning out quite the way I planned."

Maggie remembered Amy's lists and plans in their college days.

"Like?"

As Amy poured more wine, Maggie noticed Amy's fingernails were carefully polished in creamy pink, but badly chipped. The Amy she knew would have touched up those nails immediately. Although it would be crazy to try to keep nails polished neatly while working on an old house.

"This place has so much potential. We fell in love with it the first time we saw it, and the price was right. The owner was leaving the country and wanted to sell quickly. But—I know this is all going to sound very strange, Maggie. And not like me at all. But right after we moved in, I felt something was wrong. And the woman next door, Shirley Steele, who is also the hairdresser in Waymouth, told us there have always been stories about this house."

"Stories?" Maggie's wine was slightly dry, just as she liked it, and she couldn't imagine any stories that would make this house less lovely. "You mean you have ghosts? What fun!"

"Sometimes at night I swear I can hear a baby crying. But it stops almost as soon as I notice it. And one night Drew and I both saw shadows that looked like a woman in a long dress, moving across the moonlight on our wall."

"A house that has been home to as many people as this one has, over so many years, must be filled with memories," Maggie answered. "And it's so different from your apartment in the city, or from Short Hills, that you're probably just very conscious of everything. Plus"—she paused for a moment—"it's so quiet here! You can hear the birds. Those are chickadees, aren't they?" She listened again. "And I think mourning doves."

"And we can hear every car that goes by, and every lobsterman who checks his traps on the river at five in the morning. Yes; you're right. At first we thought maybe our imaginations were just filling the silences. But that's not all."

"What else?"

"There are the accidents." Amy looked down at her arm. "This one happened yesterday. I opened one of the windows, to try to wash the outside. Most of the windows are the old blown-glass kind, with bubbles in it. We don't want to replace any that aren't broken. But suddenly the glass shattered, and I jumped a little, and the window came down on my arm. It took an hour in the emergency room to take out all the little pieces of glass and stop the bleeding. My arm is pretty badly bruised."

"A nasty accident," said Maggie. "But it's an old house. Things do happen. It looks as though no one has done anything to maintain it recently. The ceilings in a couple of rooms look pretty precarious. But that isn't ghosts. It's just part of fixing up an old house." Maggie tried to sound knowledgeable. Several friends had restored Victorian homes near hers in New Jersey, but she couldn't begin to imagine the time and money they'd spent. She usually got involved only when the owners had reached the point of decorating and wanted authentic Victorian prints to match their furnishings. One couple had hung Currier & Ives prints in every room of their house. Maggie was happy to have them as customers, but she preferred a more eclectic look for her own home.

"It's not the only accident," Amy continued. "There are the shingles that keep falling off the roof. You saw some today."

"But the roofer, Giles? He said he was sorry. He must have dropped them."

"He always apologizes. But they fall even when he's not here. Even when we know he has checked and assured us they're not loose. And the lights flicker at strange moments. And there are noises in the pipes."

All just part of owning an old home, Maggie thought.

"And then there was the fire."

"Fire?" Maggie sat up straighter.

"Thank goodness we had installed smoke detectors as soon as we moved in, so we knew, even though it started in the middle of the night. It was in one of the empty rooms in the ell. I called the local volunteer fire department, but luckily we had two fire extinguishers in the kitchen. Drew was able to put out most of the fire before anyone got here. A fireman told me we were lucky; a house this age can go up quickly."

"What started the fire?"

Amy shook her head. "That's one of the scary parts. There was no wiring involved, and no one had even been in that room recently. We had cleaned it out and left it empty. We thought we'd eventually use it for storage. We're working on the main house before we get to the ell. There's no heat there, no gas lines, no materials to catch fire. In fact, one of the walls in that room is brick."

"Strange."

"The firemen thought so too. One of them asked Drew if we knew anyone in the area who would want to make trouble. Of course, we just got here. We haven't been here long enough to make many friends, and certainly not long enough to make any enemies." Amy smiled weakly at Maggie. "After that we started getting weird hang-up calls. The phone would ring, we'd answer, and whoever was on the other end would hang up immediately."

"Heavy breathing?"

"Nothing. No background noise; no voices. Some days we'd get a dozen calls. The ones in the middle of the night really freaked me out. Last night I was having trouble sleeping; my arm was throbbing, and it was hard to get comfortable. I had finally gotten to sleep at two-thirty when one of those calls woke us. And then after the call we both heard the baby crying. Drew hadn't heard it before; he thought I'd been dreaming. We looked everywhere; we don't know where the sound comes from. It lasts about thirty seconds. One night I timed it by the minute hand on our clock. It's a horrible sound. Almost an echo. As though the baby was crying a long time ago, and we're just hearing it now." Amy took more than a sip of her wine. "I'm sure you think I'm crazy. But I couldn't sleep after that, and I couldn't face being in the house alone tonight. Drew had to fly to the city to talk to one of his old clients. The guy wanted his old financial adviser, and Drew's company was glad to pay to keep the man happy. Drew will be back tomorrow. That's why I called you."

"It does sound awful," Maggie said. "But I assumed you were just here for the summer. Has Drew left the brokerage house?"

"Didn't I tell you? We both left our jobs. We decided a less stressful lifestyle would be best for us, and for our children. Someday," Amy added quickly. "Drew is thinking about teaching, and maybe I'll write the great American novel."

"Whew. You've taken on some major lifestyle changes." Amy had always loved the city; the pace, the excitement, the theaters, the clubs.

"And the changes will work. I'm sure they will. I've planned it all out. But something, or someone, is making the transition harder than we imagined." Amy took another gulp of wine. "I was the one who suggested this move; Drew was always reluctant. Expenses are higher than we thought they'd be, and with the strange noises, and the fire, and the telephone calls . . . Drew's been drinking a bit more than he should and is beginning to talk about going back. That's one reason he stayed over in New York tonight. I'm sure he could have flown down, had his meeting, and come back today. But he's meeting some friends for dinner."

"He'll probably have a wonderful time, miss you terribly, and be home tomorrow. And tonight I'll be here to help cope with telephone calls and crying in the night. Have you called the telephone company about the mysterious calls?"

"The lines out here are old; we can't get caller ID. And the caller never hangs on long enough for them to trace anything."

Maggie poured herself another glass of wine. She was glad Drew would return tomorrow. There must be more to this story than Amy was sharing. Maybe Drew would have more answers.

The phone rang.

Maggie and Amy looked at each other. One of them would have to answer it.

Chapter 2

—❦—

A New England Home, *hand-colored lithograph published by Currier & Ives, c. 1850. Elegant white colonial home on hill, surrounded by tall trees; horse-drawn carriage and children in drive in front; barn and animals to right, bottom of hill. 8 x 12.8 inches (small folio). Price: $375.*

The phone call had been from Drew, checking to see that Amy was all right. There were no more telephone calls that night, and although Amy seemed more relaxed by the next morning, Maggie was still concerned. Ghosts? A baby's cry in the night? Perhaps Amy's imagination was merely working overtime. Shingles falling off the roof and the window's shattering could be put in the "challenges of living in old houses" column. But the fire and the telephone calls should be investigated.

"I've been meaning to have my hair trimmed. Did you say your neighbor had a salon?" Maggie put down the *Portland Press Herald* as Amy debated her agenda for the day. Amy had also said the neighbor knew this house's history.

"Shirley Steele. Her salon is Cut 'n' Curl, across the river in Waymouth. She's not bad. Everyone goes there."

"I think I'll give her a call. You sound as though you have some things to do. And then, if you don't mind, I see that tomorrow there's an auction at a place called Walter English Auctions, and the preview is open today. I'd like to check it out." Maggie paused. "I know someone who may also be visiting near here, but we missed calls before I left for the Cape, and I'm not sure about the exact dates he'll be in Maine. Sometime while I'm here I should call him."

"'Him'?" Amy looked up. "Who?"

"Will Brewer, an antiques dealer from Buffalo. I met him when we were both doing the Rensselaer County Antiques Fair in May." Maggie hesitated. It probably wasn't the right time to mention the two dealers who had been murdered at that show. "In July, Will and I met in New York to see a museum exhibit. He's nice." She held the paper up so Amy couldn't see the faint blush she couldn't control.

"'Nice'? Maggie, *nice* is for maiden aunts. I assume this man is a possibility? You're a widow now, and you're still young. Keep your options open!"

"He has an aunt in Waymouth, and thought he'd be in Maine in August. I have her number; maybe I'll call in a couple of days."

"If you don't, I'll remind you. For sure. In the

meantime, have your hair done and get prettied up. This morning I'm going to talk with Giles about his progress on the roof, and then I need to get some groceries. Drew should be home by early afternoon, and I wouldn't want to cause a crisis by being out of his favorite brand of chocolate milk. Or vodka." Amy went back to her list, then looked up. "If you go to the auction preview, would you keep an eye out for a pine corner cupboard for the living room? I'd like one that is late eighteenth or early nineteenth century, the same period as the house."

"Does the living room have corner beams?"

"Yes. So the cupboard would have to have a straight back or a corner cut out. Not fit directly into the corner the way later ones sometimes do."

"I'll look, and if I see any possibilities, I'll report back so you can check them out for yourself. Depending on what's in the sale, I might or might not go to the auction tomorrow, if that's okay with you?"

"You're on vacation! Whatever you want to do is fine with me. Are you looking for anything in particular?"

"I could always use some more copies of *Harper's Weekly,* especially from the early 1870s. Eighteen seventy-three is the most valued year for print dealers because Winslow Homer's Gloucester Series was printed then. And I could use some good Curriers, or any pre-1850s books with hand-colored botanical or zoological prints. My inventory is low on astronomy and astrology just now. And sometimes I'll buy a drawing or painting, or even a dramatic early-twentieth-century print or lithograph, or some folk art. Something that catches my eye and that I think might catch a customer's. It's hard to predict. So many prints were produced and hand-colored in such small editions that there are few records of them, and even a dealer may only find them once."

"I'd like to look through your portfolios. I'll need some prints for these walls. Maybe fruit, for the kitchen, or butterflies. It's hard to say until I decide exactly what our color scheme will be."

"Better to wait then. But looking at the prints could give you ideas too. I'd love to show you some of my things. And they're right out in the van. No problem."

"Another day, then. Definitely. When Drew is here. I think he'd find them fascinating, especially since this house has reawakened his undergraduate interest in American history."

"'Prints are a keyhole to the past.' That's a Maggie Summer quote, from my Introduction to American Civilization course. I use a lot of prints to illustrate the way America saw itself, especially in the mid– and late nineteenth century."

Amy looked down at her list again. "Is there anything special you'd like me to get at the store?"

"As long as you have diet cola, I'll be set."

Amy made another note. "Will do. If only all of life were that simple!"

Cut 'n' Curl was easy to find, just off the main street (conveniently called Main Street).

Shirley Steele was a middle-aged blonde whose pink hairdresser's smock stretched across her ample front. "So, are you visiting in Waymouth?" she asked as she tied a gray plastic coverall around Maggie's neck and tucked in a towel to prevent leakage. "How much of this do you want off?"

Maggie resisted the urge to jump out of the chair before Shirley picked up her shears. "Just even it out and take off the split ends. Maybe an inch."

Shirley backed up and looked at Maggie's hip-length, wavy brown hair critically. "Short hair's more the style now, you know. Most people stopped wearing it this long in the sixties." She picked up a few strands. "But you've got good, thick hair; you can carry it off."

"Thank you."

Shampooed, conditioned, and seated in front of a mirror, Maggie tried to focus on the conversation and not watch Shirley circling her chair and assessing. "I'm visiting an old friend, Amy Douglas. She recommended you."

Shirley grew at least an inch. "Amy's such a friendly woman. She and Drew—that's her husband, but you already know that—moved in next door to me a couple of months ago."

"It's an interesting house. Amy mentioned it has a history."

"Like any house over two hundred years old."

"Do you think there could be ghosts there?" How much more direct could she be?

"Has Amy seen one?" Shirley knelt unsteadily to reach the ends of Maggie's hair.

"Not exactly. I just wondered, since the house is so old."

Shirley focused on a strand of hair and then snipped. And snipped again. "I'll tell you what I told Amy. What everyone knows. For the last hundred years only unmarried women have lived in that house. No men. Until Amy's husband, of course."

"Interesting." Maggie covered her naked left hand. Michael's death in a car accident last December had not erased his infidelities, and she did not feel that wearing her wedding ring or playing the bereaved widow accurately reflected her current status. Or state of mind.

"Of course, there were men living in the house in the nineteenth century. Sea captains, mostly. Most of them outlived at least a couple of wives."

How cheering. "Then there are no ghosts?"

"Never heard of a murder there, or a suicide. Folks say ghosts stay with a house after an unsettling death. Of course, Charlotte did once tell me—Charlotte Leary lived there until she died last year—a natural death, she was eighty-two—she did tell me the house creaked and moaned a lot, and sometimes the wind cried in the chimney. Does in our house too. Nor'easters come right across the river and up the hill and hit those two houses." Shirley snipped again. Maggie wished she could see her back and monitor what Shirley was cutting. "Charlotte was a dear woman; very active in the church. Can't think of any reason a ghost would bother her."

So ghosts only bothered certain people. Say, nonchurchgoers?

The tiny woman sitting in the chair next to Maggie's, her blueing hair standing straight up with coloring formula, was clearly taking in the conversation. "Shirley, tell the woman what she's wanting to hear. Can't do much harm now. Those New York folks bought the house right and proper and they've got a right to know what they've got themselves in for."

Maggie tried to look at the elderly woman, but couldn't move her head while Shirley was measuring her hair. "Do you know the house I'm talking about?"

"The old Brewer house has been there as long as any, and a lot of people who live here have roots there. A few folks . . ." The woman paused. "A few folks were a bit peeved that it was sold out of the family. But that wasn't anything to do with you, or your friends. That's family business."

Shirley's scissors snipped loudly and rapidly several times.

"So does the house have ghosts, then?" Maggie asked.

"Some say it does. But Shirley's told you straight. No murders or suicides anyone can remember, and there's folks here should know. I'm the oldest now, I'd wager, but I can't think of any violence done in that house outside the usual family squabbles and a couple of women died in childbirth. But that used to be pretty common. Captain Eben Brewer, back in the fifties"—Maggie realized the woman meant the 1850s—"he lost three wives in birthing. Couldn't hardly find a fourth to marry, but my grandmother, Becca Giles, she said, 'Three's a charm; no point in looking to the past,' and she married him and had seven children and outlived the captain."

"So there are ghosts?" Maggie tried to get back to the point before it was totally lost in memories.

"Some say there's a woman who walks the halls. A woman with a baby. Haven't heard the story in years, though. I don't think Charlotte paid the two of them any heed."

Maggie shivered slightly. Maybe Amy wasn't crazy. "Maybe the ghost is one of those women who died in childbirth."

"Could be. Might be. That's as good a guess as any. But you tell your friend that those ghosts ain't never bothered no one. That woman and her baby, they're quiet spirits. Some woman over to Brunswick I heared had some force in her house that knocked pictures off the wall and dishes off her cabinet shelves. Brewer house ghosts are civilized. Never bothered no one."

"Nettie, that's nonsense. Ghosts can't be civilized. It's against their nature." Shirley stood up and surveyed the ring of dark brown hair now surrounding Maggie's chair.

"Some are the kind to bother folks, and some are not. Brewer ghosts ain't the meddlin' sort."

Shirley looked at the older woman. "Those ghosts wouldn't bother kinfolk, I believe. But these people from New York ain't kinfolk. They're from away. Ghosts might be uncomfortable living with them."

Nettie looked directly back at Shirley. "Well now, Shirley, I'd say those ghosts should just calm down and accept what has to be accepted. Lizzie made her decision. Nothing to be done about it now."

"Who's Lizzie?" asked Maggie. Why did she have the feeling a couple of different conversations were taking place at the same time?

"Lizzie Colby. She's the one sold the house to your friends." Shirley took out the hand dryer and started blow-drying Maggie's not-quite-as-long-as-it-had-been hair. With the noise of the dryer no further conversation was possible.

Her hair had survived the trim. Actually, not a bad job, Maggie thought as she looked in the mirror. And both Shirley Steele and this other woman had agreed there might be ghosts in the house. Maybe Amy wasn't crazy. Or, maybe everyone was. With that many women dying in childbirth it made sense for the ghosts to be a woman and a baby.

Maggie shook her newly trimmed hair a bit as she headed to the auction gallery. Had she just rationally justified the existence of two ghosts? She had been in Maine for less than a day. No wonder people whose families had lived here for generations seemed able to coexist comfortably with the spirits of the past.

The auction preview was crowded. August was not the best time of year to look for bargains at a Maine auction. Usually auctiongoers were dealers, collectors, or individuals furnishing a home. The more dealers the better, since collectors would pay high prices for particular items to complete collections, as would someone looking for the perfect bureau for their guest room. Dealers wouldn't usually bid over 50 percent of retail, since they would have to price the item so they could make a profit. Auctions were basic hunting grounds for antiques dealers.

But this crowd of preview lookers was heavily laced with vacationers. The plaid shorts, dramatically manicured nails, and T-shirts emblazoned with puffins, lobsters, and moose were dead giveaways. An elderly man to her left was leaning on a wooden cane covered by stickers that told the world he had visited YELLOWSTONE, DISNEY WORLD, GRAND CANYON, and ACADIA.

Maggie looked briefly at two aisles of pine and cherry furniture and at three small tapestries hanging on the wall in back of the furniture. No corner cupboards of any kind, and she wasn't interested in the vintage chandelier or milk-glass light fixture hanging from a beam overhead. Oak Victorian furniture was in a corner and included a nice ornately carved pump organ labeled "From First Congregational Church." Interesting, but not for her. Maggie paused at three glass showcases filled with estate jewelry. Sometimes she splurged and bought something for herself; at auctions pieces of jewelry might sell at a small percentage of appraised value. Her favorite sapphire and pearl ring had come from an auction like this one.

Today none of the jewelry held her attention, and she wasn't interested in silver or glass or majolica. There were several cartons of books on a side table that she would check out, and one wall of framed items. So far she hadn't seen any reason to sign up for a bidding number.

The first carton of books was full of mid–twentieth-century bestsellers. Nothing she wanted to read, and certainly nothing for her business. The second carton held some of the same, but also included five late-nineteenth-century illustrated children's books.

She pulled each out and looked at it critically. The Kate Greenaway had been much loved and much scribbled in; only three of the plates could be removed and sold as prints. The Aunt Louisa book was beautiful, and the lithographs were in excellent condition, but there were paragraphs in the middle of the artwork so they wouldn't frame well. If the story hadn't been consecutive, so illustrations were on the reverse of others, some pages could have been have framed as a nice series grouping. But this book would best be kept intact and sold to a book collector. Gussie might be interested; her shop featured dolls and toys, but she carried a few beautifully lithographed children's picture books. This one would retail between $100 and $200. That meant a dealer might pay $50 or $60 for it.

Maggie made a mental note and went on. One early-twentieth-century Volland nursery rhyme book with torn pages. No. One linen book. No. One book of animal stories that included four usable lithographs: one pig, one goat, one pony, and one dog. The dog would definitely sell, and probably the pony. The other pictures were nice, but would be slow sellers. If she were to bid on this

box, she'd be bidding on perhaps seven prints, plus
the Aunt Louisa she might be able to resell. If the
carton went for $60 or less, she quickly decided, it
would be worth the effort. But she wouldn't pay
more, and she wouldn't go to the auction just for
that carton. One more carton to check. Maggie
waited a moment as the man ahead of her finished
his perusal. At least one early atlas, Maggie could
see over his shoulder. She wondered if it included
any astronomy prints. Sometimes early atlases
included maps of the heavens.

"Maggie Summer!" The voice was close, and the
hand on her shoulder was gentle and familiar.
Maggie spun around quickly, smiling at the face
sporting a soft graying blond beard and a grin.

"Will Brewer!"

"Why didn't you call? You never told me exactly
when you'd be in Maine!"

"I just got here late yesterday afternoon." Why did
she always feel like smiling when she saw Will? She had
only known him a short time but she felt as though they
were old friends.

"And, of course, the first thing you did was go to
an auction preview!" Will grinned. "What else
would a dealer do? Certainly not call a friend." He
looked around. "Is the college roommate you're
staying with here?"

They stepped away from the tables to leave room
for other people checking out the lots.

"No; she had some errands to do, so I just took
off." Thank goodness she had stopped at Cut 'n'
Curl on the way. "How long have you been here?"

"In Waymouth, about ten days; at the preview, about six minutes. My aunt is quite elderly now, and every year she saves up an assortment of small jobs for me. I've already reglued four chairs, replaced two cracked windowpanes, found a small leak by the chimney and retarred and reshingled that part of the roof, made several trips to the dump, and pruned a dozen rosebushes. I spent most of yesterday unsticking windows."

"You're a handy man to have around. Do you charge by the hour?"

"I've been visiting Aunt Nettie each summer since I was little; Maine is a great place to vacation, and Nettie became a 'summer mother' to me. She's ninety now, and still living alone. We both look forward to my visits."

"And to a little buying for the business?"

"In this case, mixing pleasure with pleasure. Not to speak of running into an attractive print dealer."

Maggie's cheeks blushed even more. "Seen anything here worth coming back for tomorrow? I'm not enthused so far. But I haven't checked everything out yet."

"I haven't either. The preview ad listed several fireplace sets and a box of tools, so I'll know after I find them." Will specialized in early fireplace and kitchen equipment, and tools. "That shouldn't take more than another fifteen minutes. There's a great place for totally evil fried clams and scallops down the road. Would you be free for lunch?"

"I'd love that."

Maggie hummed to herself as Will went on his

way and she looked through the last lot of books. The atlas didn't include any astronomy prints, and only about a dozen maps quickly salable to her customers. The others were of Europe and Asia, not fast sellers, and states in the Far West. She only did shows in Pennsylvania, New York, New Jersey, Connecticut, and Massachusetts. She had just about given up hope of finding any treasures when, underneath two leather-bound family Bibles—sadly, valuable only to the families whose records they contained, and who must have discarded them—she found a volume that had once been leather-bound and complete. She recognized it immediately, scanned through it quickly, and put it back under the Bibles. She was definitely going to attend this auction tomorrow.

It was half of an 1832 edition of Alexander Wilson's *American Ornithology,* printed in Edinburgh. Although it was a breaker, a book whose binding was broken or missing and therefore of limited value to a book dealer, the half that was still there contained eighteen of Wilson's hand-colored, steel-engraved American birds. More people today recognized the name John James Audubon, but Audubon had come after Wilson and, in fact, was said to have based some of his drawings on Wilson's studies. An Audubon portfolio was way over Maggie's budget. She'd seen in *Maine Antique Digest* that a complete Bien 1859 edition of his *Birds of America* had sold for over $300,000 at a recent auction. Of course, Mark Catesby had been the first artist to record the birds of America, in the early eighteenth century. But his prints were even beyond Audubon's in price, if, indeed, anyone was ever lucky enough to find any. Wilson had been next, almost a hundred years later, a weaver and peddler who met naturalist William Bartram in 1802 and started drawing birds. His first volume was published in 1808, twenty years before Audubon's. More people were discovering Wilson's work every year. These were his small folio prints, but she could easily price them at $80 to $100 each, depending on their subject. The auction gallery's staff must not have recognized the book, since it was stuck in a lot with books of considerably lower value.

Maggie smiled to herself and checked out the wall of framed prints. One primitive watercolor of an egret was interesting. The Currier & Ives the auction gallery had advertised in the paper was a repro, she saw at once. It was a large folio, about fourteen by twenty inches, and she knew without checking that *Winter Morning in the Country* had only been printed in a small folio. It might be an early reprint, but it definitely was not an original.

The registration desk where she and Will had agreed to meet was over in one corner. Maggie pulled out her resale tax information and went over to set up an account and get a bidding number.

Within half an hour she and Will had settled themselves in the blue, plastic-covered seats of a booth in a singularly unimpressive-looking restaurant filled with the wonderful smells of fried seafood.

"I started coming here when I was about twelve," Will said, smiling. "Maine's version of fast food."

"I noticed most of the cars in the parking lot had Maine license plates."

"This place is open year-round. Fried haddock, fried scallops, fried clams, fried chicken, fried potatoes, and fried onion rings. Plus the requisite lobster or crabmeat rolls. Clearly a restaurant valuing taste over concerns about cholesterol. Although a couple of years ago they did add a salad to the menu."

"And I noticed peanut butter sandwiches and vegetarian vegetable soup on the list."

"Something for everyone."

Their seafood platters arrived quickly, along with a diet cola for Maggie, an iced tea for Will, and a dish of coleslaw to divide. They both dug in and it was several minutes before Maggie raised her head and grinned. "I haven't had fried clams this good in years. Not even on Cape Cod."

"Of course not. These are the best. Trust a man with Maine roots who has summered here for more years than I care to divulge." Will's eyes reflected the blue of his shirt.

"Then your family originally came from Maine?"

"My father's family did. Maine sea captains back into the mid-1700s. My grandfather was born here; Aunt Nettie is his sister. But the family was hit hard by the Great War."

"We're talking World War One?"

"That's the one. Nettie's husband was killed, as

was my great-uncle William, who was very close to my grandfather. My grandfather survived, but couldn't face the empty place at the dinner table. He moved to Buffalo and got a job in the hydro-electric plant at Niagara Falls. Met a local girl, married, and stayed in Buffalo. He named his one child, my father, after his brother. I'm named after both of them. They're all gone now, but Nettie tells me at least once a year how proud she is there's still a William Brewer in the family."

"Nettie. That's an unusual name." Maggie suddenly thought of the blueing woman at the beauty shop.

"It's really Jeannette, but she's always been 'Nettie.'"

"Is Aunt Nettie a tiny little woman, with white hair?"

"And enough gumption and sass for the whole town. That's her. How did you know?"

"I think I met her this morning at the beauty salon."

"It's Thursday morning . . . it must be Cut 'n' Curl." Will grinned. "She's been having her hair done there once a week for years. What she doesn't hear at church she picks up there. Did you get an earful?"

"Actually, yes. I was asking about the house my friends bought. She was talking about possible ghosts there."

Will paused between bites. "Your friends didn't buy Charlotte's house by any chance?"

"Charlotte. That name sounds familiar. But your

aunt also said something about a 'Lizzie,' I think."

"I should have guessed it! Your friends are the ones who bought our family home. Why do outsiders come in and think they can just buy anything!"

Maggie frowned. "The house was for sale. They bought it. I don't understand."

Will sighed. "I'm only an out-of-state member of the family. I wasn't involved. But I sure heard about it. The family felt strongly that the house shouldn't have been put on the market at all. It's been in the Brewer family since it was built in the late 1700s."

"Whoa, Will. Amy and Drew bought a house. That's all. And they're going to fix it up. Whoever lived there before, Charlotte, may have been from the right family, but she clearly hadn't done a lot of work on that house in fifty years. And I don't think her name was Brewer. I would have remembered that, since it's your name."

"Charlotte's mother was my great-aunt Sarah, Nettie's only sister. Sarah married Silas Leary, so Charlotte's last name wasn't Brewer. But that doesn't mean she wasn't part of the family. There are Brewers living all around here who don't have the Brewer name. Cousin Charlotte lived in that house all her life."

"And then?"

"Everyone thought she would leave it to Shirley, her niece. You met Shirley at Cut 'n' Curl. Shirley took care of Charlotte at the end and didn't have a house of her own after her husband headed north to fish in Alaska and didn't take her with him."

Maggie shook her head. "That's far too much family for me to keep straight. And I thought Shirley lived in the house next door to Amy and Drew."

"She does. She and her twins, Sorrel and Sage, moved in with her brother Tom after her husband left. It was convenient for her to help Charlotte, and everyone just expected the house would be hers someday. I'm sure Tom thought her moving in was temporary. For the last hundred years or so the house has always been owned by an unmarried woman in the family. Traditions are strong in Maine."

"So what happened?"

"Charlotte must have decided Shirley didn't qualify, since she had once been married. She left the house to Lizzie, Shirley's older sister, who worked at the town office. The will came as a surprise to everyone. No one had ever paid much attention to Lizzie. She was quiet, about fifty, never married, and owned a small house in Waymouth."

"And?"

"Lizzie didn't tell anyone what she was going to do. It's a great family scandal. Last spring, right after the estate was settled, she advertised the house in *The New York Times*—not even in a Maine newspaper!—and sold both that house and her own before anyone in the family knew what she was doing. You'll love this part. Lizzie took the money from both houses, flew to New Zealand, and married a sheepherder she'd been writing to on the Internet."

Maggie grinned and raised her fist in solidarity. "Right on for Lizzie! But let me guess: Shirley hasn't been too happy about all of this."

"To put it mildly. The only person less happy is Tom, who had hoped to have his quiet bachelor's hideout back. I got here a couple of weeks ago and have heard the whole story from at least seven people. The town has been buzzing, as they say."

"It all sounds pretty silly to me. I'm sorry Shirley didn't get her house, but Lizzie got her heart's desire, and Amy and Drew love their home. Except for a few problems they seem to be having with it."

"Leaking gutters and roof?"

"Fires and phone calls. And a couple of ghosts."

Will put down his fork.

Chapter 3

———✎———

News from the War, *wood engraving by Winslow Homer published in* Harper's Weekly, *June 14, 1862. Sketches illustrating ways people got information about the Civil War: woman receiving letter, sailors and army staff reading dispatches, boys racing to "the newspaper train," wounded veteran telling news "from Richmond"; and one of Homer's few self-portraits, of a man sketching soldiers, captioned "our special artist," the title given Homer by* Harper's Weekly. *20.25 x 13.25 inches. Price: $325.*

A new, bright red Jeep—perhaps Drew's—was in the driveway when Maggie got back after lunch. The truck next to it, plus the hammering, meant the roofing was still in progress. The young roofer—Brian, she remembered—waved from the peak of the ell, and she smiled and waved back. The sky and water were both dark blue, sunflowers were blooming in the field beyond the lawn, she and Will would meet at the auction tomorrow, and she felt happily full of Maine seafood. Amy must still be grocery shopping.

She knocked on the screen door by the kitchen, but no one answered, so she walked in. Dishes were draining, newly polished silver flatware and kitchen knives were drying on a towel, and a blueberry pie was cooling. Amy, or maybe that girl who helped her, Crystal, had been at work. As always, Amy's kitchen, even this kitchen that could definitely use at least a coat of paint, was immaculate. Maggie noted a box of disposable gloves by the sink. Typical Amy.

She'd get the mystery she was reading and perhaps a light sweater for river breezes and settle on the porch until Amy got home. Perhaps Drew was in his study.

As Maggie walked up the front staircase toward her room, she became increasingly conscious that she was not alone in the house. And the sounds she was hearing were not ghostlike. They were coming from the master bedroom. Amy must have left her car somewhere, because the sounds were definitely not conversational. Maggie walked as lightly as she could. This did not sound like a good time to make her presence known. She had to walk past the bedroom door on the way to her room, and the door was only partially closed. She took a deep breath, smiled to herself, and started to tiptoe by.

Even with her eyes averted, she couldn't miss the discarded shorts and bra in the doorway.

Amy had been wearing jeans that morning.

Maggie flushed red, but she couldn't stop herself

from glancing through the doorway as she passed.

She hadn't seen Amy's husband since their wedding, but the slender build and the slightly tousled black hair were definitely Drew's. Equally certain, that was not Amy on the bed with Drew. That was Crystal.

Maggie cursed the pine floor that creaked, but she got to her room and closed the door as quickly as she could. They had probably been too occupied to hear her.

She sank down onto the bed. Poor Amy! Here she was, coping with ghosts and annoying phone calls, and planning a family with that bastard, who was taking advantage of a girl barely old enough to legally consent. And in Amy's own bedroom!

Had Michael done the same thing? The thought consumed her with anger. Maggie's husband had other women, but she had never imagined that betrayal could be so flagrant. Were all men pigs? Selfish idiots? What if she just walked back there, flung open the door, and denounced them both?

And then what?

She paced the room, not caring if her footsteps were heard all over the house. Did Amy know? Had this happened before? Should she tell Amy? How could she *not* tell Amy? How could she face Drew after what she'd seen?

Part of her wanted to throw her clothes into her suitcase and leave. Let Amy cope with her own ghosts. Forget the auction, forget Will. Just get out of here.

But how would she explain leaving so suddenly?

Maggie's fingernails ground into the palms of her hands as she walked up and down, her thoughts swirling.

She was startled when there was a light tap on her door and she realized she'd been pacing over half an hour.

"Maggie? Are you resting?"

Maggie took a deep breath. Stay calm. Being upset wouldn't help Amy. "Come in, Amy."

"I just got home and saw your car, so I was sure you were here. How was the auction preview? And your lunch? I got the message you left on the machine. What fun that you ran into your friend!"

Had Amy seen what was going on? How could she not have? How could she be so calm? "Not a spectacular auction, although there are a couple of lots I might bid on. I asked them to reserve a seat for me for tomorrow morning. No corner cabinets of any sort, though."

"Just my luck. But keep looking for the cabinet when you're antiquing. You never know where there might be one."

"They're not that unusual. I'm sure you'll find one you like somewhere." Should she say anything? How could Amy have missed what was happening?

Amy sat on the other side of the bed. "And how was your friend?"

"He's fine. He's been here a couple of weeks." Should she tell Amy all she had learned about this house at the beauty salon and from Will? Now none of it seemed very important. "His great-aunt lives in Waymouth, and he's doing some repairs for her. He used to teach woodworking at a school near Buffalo, before he went into the antiques business full-time."

"He's a competitor of yours, then."

"No. My prints are a long way from the fireplace equipment and early kitchen tools he specializes in. No competition there. In fact, we're going to meet at the auction tomorrow."

"Then you must invite him for dinner tomorrow night! And his aunt too. I'd love to meet him, and the more people Drew and I know locally, the faster we'll feel we belong here."

Would an invitation to dinner at the old family home be considered friendly, or infuriating? "I'll ask Will tomorrow at the auction. I don't know if he has any plans."

"No problem either way. We'll just barbecue, and make sure we have extra steaks."

Maggie and Amy looked at each other in strained silence. Amy broke it. "I'm going down to my study to pay a couple of bills. You're probably tired. You had a long trip yesterday, we were up late chatting, and you've been out today. Rest a little, and then come down to the porch when you're ready for some afternoon libations. Take your time." Amy got up.

Was she telling Maggie to stay in her room? "It's such a beautiful day, I thought I might take a walk."

"Why not wait until a little later, and I'll join you. I just have to handle a few things. It won't take more than thirty minutes or so." The door clicked as Amy closed it.

What was going on? Why did Amy want her to stay in her room? Maggie walked to the window, feeling less like lying down than she had all day. Her room faced the back of the house, away from the river. She could see the roof of the ell. Giles and Brian Leary must have finished for the day. They were gone.

It was a beautiful day, but Maggie sensed a large, dark cloud over the house.

She decided to lie down after all.

Chapter 4

—❧—

The Fore and Aft Sails of a Twenty-Gun Ship, *copper engraving by D. Steel, London, September 1, 1794. Detailed rendering of ship at sea, with identifying notations on sails. One small fox mark in sky. 7.5 x 10 inches.* Price: $225.

Forty minutes later Maggie gently opened her door. There was no sign of Drew or Crystal, and Amy was happily sorting papers in her study.

"Thank goodness you've come to rescue me!" Amy dropped the pile she was holding.

"Can I be rude and ask what you're looking at?" Maggie peeked over at the desk. The papers Amy had put down appeared to be covered with pictures of children.

"We'll talk and walk," Amy answered, as they headed out the door. "Isn't this day wonderful?" She took a deep breath. "We're far enough upriver so you can't always taste the salt in the air, but today the wind must be from the ocean."

There was definitely a salt smell in the breeze. "A

perfect Maine day," Maggie agreed. An August day at home in New Jersey would no doubt have been sweltering: high temperatures, high humidity, tempers flaring, cars overheating, mosquitoes buzzing. Here all was cool and peaceful. No wonder people moved to Maine.

"I can hardly wait for our first winter here," said Amy. "Locals say we won't get as much snow on the coast as most people imagine, and the tourists all go home, leaving lots of parking spaces and peace."

Wasn't Amy complaining about the quiet just last night? "You can probably see even more of the river when the leaves are off the trees." Contrary to what many people imagined, there were lots of trees in Maine that were not evergreens. "But those temperatures will be pretty low, I've heard."

"I'm not worried. We have central heating. People have lived in this house all year round since the eighteenth century; there's no reason Drew and I can't too. And we'll have a woodstove by then, and bottled water, in case we can't get out for a couple of days, or lose power for a while. There were some bad ice storms here a few years ago." Amy pointed at some birches that were still bent over. "You can tell which ones were damaged. Some have never recovered."

They walked down by the river on the road below the ninety-degree turn. Two people in a red kayak paddled by and waved. Farther out on the river a small motorboat sped toward Waymouth. Only a few cars passed them. "This road dead-ends about three miles down the peninsula," Amy explained. "We have about five acres but most of it goes back from the road. Shirley and her girls and her brother live up there." She pointed at a yellow Victorian house with rust-colored trim up on the hill, parallel with hers. "Our neighbor in the other direction is too far away to see, but Shirley and Tom's lights are clear through the trees, which is nice. There's even a rough stone path between the two houses."

"My friend Will is some sort of cousin to Shirley and her brother. He told me Shirley helped take care of the woman who lived in your house last."

"Charlotte Leary. I know. Shirley told me. Charlotte was her aunt. Everyone up here seems related to everyone else. Giles and Brian, who are doing the roofing, have the last name Leary too. I guess that's one of the charms of these old Maine communities."

If charms included people angry because you'd bought their family home.

"And who is Crystal, that girl I saw in the kitchen yesterday?" Maggie looked determinedly out at the river so her face wouldn't give away any emotions.

"Crystal and her mother, Rachel, live in a small house on the other side of our property, up on the next road. Rachel works at the library. I met her when I started doing research about the history of our house. Crystal was looking for a summer job, so I suggested she come and help Drew and me. There was so much unpacking and sorting to do when we first got here."

Ah. That's what Crystal was doing. Helping. So why didn't that make total sense? Maggie changed the subject.

"What have you found out about the house?"

"Lots of great stuff! It was built in 1772, but then it burned down and had to be built again, in 1774. And it was built on an island." Amy walked ahead a little and pointed across the river. "That point, over there? It's really the tip of an island. Our house was built there, and then moved to the mainland in the 1830s sometime. I can't pin down the date."

"Moved? How could such a big house be moved?"

"The records say twenty yoke of oxen pulled it across the Madoc River, which was frozen that year, and up the hill to where it stands now. It was set as a channel marker for ships turning at the north eastern end of the island toward Waymouth harbor. The ell and barn were built at the new location."

"Wow. What a job." Maggie looked up at the hill and then across the river. "So the river freezes in winter?"

"Not for maybe a hundred years. Global warming, I guess. But I found references to boats iced in for the winter back in the late eighteenth and early nineteenth centuries. We don't think about weather changing that much, but it must have."

"James Fenimore Cooper wrote in *Satanstoe*, which is set in eighteenth-century Albany, that young couples would race sleighs on the Hudson. No one is trying that now!"

"For sure. Anyway, the house must have been

empty for a while in the early nineteenth century; I couldn't find any records for that period. Then it was owned by several captains. At least one sailed ships to the Far East. I'm sure there is more in the Waymouth Courthouse Archives, but I haven't gotten to them yet."

"Change of topic. Amy, I have to ask! Are you and Drew adopting a baby? I saw the nursery, of course, and those pictures of children on your desk." Maggie hesitated. "If that question is out of line, say so. But I'll admit I've thought about adoption myself, and I'd love to know more."

"You? Adoption? Maggie, you'd make a great mom! You don't have to be married to adopt now. And there are so many children who need homes."

"So what are you and Drew doing?"

"It's a long story. Both Drew and I really, really want to be parents. Drew was adopted himself. He was left on the steps of St. Patrick's Cathedral when he was a baby. His adoptive parents are wonderful people, but Drew has always wanted to have someone in his life who was biologically related to him. His two brothers were also adopted, but they don't feel that way. They're just fine with who they are, and with the little they know of their history. But Drew has always wanted what he calls a 'real' family."

"Did he try to find his biological family?"

"For years. It wasn't just a matter of records being sealed. There were no records. He knows the date he was found at the cathedral, and how he was assigned a birth date, and even why he was given the name

Andrew. The name came from an alphabetical list of names at the New York Foundling Hospital, where he lived until he was adopted when he was six months old. But there's no way he can locate a mother who couldn't be found forty-two years ago. That's why it's so important to Drew that he have a child of his own."

Maggie nodded. "I've never thought what it must be like never to know anyone biologically related to you. You'd have curiosity, if nothing else. To know whether someone else's eyes looked like yours." Involuntarily she thought of Will's eyes, and flushed a little.

"At first Drew and I thought it would just take time for me to get pregnant. I did everything I'd heard of from protein diets to taking my temperature every morning to find the right time of month, to convincing Drew to give up his Jockey shorts. You don't know what we tried!"

And Maggie really didn't want to know.

"Nothing worked. And we're getting older. I tried to get Drew to think about adoption; that's why we have all those pictures in my office. I got on the mailing list for every domestic and international agency I could find, and they keep sending me pictures of 'waiting children.' Drew doesn't even want to look, but I keep thinking maybe I'll see a face that looks like Drew's, and that he'll change his mind and decide adoption is all right."

"He doesn't believe in adoption?"

"He believes it's a good thing. He loves his adoptive parents. He just wants at least one child that is 'really his.' After that, he says maybe we could adopt. But time is passing."

Amy was the same age as Maggie. Thirty-eight. "And you tried all the infertility treatments?"

"Some of them." Amy hesitated. "It's my fault, Maggie. When I was in high school, I got pregnant. Believe me, it was not my fault. But I couldn't have a baby. Not at fifteen."

"You had an abortion."

Amy's voice dropped. "My stepfather arranged it. It was supposed to be clean and easy. Only it wasn't." She paused. "I was all right in a few days. But my fertility doctor told me the abortion created scar tissue, which is probably one reason I'm having a problem getting pregnant. Plus, of course, being over thirty-five doesn't help."

Maggie felt old and wrinkled just listening to her. This was a side of Amy she had never guessed at. The young Amy had made a mistake. The Amy she knew had always been in control.

"How did Drew react when you told him?"

Amy walked a few steps before answering. "I couldn't tell him, Maggie. How could I tell someone whose mother had chosen to have him even if she couldn't take care of him that I had chosen to kill my baby? He would never forgive me. He's not dealing well with my not getting pregnant. Telling him I'd had an abortion that prevented my conceiving could end our marriage." She hesitated. "Sometimes I think the only reason he married me was to have a child." Amy walked a few steps toward the river and then turned around. "I'd do anything to make this marriage work, Maggie. If Drew knew it was my fault we haven't had children, if he thought I couldn't conceive, he would divorce me."

"Oh, Amy, you can't believe that," said Maggie, but then she remembered the scene in the bedroom. And the baby's room just down the hall. "What about the nursery? It's so perfect!"

"Drew bought the crib for me as a wedding present, and then the other things we bought because we really thought it was just a matter of time until I got pregnant. Oh, Maggie, I don't know what will happen if we don't have a baby!"

"Have you been to a doctor in Maine yet?"

"I went last week. Of course she wants all my medical records transferred from New York before she can make any recommendations. She just suggested all the same things everyone suggests and mentioned several times how fertility begins to decrease at age thirty."

"You can't give up hope, Amy. Someone I work with was told she could never have children. She and her husband adopted two cute little boys from Korea. Then she got pregnant and had a little girl!"

"People keep telling me stories like that. Maybe that's one reason I wanted us to apply to adopt. But we're getting too old even to apply for an infant. So many people want to adopt healthy babies that agencies are really selective. They don't want parents over forty. We'd have to adopt a baby with a medical problem, or an older child, or a child from overseas."

"My friend's Korean sons are terrific."

"I'm sure. But that isn't what Drew is looking for, and I'm not sure I could handle having children who didn't look like us. And I've read information on dozens of children. Most of the older ones have emotional problems of some sort."

"But their major problem is not having someone to love them."

"I'm just not ready for all of that. I want a perfect baby who looks like Drew, and maybe even like me, to go in that canopied crib."

Maggie tried not to hear the growing hysteria in Amy's voice. "Why don't we turn around and head for home and a glass of wine? I'm glad you told me, Amy. I understand what it is to want to be a mother." And, suddenly, Maggie did understand. As they headed back, she found herself wondering about all those children in the pictures on Amy's desk. Children no one wanted. Children who might not fit perfectly into a white, canopied crib. She shivered, wrapped in her own thoughts.

Chapter 5

———✎———

The Mirror Carp: Cyprinus carpio, *lithograph, dark green background; brown fish with gold markings. From oil painting by American artist John Petrie, of a "specimen—weight 1½ pounds—caught and painted at the New York State Hatchery, Mumford, New York." From 1895 limited-edition portfolio* The Fishes of North America That Are Captured on Hook and Line, *by William C. Harris, editor of* The American Angler. 11.5 x 18.5-inches. Price: $160.

Drew had already opened the wine by the time they got back to the house. At least that's what Maggie thought until she realized he was filling his goblet with vodka instead of white wine. And he had clearly been doing so for a while. He was more dressed than when she had last seen him; he was wearing a pair of pressed jeans and a dark gray polo shirt. And his black hair was not as tousled.

"I finally get to see the mysterious guest!" Drew's hug was encompassing, although he didn't put down his glass. Maggie felt a chill of liquid seeping through her T-shirt down her back. "Amy says you've been here since yesterday."

"You were away last night and I guess I missed you today." Maggie turned and poured herself some red wine. She didn't want her glass to get mixed up with Drew's, although it didn't seem likely he'd put his down anytime soon.

"So how's the antiques business? Outperforming the stock market these days?"

"It's doing all right. No business is doing what it was in the nineties. But investing in any limited commodity is never a bad idea, and that's what antiques are."

"True. Before you leave, Amy and I want to take a look at some of your prints. Do you have many from 1774? That's when this house was built."

"I have a few from that period, but not many, and they'd be European. Even American artists had most of their engraving done in Europe until the middle of the nineteenth century. Printing techniques and equipment were much more sophisticated abroad. Paintings and folk arts like embroidery were more common in America than prints until Currier and Ives proved prints could be commercially successful. I do have some wonderful American engravings and lithographs from 1850 on. And a few from before. I'd be happy to show you."

"Since we're now Mainers, I suppose we should be buying Winslow Homers, or one of the Wyeths. Or— who is that man who did wood engravings and paintings on Monhegan, Amy?"

"You're thinking of Rockwell Kent." Amy turned to Maggie. "We saw an exhibit of his at the Metropolitan Museum last winter. Very powerful."

Maggie nodded. "I have quite a few Winslow Homer wood engravings, and some N. C. Wyeths. Andrew and Jamie Wyeth are too recent for my business, although I certainly admire their work."

"We'll look at them soon. Winslow Homer sounds good. He did some Civil War stuff too, didn't he?" Drew poured himself some more vodka.

"Quite a few. He was the 'special artist' for *Harper's Weekly* during the Civil War, although there were also a half dozen other artists reporting with their pencils from the battlefront. He and Thomas Nast are the best known today. I have some Nasts too."

"I've always found the Civil War period fascinating. Did Amy tell you I majored in American history in college?"

"She mentioned that you were a history buff." She had also mentioned Drew had been drinking too much recently.

"I'm thinking of teaching up here in Maine. They need teachers everywhere, and I suppose I could pass a test or take courses or whatever it takes to get certified here."

"That would be a major change of profession for you." Maggie couldn't imagine this former stockbroker in charge of a group of children. Especially after the interaction she'd seen him having with one teenager a couple of hours ago.

Amy rose. "I think we need to get dinner started. I'm going to put some chicken breasts and potatoes in the oven. Drew, I told Maggie that tomorrow we'd have a barbecue. She has a friend who is visiting in Waymouth, and I thought it would be fun to invite him over."

"Do you need help, Amy?" Amy's arm was still bandaged. In fact, Maggie noticed a little blood seeping through the gauze.

"I'll be fine. Crystal fixed everything earlier so all I have to do is put it in the oven. You relax and keep Drew company." Amy left the porch.

"So your friend is vacationing Down East too, Maggie."

"He has an aunt in Waymouth. He's also an antiques dealer; we're going to an auction tomorrow morning."

"That's nice." Drew pulled his chair closer to Maggie's. "While you were on your walk, did Amy tell you all our family secrets?"

Maggie hoped Amy's trip to the kitchen would be a quick one.

"All about the crying baby and the ghost woman?" Drew added.

Thank goodness it was those secrets he was talking about. "Yes, she told me. The telephone calls sound awful. And the fire must have been frightening."

"It's all nonsense. The fire was just an accident. And everyone gets some wrong numbers. Amy is a little high-strung."

"I never thought of her that way."

"Well, think, then. She gets uptight when everything doesn't go her way."

Amy had always wanted life to be controllable, Maggie agreed silently. And a lot of aspects of Amy's life right now were not under control. That was becoming clearer every hour.

Drew topped off his glass.

In the distance, Maggie heard the telephone. She hoped it wasn't one of those hang-up calls. Amy had enough to deal with tonight.

Amy was in the doorway. "Drew, do you know when Crystal left this afternoon? Her mother is calling. Crystal hasn't gotten home yet."

"I don't know when she left. A while ago. Plenty of time to walk home. Or maybe that Leary boy gave her a ride."

"But you don't know for sure when she left."

"Hell, I don't keep track of all the help. Tell her mother to relax. She's a teenager. She'll be home when she's ready to get there."

"She must not be with Brian Leary. Her mother says she had a date with him tonight, and he's there at her house now, waiting for her."

"I don't know anything."

"Rachel seems very upset. Maggie, would you mind taking another walk? I'd like to follow the path Crystal takes from our house to hers and make sure she didn't fall or something."

"A good idea," Maggie agreed. Crystal might just be lollygagging, but it was strange that she would be this late. Could something have happened to her?

Chapter 6

———◦———

*In the Bath, one in a series of French steel
engravings illustrating the 1838 memoirs of
Casanova (1725–1798), an Italian adventurer
who traveled throughout Europe as a preacher,
alchemist, gambler, violin player, and spy. His
memoirs tell of his rogueries and amours.
Some engravings in this series are overtly
sexual or scatological. This one depicts an
unwilling woman, undressed except for her
cap, being forced into an early-nineteenth-
century bathing tub by a fully dressed man.
3 x 4.25 inches. Price: $50.*

Amy and Maggie headed past the ell and barn and
driveway and small garden, across the lawn, and into
a field. At first, Maggie couldn't see any path. There
certainly wasn't a path by suburban standards, but in
places the tall grasses and goldenrod had been stepped
on, breaking some of their thick stems.

"This is our land," Amy said, turning her head
toward Maggie as they pushed their way through the
waist-high grasses. "Used to be hayed, I'm told. We

may get a small tractor and turn part of it into lawn next year." The field was a couple of acres of difficult walking. Two crows screamed their indignation at the women invading their territory.

"Are you sure this is how Crystal gets home? Why doesn't she take the road?"

"There are no direct roads from her house to ours. Cutting through the fields and woods leads her straight home. Crystal!" Amy's voice was loud.

As the crow flies, Maggie thought. But—crows could fly. Maybe Crystal was light enough that her footsteps didn't always break down the grasses. They crossed a damp section of ground, perhaps over an underground spring, and Maggie brushed aside a thick milkweed stem. An orange-and-black monarch butterfly fluttered away.

"I've been this way a few times," said Amy. "Just to see our land. The borders of our property are pretty narrow. In the eighteenth century, when most of the property lines were drawn, lots by the river often were narrow and deep, so as many people as possible could have water access. There was no bridge across the Madoc to Waymouth then. Everyone had a boat. Most lots go back, as ours does, almost to the next road, which is Egret Point, where Rachel and Crystal live, on another little peninsula. Their house isn't near the water, but houses on the end of their point are."

Emerging from the field, they entered a smaller area of woods. "Crystal? Can you hear me?" Amy called. They stood and listened, but there was no answer.

"This feels as it must have when Native Americans lived here," Maggie said quietly. The only sound was their footsteps crunching on the fallen pine needles and mosses and some gulls crying high above them.

"There haven't been many Indians here since the early eighteenth century. The early settlers and the Abenakis weren't the greatest of friends. After the French and Indian Wars the Abenakis who were left went north or west, leaving this section of the shoreline to the whites." Amy stopped and looked around, as she had several times before. "There's no sign of Crystal. I thought she might have fallen, or was walking very slowly, and we'd catch up with her. Let's hope she's already safe at home."

"Does she walk back and forth every day?"

"She works five days a week, but not always the same days, depending on when I need her to help me. Sometimes Brian or Giles drive her home in their truck."

"I take it Brian is her boyfriend."

"Could be. They spend a lot of time together. But Crystal has ambition. She doesn't want to settle in Madoc, the way her mother did. She wants to see the world."

"She looks pretty young to be making major decisions about her future." Maggie couldn't get the picture of Drew and Crystal out of her head. "How old is she?"

"Eighteen. Old enough to know what she wants and do something about it." Amy stepped over a fallen branch that was blocking the way.

"When I was eighteen, all I knew was I had to finish high school and go to college somewhere. Everything else seemed very far in the future."

"I don't think Crystal is the college type. She's thinking of becoming a model. She's been borrowing my copies of *Vanity Fair* and *New York*."

"She is pretty," Maggie had to agree. "But aren't most models almost emaciated? And taller." Crystal was only about five feet four inches and parts of her were definitely not emaciated.

Amy shrugged. "Maybe. That she'll have to find out on her own. She's just thinking about different possibilities now." She stepped over a large rock in the path and moved another branch out of their way. "I've been trying to give her some mentoring advice. Teenaged girls never listen to their mothers anyway. She's very impressed that Drew and I are from New York."

Maggie pointed ahead. "Is that her home?"

Just beyond the end of the tree line was a small, brown-shingled cottage, perhaps a third the size of Amy's house, nestled comfortably between the woods to its rear and a small lawn and garden of pink and mauve and white and purple delphiniums. A police vehicle and a car were parked in front, just on the other side of a large winter-ready woodpile.

"Let's hope she's home safely by now," said Maggie, as they approached the back door. A plump, brown-haired woman opened it.

"Did you see any sign of her, Amy?"

"Not one. She still hasn't called or come home?"

"Brian took his truck and is out checking the roads and some of their friends' homes." They entered the small kitchen, where a big man in navy trousers and a blue shirt was seated at the table. "Have you met Owen Colby? He's a neighbor, and he works in the sheriff's office." Owen Colby rose and offered a strong hand to Amy and Maggie.

"I understand Crystal's been working for you this summer, Mrs. Douglas."

"Yes. Most weekdays, and sometimes on the weekend. She's been helping us get unpacked and settled in."

"And she was over at your place today."

"She washed up the dishes and cleaned out a cabinet in the kitchen while I was grocery shopping. She made a pie with the last of the blueberries too."

"Crystal's a real good cook," her mother added. "She's always liked to bake."

"When did you last see her, Mrs. Douglas?"

"I was out doing errands most of the day. So was Maggie. When I got home, about three o'clock, she was finishing up. I told her she could leave after she'd put the groceries away, and I went into my study to do some work. When I came out forty minutes later, she was gone. I assumed she'd gone home."

"And your husband doesn't know exactly when she left either."

"No. He was in his study, upstairs. Or on the

front porch. Not near the kitchen, where Crystal was working."

Maggie ground her nails into the palms of her hands, hoping desperately Owen Colby wouldn't ask her where *she* had last seen Crystal. But he didn't.

"Well, Rachel, I can't help but think Crystal will turn up soon enough. She's at an age where they just take off sometimes. Think being independent means not telling anyone where they're going." Deputy Colby put away his notebook.

"But can't I file a missing person's report or something?" Rachel Porter was obviously distressed. "She has crazy ideas, sometimes, about taking off to live in New York." Maggie noted Rachel did not look at Amy when she said that. "Or being a model. Maybe she's hitchhiking south."

"Has she mentioned any plans to travel?"

"Not right out. But her room is full of brochures about New York."

"Rachel, you keep in touch. We can't file a missing person's report on her until tomorrow afternoon, but I'll let the state police know she's gone missing, and if they see anyone meeting her description, they'll pick her up. If you hear from her, now, you let me know. I'll talk to some folks in town. Chances are someone has seen her. Or she may have just taken a long way home to think. She could walk in the door at any moment."

Maggie and Amy followed the deputy out the door, and he indicated they could sit in the back of his car. Not the best way to be seen by your neighbors, Maggie thought, but here in Madoc probably the whole town would know within an hour just what was happening.

Most likely Crystal would be home by then. Maggie hoped so. But she feared nothing would be that simple. How could a teenaged girl have disappeared during such a short country walk?

Chapter 7

—⁓—

Carrying the Flag, Good Housekeeping
cover, July 1931, by Jessie Willcox Smith
(1863–1935). Young boy, perhaps age six,
waving an American flag. Smith was a
well-known Philadelphia illustrator, the only
woman who studied with Thomas Eakins, and
then with N. C. Wyeth and Maxfield Parrish
under Howard Pyle. She specialized in paintings
of children. 8.5 x 10 inches. Price: $60.

Later that night Maggie sat in bed, looking through
a pile of the "waiting children" pictures Amy had
given her. Children not only from all over the United
States, but from China, Thailand, Korea, Colom-
bia, Russia, Peru . . . the number of faces and stories
was overwhelming, and Maggie felt torn in too
many directions to give them the attention they
deserved. All these children needed a home. Deserved
a home. And Amy and Drew had a perfect white
nursery waiting for a baby who for some reason
couldn't be any one of these children. Did that make
sense? Did anything in this house, or in Amy and

Drew's marriage, make sense? Maggie had been in Maine for just a little over a day, and she felt like Alice in Wonderland, in a strange universe with different rules.

Amy had the marriage and the house she wanted. But those things weren't enough. She wanted a child. A child for Drew. As Maggie thought back, she didn't remember Amy's focusing strongly on wanting a child for herself. The child was required to meet Drew's needs. Maggie shuddered. What a heavy responsibility both Amy and Drew were already putting on that poor unborn child's head.

How had her parents felt before they had children? Maggie wished she could pick up the telephone and ask her mother. "Mom, how did you know when it was the right time to have children? How did you know focusing your life on them would give your own life more meaning?"

It had been almost ten years since their car had crashed, but Maggie found herself wiping a tear away. It always happened like this. She wouldn't think about her parents for days, but then, suddenly, she needed them, and the realization that they were gone would hit her all over again.

Did her brother Joe ever think of them that way? She doubted it. She and Joe had never been close; he was twelve years older than she was, and he always seemed to have interests other than a little sister or parents. He'd left home as soon as he graduated from high school and, after that, called only once or twice a year. He'd worked in Wyoming, in Chicago, in Seattle. Ten years ago he'd been working in Florida. Her parents had been on their way to visit him when a car going in the other direction had veered into their station wagon. Joe had come to the funeral, but Maggie had only gotten a couple of Christmas cards from him since then. Last she'd heard, he was in Arizona.

She looked down at the pile of pictures. She had two extra bedrooms in her house. She had no ghosts. And she would love to have a child to take to the circus and to read stories with. To share Christmas and the first day of school with. Was love enough? Did these children really want a family, or would they be like Joe and escape the confines of people who loved them as soon as they could? She shook her head. She couldn't think about those things now. She needed to think about what was going on in this house.

This house that came with a heritage that was more than a history, in a community that seemed very accepting of the possibility of ghosts. There was certainly a strange undercurrent in the family who had owned the house. But even if some of them were sorry it had been sold, the sale couldn't be undone. Amy and Drew were here. Unless . . . she shook her head again. If Amy and Drew had problems, and it was clear they did, then the problems between them had started long before they'd bought this house.

And Amy didn't even seem to know about Crystal's relationship with Drew! Was she so naive? Didn't she care? Was she one of those wives who would tolerate anything to keep her husband? Or did she not want to know?

Maggie turned off the light and punched her pillow several times.

Amy had always known what she wanted, and she had never let anyone push her around. What had changed?

Maggie closed her eyes and tried to sleep. She had an auction to attend tomorrow. She was meeting Will there. She turned over abruptly. What was Will really like? She hardly knew him! For all she knew he had a woman in every city he visited. He could be at some Maine pub right now, romancing some waitress.

She punched the pillow again. Why was life so complicated? Why couldn't everyone just be honest with everyone else? How could men do this to women?

She drifted into a restless sleep, seeing photos of unwanted children turning in front of her eyes. Hundreds of children without love. Without families. Their eyes followed her accusingly. What could she do? It wasn't her fault that their parents were gone. The children started crying, at first just a few tears, but then louder, and louder. Maggie sleepily pulled the pillow over her ears. She couldn't stand the crying. Then her door opened, and the light switched on. Amy was standing there in a long white nightgown. "Maggie! Don't you hear? It's the baby!"

Maggie's fuzzy mind groped for logic as she sat up, half in dream and half in Amy's guest bedroom.

She thought she had heard a child crying. But now it had stopped.

"You heard it too! You had to! You did hear it!" Amy took quick steps over to the bed. "Maggie, I'm not crazy! There was a baby crying in this house!"

Maggie reached over as Amy sat down and buried her head in Maggie's shoulder.

"I heard it, Amy. I did. It was a baby. A baby crying so your heart would break."

Chapter 8

———❦———

Niagara Falls (from the top of the ladder on the American side). *Hand-colored steel engraving by J. C. Bentley for W. H. Bartlett showing the Falls and several elegantly dressed people observing them; 1839. Bartlett's engravings were some of the best and earliest depictions of American scenes. Published in London and hand-colored after publication. 7.25 x 5.5 inches. Price: $75.*

The Walter English Auction House was full by nine the next morning, although the auction wouldn't start until ten. Maggie wove her way between people who were making the most of the last preview hour until she reached the two chairs she and Will had reserved. Pieces of masking tape marked places for BREWER and SUMMER next to each other. She put her bottle of Poland Spring water and a navy cardigan sweater on her seat. With this number of auctiongoers there would be a lot of people standing. Better to reinforce the reserved seat with a message that said, "Don't sit here! This seat taken!" The same game was being played throughout the room; chairs were covered by jackets, newspapers, books, cups of coffee, and on the chair in front of Maggie's, a piece of needlework in progress. Like animals marking their territory, she thought. Her sweater would tell Will that she was somewhere in the crowd. Luckily she had registered and picked up her bidding number yesterday. The line for that table was out the door. She headed toward the woman who was frantically collating and stapling extras copies of the auction catalog. Catalogs were good references during the auction, and afterward, if you noted the prices items sold for. She pulled out her $3 and waited for the woman to turn around with another several copies. When the woman did turn, she and Maggie looked at each other in surprise.

"Rachel! What are you doing here? Did Crystal get home last night?"

Rachel took Maggie's $3 and handed her a catalog. "No. I left the lights on and sat up all night waiting. She didn't even call. She's never been out all night before. Not without calling."

"I'm so sorry. Maybe today you'll hear from her."

"Johnny promised Walter I'd help out this morning, and I couldn't stand just pacing the floor and doing nothing, so I came. I'm going to the sheriff's office as soon as the auction starts to see if now they can officially list her as missing. This isn't like Crystal."

"Hey, hurry up there. People are waiting for catalogs!" called an impatient voice behind Maggie.

"If Amy or I can help," Maggie said, looking into Rachel's brimming eyes, as she moved away, "call. Really."

Rachel smiled weakly as she turned to her next customer.

Crystal's mother was not coping well. But, then, why should she? If only that girl would come home! Did she feel guilty about yesterday afternoon? Did she sense that she and Drew had been seen? There was certainly no hint that what was happening in Amy's bedroom was not consensual, but who knew what an eighteen-year-old girl would think. Maggie felt very old; as though she had been born eighteen centuries ago. And she didn't think she had ever been the kind of eighteen Crystal was now. She thought of all the young women she had taught over the years. For some reason, Crystal seemed different.

Maggie shook her head slightly and focused on the scene at hand. There was nothing she could do about Crystal here. She decided to take a closer look at the tapestries she had passed by the day before.

She maneuvered her way through the crowd and checked them out, then confirmed the lot numbers she had noted yesterday for the boxes of books she had hopes of buying and circled them in her catalog. She also circled the number of the egret watercolor. Good; all the numbers she was interested in were under three hundred. There were six hundred lots in this auction, and she didn't want to spend a full day sitting on a hard folding chair inside a country auction house. Especially with a missing girl on her mind. She had hardly met Crystal; she had certainly not been impressed with her behavior. But Crystal was eighteen and she was missing. Maybe she and Amy could think of or do something that would help.

She glanced over at where Rachel was working. Being a mother was not easy.

Will put a cup of coffee on his seat as she approached. "Good morning, print lady! How was your evening?"

Maggie grimaced. "Memorable. We can talk later. Do you have to check anything out before the auction starts?"

"I want to take another look at one set of brass andirons. I looked them up last night and there should be a maker's mark if they are what I think they are." He spoke quietly, as did most dealers at auctions, for the same reason Maggie was holding her catalog close to her body so no one could see the circled lots she planned to bid on. No one wanted to advertise their particular interests before the bidding. It might encourage—or discourage—others if they knew what specific dealers thought was worth bidding on.

Maggie sat, turned over her auction catalog, and opened her bottle of Poland Spring. Water was fine, and this was Maine, but she would rather have diet cola.

"Dear," interrupted an older woman on her right. "Have you ever been to an auction before?"

"Yes," replied Maggie. "A few." A few hundred, at least.

"This is my very first," said the woman in the blue dress with matching pocketbook. The friend next to her nodded. "We've been watching *Antiques Roadshow* on the TV, and we wanted to see what it was all about."

"Have you registered, so you can bid?"

"Is that how you get those cards with numbers on them?" The woman pointed at Maggie's bidding card.

"Yes. You can get them over at the registration desk. You can't bid without one."

"Then I guess we'd better register." The woman rose and squeezed her way past Maggie. "I'll be right back, Flora. We don't want to miss anything."

"Are there always so many people here?" asked Flora. "And so many—sorts—of people."

"It all depends on what's in the auction, and on the time of year," Maggie answered. "A Maine auction in August is bound to attract a lot of people."

"Oh, yes. You know, I was afraid we weren't quite dressed up enough for an auction. I've seen auctions in movies. Everyone looks very elegant. But Sophia said we didn't have to dress that way for a morning auction, and I see there are even people here in shorts!"

Maggie smiled to herself. Heavens. The woman would probably have worn her tiara for an evening auction. Of course, auctions were like any other events: they varied considerably. Those attending a farm auction on a Saturday night in Maine would probably not dress in precisely the same way as would those in New York at Parke-Bernet. Although the basic procedures were the same. She hoped these two ladies wouldn't ask her to explain every term used during the day.

Will returned and sank down, opening the top on his coffee. "I'm interested in three lots. And one more, if it goes low enough. You?"

"About the same. How fast does this auctioneer go?"

"He's one of the faster ones. About one hundred lots an hour."

Maggie nodded. Thank goodness. Some auctioneers took forever and only got through perhaps fifty lots an hour. Again, of course, a gallery like Sotheby's wouldn't even be in the same ballpark when it came to speed. Elegance and big dollars were expected to take time. It was part of the show. "I'd like to be out of here by one."

"Your highest lot number?"

"Two sixty-six."

Will nodded. "It'll be close, but I think you'll make it. I have one item higher than that. We'll see how the prices go in any case. It looks like a liquid crowd."

They both looked around. It definitely felt like a tourist crowd with money. The question was, would they spend it here or bore easily and take their wallets off to an antiques show or gift shop? Lots at the end of the auction would no doubt bring less money than those in the first couple of hundred numbers, as this crowd inevitably moved on to other amusements.

"Lunch again today?"

"I don't think so, Will. But Amy and Drew would like you and your aunt Nettie to come for a barbecue tonight if you can."

Will hesitated just a moment too long and then shrugged his shoulders. "Why not? It will give the old girl more to talk about."

"Will she feel awkward, visiting a house that was once in her family?"

"Oh, she'll love that part. She'll report back exactly what they're doing wrong with it." He hesitated again and then grinned self-consciously. "I was thinking of what she'd say about you. She's been trying to match me up with women ever since my wife died eight years ago. And here's a pretty lady just arriving out of nowhere."

"If it would be too embarrassing . . ."

"Hell, no. The more I think about it, the more fun it will be." He reached over and squeezed Maggie's hand. "I'd like you to meet Aunt Nettie officially. And I think she'll like you."

Maggie smiled, but then gently removed her hand. She liked Will. She wanted to trust him. But the memories of Drew and Crystal were still too clear.

"Will, you don't happen to know a Crystal Porter?"

"Sure. Rachel's daughter. She must be ten or twelve by now."

"Try eighteen." Did everyone in Maine know everyone else?

"Where did you run into her?"

Why did a direct question feel so filled with implications?

"She's been helping Amy and Drew around the house this summer. But yesterday afternoon she didn't come home. Her mother is really worried about her."

Will glanced quickly over at the table where Rachel was still stapling and selling auction programs. His voice lowered. "So she takes after her mother, eh? I guess I haven't kept up-to-date with that part of the family."

"The family? You mean they're related to you too?"

"Pretty distantly. I couldn't figure it out without a diagram. Rachel and I share the same great-grandmother or something like that."

"And Rachel has a past."

"Pretty far distant. About eighteen years, I'd say, if Crystal is that old now."

"And Crystal's father?"

"As I recall at the time there were a number of candidates for that honor, but Rachel just shut her mouth and raised Crystal alone. She got pregnant just after she graduated from high school."

"And she never married?"

"Don't think so." Will lowered his voice even further. "Although rumor has it she's been spending time the last couple of years with Johnny Brent."

Johnny Brent. "I've seen his name on the roofers' truck at Amy's house."

"He has a good-sized construction company now, maybe a dozen trucks and crews. Not new homes, for the most part. He specializes in fixing up older homes, adding rooms, replacing roofs, doing interior work. That sort of thing."

The crowd parted as a tall, burly man strode to the front of the room and stood at the lectern. He banged on it with a worn mahogany gavel as people found their seats. "Good morning. I'm Walter English, and welcome to this morning's auction. Be sure to read the terms and conditions of the sale on your bidding card. A twelve percent buyer's premium will be added to the total of all purchases, with a two percent discount for cash or checks. We reserve the right to hold your purchases until the check clears. Sales tax will be added unless you have a valid resale number on file with us prior to the sale. You must be registered and have a number to bid. I'll tell you what I know about any item coming up, but if you haven't looked it over before the sale, I suggest you don't bid on it. Everything is sold as is, where is. All sales are final. Small items will be brought to your seat. Empty cartons and newspapers are in the corner for you to use in packing. Larger items will be put outside the door. As soon as I say 'Sold!' the item is yours. You are responsible for making sure it is safe, and that it is paid for and removed from this property. In that order. If there are no bids commensurate with the value of an item, I reserve the right to pass it. If an item is passed, it will not come up again in this sale. My assistant"—he waved at a woman sitting at a table to his left—"will be placing absentee bids." He took a breath and looked around the room. "Are there any questions?"

Silence.

"The first item up for bid today is this fine maple sideboard. Been refinished, and brass hardware on the drawers has been replaced. Excellent condition, though, all of it. Who'll start the bidding at three hundred dollars? Two hundred dollars? One hundred dollars? All over the house. Who'll give me one-fifty!"

There was no time to talk. Even the two women sitting next to Maggie seemed transfixed as they watched the wide assortment of goods come to the block. A set of tools, maybe twenty years old. A Victorian oak footstool with a modern needlework cover. A copy of the Mona Lisa in charcoal. A box of Christmas decorations from the 1930s. An oil painting of Boothbay Harbor signed by somebody no one had heard of. A wooden carton filled with glass apothecary bottles. A carton of chipped silver overlay glass from the 1920s. A gold watch. A cherry sideboard. Four boxes of well-used kitchen pots and pans.

Maggie smiled to herself. When people out of the trade thought of "estate auctions," they seldom realized that meant *everything* in the estate, including the old paint cans in the basement, should the owner or auctioneer think anyone would value their labels. A true estate auction meant everything in the estate had either gone into the Dumpster or into the auction house.

Will bought a set of iron fireplace implements

with owls on the handles. Maggie decided not to bid on the box holding the children's books when it went for more than $60. Flora was delighted to purchase a shoebox full of costume jewelry for $35. "For my grandchildren to play with!" she whispered to Maggie with excitement, as a dealer two rows back sighed in exasperation. Maybe he'd hoped to buy the box and sell the jewelry piece by piece on eBay.

Will stopped bidding on a box of tools when it went over $200. And Maggie delightedly bid $70 for the box of old Bibles and the Wilson birds and won it. The egret she liked was too popular; a well-dressed tourist bid it up to $400, which was way over its retail value. He seemed pleased, and Maggie shrugged. That would have been an extra for her and certainly wasn't worth that price. She had the carton she came for. It had been a good auction.

"I'm going to sign out," she whispered to Will. "See you at about five this afternoon?"

"I'll be there, with Aunt Nettie. Enjoy the afternoon!"

It took just a few minutes to turn in her bidding number and pay the $70 plus $7 buyer's premium for the carton of books. No sales tax for a dealer. Another auctiongoer held the door for Maggie as she carried the heavy carton of leather-bound books to her van. She put it on the front seat. The cargo section of the van was filled with prints. She'd have to repack before she headed back to Jersey.

What a beautiful afternoon! She glanced at her watch. Just a little past one o'clock. She'd check in with Amy, and maybe they could drive down to Pemaquid Point to see the breakers. She'd been on the coast of Maine two days now and hadn't even seen the ocean.

Chapter 9

———✆———

August in the Country—The Seashore. Wood engraving by Winslow Homer, published in Harper's Weekly August 27, 1859. Beach scene with many (fully dressed) people enjoying the sunshine. Includes man trying (unsuccessfully) to scare ladies by waving a lobster at them, and a boy whose finger has been caught by a crab. An early Homer, less dramatic than his later work, but already showing his sense of humor and ability to depict people's faces and elaborate fashions. 13.75 x 9.12 inches. Price: $325.

"How was the auction?" Amy was settled comfortably on a porch lounge chair overlooking the river, a glass of iced tea in her hand. "Before you tell me, there's a plate of sandwiches in the refrigerator. And take some iced tea or diet cola."

"Have you already eaten?" Maggie suddenly realized a sandwich was just what she needed.

"I was hungry, so I ate early. But you and Drew

weren't home, so I just kept creating. Take what you'd like."

Maggie found a plate and chose half an egg salad sandwich and half a tuna. They looked so good she added half a ham sandwich too. Amy had made enough sandwiches for the neighborhood. And diet cola was definitely Maggie's drink of choice. She was back on the porch with her plate in less than three minutes.

"Now, how was the auction?"

"Crowded. Noisy. Things went a bit higher than I would have liked. But I got the carton I was hoping for at a good price."

"Congratulations! I told you Maine was a wonderful place! And how is your friend Will?"

Maggie finished chewing her bite of tuna salad sandwich first. "This is delicious. You added sweet pickles?"

"And a few chopped olives."

"Nice touch. Will's fine. I left him there. He was waiting for another lot or two to come up. But I didn't want to miss this beautiful Maine afternoon."

"Did you invite him for dinner?"

"He and his aunt Nettie. I said 'barbecue at five,' and he promised to come. I did tell you they're from the original family to own this house, right?"

"You told me. But that's true of half the state of Maine, it seems. The only difference is that Will's last name really is Brewer."

"Where's Drew?"

"He took off somewhere with Tom Colby,

Shirley's brother, from next door. I think Tom said something about checking out a cemetery."

"A cemetery?"

"Tom's on the board of the Madoc Historical Society, and one of their projects is recording the names in all the old family graveyards and restoring the headstones. He teaches history at Waymouth High and is a Civil War reenactor. Drew is a Civil War buff too, so they especially like locating the resting places of Civil War veterans. They clean off the mosses and put up small flags and so forth."

"Sounds like a good thing to do."

"It keeps them busy. Drew said he'd stop for steaks on the way home. If he forgets, we have some in the freezer."

"I'm not worried." Maggie put down her plate. It was embarrassing how fast those three half sandwiches had disappeared. "And I'm certainly not hungry now. Have you heard anything more about Crystal?"

"Nothing. I'm sure she's just staying with a girlfriend. Maybe she had an argument with her mother. Teenaged girls do."

"I saw Rachel at the auction this morning, and she still seemed pretty upset."

"Rachel was at the auction?"

"She was putting auction catalogs together and selling them. She said something about 'Johnny' asking her to help."

"'Johnny'? Oh, probably Johnny Brent. He owns the construction company Giles and Brian Leary work for. Rachel and Johnny are pretty close."

"But how would that explain her being at Walter English's auction?"

Amy frowned a bit. "I'm not sure. I heard something about Walter English and Johnny Brent doing something together." She threw up her hands. "Or maybe they're just friends. Everyone up here seems to know everyone else."

That was for sure.

Maggie took a last drink of diet cola.

"It's such a beautiful afternoon I thought maybe we could drive down to Pemaquid Point for an hour or so. I was there years ago, when Michael and I vacationed in Maine." Maggie stopped for a moment, remembering the good times. "It was such a beautiful spot. Do you have time?"

"Sounds like a great idea." Amy looked at her watch. "The roofing guys won't need us. It's a little past two. We can easily be back in a couple of hours to turn on the grill if Drew isn't home by then. And he should be. It would be good for me to get out of the house for the afternoon too."

"I left a sweater in my car. Do I need anything else?"

"Nothing. But the sweater is a good idea. Sea breezes can be cool on an August afternoon."

"Last night I started looking at some of those pictures of children needing homes. Do you have any books on adoption I could borrow while I'm here?"

"Stacks of them. Just check in my study while I run upstairs to get a sweater. Take whatever seems interesting. I'll write a note to let Drew know where we've gone."

Amy's study was neat and orderly. The bookshelves were divided between books on Maine history and books on children. As always, Amy was organized. One entire shelf on baby and toddler care, authors alphabetized. One shelf on infertility and pregnancy. The adoption books were down lower. She pulled out one on "open adoption." What was that? And *Adopting the Older Child*, and *Today's Options in Adoption*. The bottom shelf was stacked with copies of *Adoption Today* magazine, and another pile of what appeared to be booklets and brochures from adoption agencies. She'd look more carefully tomorrow. She had enough for now. Maggie stepped back and stumbled against Amy's wastebasket. She reached to push it farther under the desk.

She couldn't help noticing a box pushed loosely underneath an assortment of what looked like junk mail. An empty home pregnancy kit.

Maggie winced. Amy would have said something, she was sure, if it had been positive. But she clearly was still trying. It would definitely be good for her to get out of the house for the afternoon.

The shelves of gray and black rocks leading into the crashing surf at Pemaquid Point were as dramatic as Maggie had remembered, although she hadn't remembered the three tour buses full of Texans who were also climbing on the rocks and admiring the view.

Maine was beautiful, with or without people in

Stetson hats. She and Amy didn't talk much as they relaxed and enjoyed the ocean view, the lobster boats, the herring gulls, and rafts of eider ducks. Neither of them mentioned Drew's drinking or pregnancy tests or crying ghosts in the night. We've been friends for a long time, Maggie thought. Amy's going through some difficult days. I'm glad I'm here.

A little girl, perhaps six years old, tentatively walked on the rocks not far away, holding tightly to her mother's hand. The two stopped and bent down to look into a tide pool. There were so many wonders for a child to discover.

Maggie stretched and felt the warm sun all through her body. She hadn't needed her sweater after all.

The peace didn't last long. Five vehicles were already in Amy's driveway when they pulled in. Maggie had left her van there. The Brent Construction truck meant Giles and Brian Leary were still working on the roof. Drew's Jeep was easy to identify. An old Ford truck was parked next to it. But, most dramatically, a police car with its radio left on was next to the Ford. And then an ambulance pulled in behind them.

A man in uniform walked quickly out from the kitchen door.

Maggie felt as though she were in a time warp: the uniform was that of a Civil War soldier.

The ambulance driver called out, "Where?"

"Field in back of the barn," replied the Union soldier.

"Drew?" Amy paled, as a woman from the ambulance ran past her and around the barn. "What's happened to Drew?"

"It's not Drew," said the soldier, coming up and touching her shoulder. "Drew is fine. He's in back of the barn with Giles and Brian."

"Then?"

"It's Crystal Porter. Brian Leary found her over in the grasses behind your barn. Drew and I had just pulled in when Brian came running, and Drew called 911."

"What happened? How is she?" Maggie and Amy both started running toward the barn.

"No need to run," the soldier called after them. "She looks pretty dead."

Chapter 10

———×———

The Lobsterman (Hauling in a Light Fog).
N. C. Wyeth illustration for Kenneth Roberts's
Trending into Maine, *1938. Lobsterman in*
traditional wooden dory, checking a lobster
trap in a rough sea. Gulls follow dory in the
fog. Wyeth and Roberts were close friends,
and both had homes in Maine. 5.5 x 7 inches.
Price: $75.

Brian Leary stood on the border of the field, his face
as pale as the faded white paint on the barn. His
father was next to him. Perhaps twenty feet out in the
high grasses that separated the Douglas home from
the one where Shirley and Tom lived, Maggie could
see a policeman and the woman from the ambulance.
They were talking quietly, but no one seemed to be
taking any sort of action. Not a good sign.

Amy suddenly burst into tears and sat on a large
rock that looked as though it had been part of a
stone wall many years before. Maggie walked up to
the Learys. "The man in the uniform said you'd
found her, Brian."

"Dad and I were up on the roof, working on that corner of the ell." He gestured somewhere above where they stood. "I noticed half a dozen crows making a racket over there. When I came down for more shingles, I went over to see. I thought maybe a dog or cat had been injured. It wasn't a dog or cat." Brian turned suddenly and ran a few steps back toward the edge of the field. He bent over and vomited.

"Brian and Crystal were friends," his father said quietly, as though an explanation were needed. "And she was so young."

Maggie nodded. Drew was sitting next to Amy, rocking her gently in his arms. The soldier came up to Maggie.

"I don't believe we've met," he said, extending his hand. "Drew says you're an old friend of Amy's. I'm glad you're here."

"Thank you," said Maggie. "And you are?" His uniform certainly looked authentic.

"Tom Colby. I live next door." He pointed in the general direction of the house just visible on the other side of the high grasses. The high grasses where Crystal lay.

"You're Shirley's brother." Maggie suddenly connected. "The Civil War reenactor."

"Yes."

"You had me a for a moment. Are you with the Twentieth Maine?"

"No, ma'am." Even under the circumstances Tom straightened up and smiled slightly. "I'm with Company D of Berdan's Second Regiment."

"A sharpshooter."

His eyes opened in amazement. "Almost no one knows about Berdan's Second anymore. Are you a Civil War buff?"

"No; just an antiques dealer and American civilization professor. Tom, you were here with Drew when Brian discovered Amy. What happened?"

"I don't rightly know. Drew and I had just pulled in. We went to work on some local graveyards this afternoon. We had been to one of them before, and I had done some research and verified that three of the men buried there had fought in Maine regiments."

"In the Civil War."

He nodded. "When I find that, I usually try to have a quiet ceremony for them, after I clean off the grave and record the information for anyone seeking relatives. I put a small flag near their stone to honor them. When I can, I like to wear my uniform. Seems fitting."

"So then you and Drew came back here."

"I'd left my truck around the other side of the barn; we'd taken his Jeep. As we pulled into the driveway, Brian came tearing around the side of the barn. We figured out pretty fast we needed help. I stayed with Brian until Giles came down from the roof, and Drew called 911. I was just calling my sister to say I'd be home a little late. The police got here just before you and Amy did."

"Did you see Crystal?"

"I didn't touch her or nothing. I did go to see if what the boy said was true."

"And?"

"She was dead, sure enough. I'd say for some time. A body in a field attracts all sorts of—"

"That's all right, Tom," Maggie stopped him. "I believe you. But how did she die? And why was she over there?" Maggie looked at the area. They were in back of the Douglas barn. Farther down to her left she saw an open stone path. "Is that the path to your house?"

"Sure is. Been there for a hundred years, most likely. This was the old Brewer home, you know, and Captain Eben's cousin built the house I own about 1870. That's when the path was first laid. Shirley and I kept it clear. She used to come over each day to check on Charlotte. Until last winter, of course."

When Charlotte had died. But Crystal wasn't anywhere near that path. Nor was she near the much less formal path Amy and Maggie had followed yesterday between the Douglas home and the Porters'. The path to Tom and Shirley's house went north, paralleling the river. The path they had followed yesterday had led east, across the field beyond the barn. Crystal's body lay somewhere in between.

"How?"

Tom shook his head. "Couldn't tell right off. I didn't touch her. Didn't want to. She could have fallen, I guess. The field is pretty uneven out there. Hard to tell what happened. As I said, the creatures hadn't left her alone."

Maggie shuddered. She didn't want to think about the condition of Crystal's young body, which she had seen alive and full of life just yesterday. The policeman was on his cell phone. The whole scene suddenly reminded her horribly of the antiques fair last Memorial Day. The fair where there had been two murders. The fair where she had met Will.

Will. Will was invited for dinner, with his elderly aunt. This was no time for visits.

"Tom, I'm going to make a phone call. I'll be right back." She stopped briefly to tell Amy and Drew what she was doing. Neither paid attention to her. Their minds were far removed from an evening barbecue.

In the house she dialed the number in her wallet and let it ring ten times. No answer. Darn. And no answering machine, either. She couldn't even leave a message.

As she walked back outside, a Maine State Trooper's car pulled in. Reinforcements. Within minutes crime scene tape was circling a large section of the field, and pictures were being taken. The ambulance was pulling out. It was clear the services of its crew were not needed.

All was quiet. Everyone stood in groups as though waiting for a daguerreotypist to capture them. Brian and Giles Leary. Amy and Drew. The Union soldier. And Maggie. The deputy who had arrived first and the two state troopers he had called were out in the field, carefully checking the ground. No one else was allowed near. Finally one of the state troopers came toward them.

"Nothing much more we can do here, folks. The girl's dead. You all know that. We don't know why, so we're securing the site. I've called for someone in the medical examiner's office to come and take a look, then remove her body. They'll probably take her to Augusta to take a look at her." He hesitated and turned toward Brian. "You found her. You know who she is?"

"Crystal Porter," he said softly. "We go to high school together. We were friends. Good friends."

"That the girl went missing last night?"

"She lives with her mother, up on Egret Point. Over there." Brian pointed. "Her mom was real worried about her."

The trooper's voice was soft. "We'll be sending someone to tell her mother. And your name is?"

"Brian Leary."

"Age?"

"Eighteen."

"And how did you happen to find her, Brian?"

"My dad and I were doing some roof work for the Douglases. Up there." He pointed at the ell. "The crows were making a fuss down in the field. I went over to see why. And I saw her."

If possible, Brian got even paler.

"Did you touch her body, Brian?"

"No! I yelled, and ran back to get my dad. To get help. I found Mr. Douglas and Mr. Colby. They were just getting in. Mr. Douglas called the police."

"And when did you last see Crystal Porter alive?"

"Yesterday, around noon, I guess. She was in the kitchen fixing some things for Mrs. Douglas when I went down to get a glass of water."

"Did you talk with her?"

"Not much. We were going over to Brunswick to see a movie last night with a couple of the other kids, and I told her I'd pick her up around six o'clock. She said she was finishing up pretty soon and would be going home. She'd see me at six."

"You didn't have any arguments, or disagreements?"

"No, sir!"

"And did she see you at six?"

"She didn't come home. I was there at six. She hadn't called or anything. I drove around looking for her all evening, and called all our friends, but no one had heard from her or seen her."

"Did you see her leave here?"

Brian looked at his father. "Dad and I were working on the back part of the ell roof, like we were today. Crystal would have gone out the back door and walked across the lawn and field on the other side. If I'd stood up or something, then I might have seen her. But I don't remember doing that. And we did leave earlier than usual yesterday. We needed more roofing paper."

"What about you, Mr. Leary?"

Giles shook his head. "I don't remember seeing her leave either. People did come and go—Mr. and Mrs. Douglas, and Mrs. Douglas's friend, here—so I heard cars. But I don't remember seeing or hearing Crystal. But, of course, I wasn't paying special attention. She was here most afternoons."

"How about you folks?" He looked at the rest of them. "Mrs. Douglas? Mr. Douglas? What time did Crystal leave here yesterday?"

Amy shook her head. "She was here until at least three o'clock. I told her she could go after she'd finished cleaning out a cabinet in the kitchen. I was in my study, and I didn't watch her. I'd say she left shortly after that."

"Mr. Douglas?"

"I was upstairs. I don't know when she left. Crystal's hours were Amy's business."

"Did you happen to notice, Ms. . . . ?"

"Maggie Summer. I'm visiting the Douglases. I was resting at about three, upstairs in the guest room. I didn't hear or see anything." Maggie crossed her fingers that the detective wouldn't ask her when she'd seen Crystal before that. But he didn't. She needed to talk to Amy before this situation got more complicated. She wouldn't lie to the police.

"Thank you all," the detective said. A man and a woman walked around the corner of the barn and he raised his hand toward them. "That's the medical examiner's team. I need to work with them. I'll be in touch with all of you." He hesitated. "At this point it's too early to tell what happened to Crystal Porter. Do any of you know whether she was involved with drugs or alcohol?"

Silence.

Amy said, "I never noticed anything, Detective. And she worked here most weekdays this summer."

"Brian?"

Brian glanced at his father in embarrassment. "I've seen her have a beer, sometimes. A lot of the kids do it. But I've never seen her take anything else."

"Okay. If any of you remember something that might be helpful, you call me." He handed out his cards. Detective Nicholas Strait. "I'll probably be back to talk with all of you as soon as we know what questions need to be asked." He looked at Brian. "I'll talk to the girl's mother." He went over to the two newcomers and started pointing toward the field.

"Why don't you two pack up your gear and go home," Drew said to Giles and Brian. "It's getting late anyway."

"I have to go too," said Tom. "I promised I'd get dinner started for Shirley and be there when the bus brings the kids home from day camp. Thanks for the help at the cemetery, Drew."

Brian and Giles began picking up the tools that had been left on the ground, and the rest of them went toward the front of the house.

Will Brewer and Great-Aunt Nettie were just pulling in.

"Oh, Lord," said Amy. "We have dinner guests."

Chapter 11

—❧—

Untitled fashion plate from Gentleman's
Magazine, *April 1852. Hand-colored steel
engraving of elegant man and woman in
outdoor afternoon attire with two small
children, one dressed in the popular tartan
plaid of the period. 7 x 9 inches. Price: $70.*

Maggie was the first to reach the car. "Will, I tried
to call you. There's a problem. I don't think this is a
good time for you and your aunt to be here."

But Drew was right behind her. "Nonsense,
Maggie. We can't just stand around feeling de-
pressed. Life has to go on." As Will looked ques-
tioningly at Maggie, Drew reached out his hand.
"Drew Douglas. You must be Maggie's friend Will.
We're glad you could come."

Amy then took charge. "I'm glad to meet you.
This is a little awkward, and we haven't had a
chance to get dinner started. But we all need to eat,
and having company would make this evening easier
for us."

Will still hesitated, looking to Maggie, and at the

two police vehicles and the car from the medical examiner's office.

"If Drew and Amy say it's fine, then it will be. And your aunt?"

Everyone turned to see the tiny woman sitting in the front seat of the car. Will hurried over to open the door for her, a gesture she had clearly been waiting for. "Aunt Nettie, we seem to have caught these people at a difficult time. But they are insisting we stay. Would that be all right with you?"

"It will be just fine, if you introduce me," declared Aunt Nettie in a clear voice. "At my age where and what I eat isn't a quarter as important as who the company is I'm eating it with."

"This is Drew Douglas," Will said, as Drew bent down and shook Nettie's hand, "and this is Nettie Brewer, my aunt."

"Might as well call me Aunt Nettie. Half the town does already. And which one of these people is Maggie?"

Maggie actually blushed as she stepped forward. "I'm Maggie. And I'm pleased to meet you. This is my friend Amy Douglas."

"Well, now that everyone knows everyone else, let's get down to brass tacks. What's this problem everyone's looking so glum about? What are all these police cars doing in your driveway?"

"Maybe it's something they don't want to talk about." Will looked from Drew to Amy and back again and tried for levity. "When I talked with Maggie yesterday, she said you might have ghosts in the house. You all look as though you've just seen one."

There was silence.

Maggie hesitated, but Amy nodded slightly. It wouldn't be a secret for long. Having decided to have dinner together, they couldn't not mention what had happened. She hoped Aunt Nettie wouldn't be too upset. You never knew how older people would react at the thought of death. Especially the death of someone so young. And a relative of some sort too, Maggie remembered.

"Aunt Nettie, this afternoon the body of one of Amy and Drew's neighbors was found in the field behind the barn. The one between this house and the one where Shirley Steele and Tom Colby live."

"The matter's with the police now. We really shouldn't be talking about it," Drew added quickly.

Will ignored Drew and looked at Maggie. "Maggie seems to get herself involved with the strangest situations. Who died?"

"Crystal Porter."

Aunt Nettie gasped. "Rachel's little girl? Dead? How?"

"We don't know. She'd been helping out at our house, and she left yesterday afternoon to walk home. She never got there," said Amy.

"But her house isn't in the direction of Tom and Shirley's," Aunt Nettie said immediately. "What was she doing over behind your barn?"

"We don't know. We don't really know anything," said Maggie. "I tried to call and suggest we cancel tonight, but no one answered."

"Will was doing some errands for me, and I don't answer the phone unless I'm expecting a call," said Aunt Nettie. She smoothed out the skirt of her cotton Black Watch plaid dress. "And I'm sorry about little Crystal, but she was conceived in error, and perhaps it was God's way." She looked around at the startled faces of those listening to her. "What are we going to have for dinner?"

Will and Aunt Nettie had brought two bottles of burgundy and a blueberry pie for dessert. They all sipped wine while Drew and Will started the grill and Aunt Nettie and Maggie helped Amy in the kitchen. Maggie cut the steak in cubes and marinated it in dressing. Finding enough green peppers, onions, and tomatoes to make shish kebab was not hard to manage, and Amy added some garlic to a package of white rice. "Voilà! Dinner."

The early-evening wind blowing across the river was cool. After Aunt Nettie asked to borrow a sweater Amy decided to serve dinner on the slightly rickety kitchen table.

"We have so many things to do in this house," she chattered, clearly eager to keep the conversation away from more weighty subjects. "The kitchen has wonderful cabinets, but so little counter space. We want to find an old pine table, and some chairs to match. Our apartment in New York was full, but the furniture we had there hardly fills two rooms in this house! And we love the old fireplaces. Before next winter I want to get the chimneys lined so we can have fires in at least the living room and the master bedroom."

"I wonder what condition the old kitchen is in," said Aunt Nettie.

"Well, you can see," said Amy, looking around.

"I don't mean this room. I mean the *old* kitchen." Aunt Nettie spoke definitively.

"Isn't this the old kitchen?"

"One of them, of course," acknowledged Aunt Nettie, speaking as if she were educating a slow child. "Where we're sitting is actually part of the oldest kitchen. But when Captain Brewer moved the house over from the island in 1833, they closed it off. It was too old-fashioned. Just a fireplace; no stove. The new 1833 kitchen was in the ell."

"Where?" asked Drew. "There's a chimney there, and a brick wall. I didn't think of it as a kitchen though."

"It was the kitchen," Aunt Nettie said. "It was the kitchen until Charlotte inherited the house in, I think it was 1931. She's the one who decided to use this room as the kitchen again, and modernized it. She said she'd fix it up good enough to last until she died. And she did."

They all looked around. Certainly the 1931 appliances were still there. And operating in some sort of fashion. "They made good stoves in those days," agreed Amy. "And refrigerators."

"Just as good as the old iceboxes," agreed Aunt Nettie. "I just never understood why Charlotte used this end of the kitchen for her appliances when she could have used the old part."

"The old part?" Drew looked around. They were sitting at one end of the kitchen. The end where the cabinets were, and the sink. At the other end of the long room was the door to Amy's study, and the door to the outside. And two blank walls.

"Over there." Aunt Nettie pointed at the empty wall beyond the cabinets. "That's where the old fireplace was, before 1833. I remember my grandmother telling me they boarded it up before they moved the house. They put the new stove in the ell."

"In 1833," said Maggie. "So the original 1774 fireplace is still there? Behind the wall?"

"So my grandmother always maintained," said Aunt Nettie. "I told Charlotte, when she was fixing up the place, but she didn't want anything old. She liked new things. She's the one put the linoleum over the brick hearth."

"There's a brick hearth?" Amy started to get excited.

Will had already risen and gone over to the wall and begun tapping on it.

Maggie smiled at him. "An old fireplace! What a temptation. Will specializes in old fireplace and kitchen equipment, you know."

"Do you know anything about the construction of these old houses?" Drew had joined Will at the wall.

"I have a degree in construction. I taught woodworking for eighteen years before deciding to go into antiques full-time."

"Do you think we could do it? Take the wall down?"

Will tapped again, high and low. "I'd be willing to bet there are beams here, supporting part of the original structure, but we could work around them." He reached down to the flowered brown linoleum. As he touched the edge, a small piece of it broke off in his hands. He looked at Drew questioningly.

"Go right ahead," said Drew. "Here, I'll help you. That linoleum had to go sometime anyway." They both got down on their knees and started breaking off pieces of the flooring. Clouds of dust rose immediately.

"Look!" Drew pointed. "There are bricks under here!"

"Just as I said. They wouldn't have disappeared in only seventy or eighty years." Aunt Nettie sneezed. "But taking up any more of that linoleum's going to be a messy job."

"Tomorrow?" Drew asked, grinning.

"Tomorrow!" agreed Will.

Crystal's death had not been mentioned in several hours. Not that anyone had forgotten.

Chapter 12

—◇—

Malay Cock. *Harrison Weir (1824–1906).*
Lithograph of rooster, published by Leighton
Brothers, c. 1855. Weir was a noted British
animal and poultry painter and illustrator
whose work was extremely accurate to nature.
He was also a friend of Charles Darwin's.
7 x 10.5 inches. Price: $60.

Maggie woke to the sound of the telephone. She glanced at her bedside clock: 1:30. The ringing stopped. It wasn't her house; the telephone wasn't in her room. But houses built in 1774 weren't insulated. Sound travels well in them. The telephone rang again at 2:00. At 2:45. And at 4:00. By the time it rang at 5:15, Maggie gave up on sleep.

Assuming that there had not been five emergencies, the mysterious caller must be back. And if she couldn't sleep down the hall from the telephone, Amy and Drew, with a phone in their bedroom, must have gotten very little rest.

She decided five-thirty was morning and pulled a bathrobe over the faded orange college T-shirt she used as a nightshirt. Maybe it wasn't time for bacon and eggs, but the craving for a diet cola was too much to resist. To her surprise, she wasn't the first one up. Drew was sitting at the kitchen table, sipping a large cup of coffee.

"Sorry about the phone calls. They woke you too?"

Maggie nodded. "Were they the hang-up calls Amy told me about?"

"Yup. Every one. I grabbed them as fast as I could, but no one was there. I finally turned the ringer off on the bedroom phone and came down here to turn this ringer off too, and the thought of coffee was too overpowering to ignore. Some for you?"

"Actually, I'm more the diet cola type. But I happen to know there are a couple of bottles in the refrigerator." She poured herself a glass and drank deeply. "There. That was almost worth missing sleep."

"There sure hasn't been a lot of sleeping done in this house recently."

"Not even mentioning your mysterious caller, and now Crystal's death. You and Amy have a lot going on in your lives."

"I don't know how much she's told you, but moving here hasn't been the stress-free experience we had both imagined. But we love this house, and we love Maine. I'm sure we'll get the house in order, banish whatever ghosts are around, and be able to re-create ourselves as normal people." Drew took a deep sip of his coffee. "It was Amy's idea to move, you know. I had my doubts. But I still think we can make it work, if only she would relax a little."

Relax? When her house was filled with ghosts, her drunken husband was sleeping with a teenaged neighbor, when she couldn't meet his need for a baby, and they had found a body in the backyard? No reason she could think of why Amy wouldn't be able to relax.

"Amy's always been so focused," continued Drew. "She's always known exactly what she wanted to do, who she wanted to be with, and where she wanted to go. I've never been that way. Oh, I worked hard enough to get through college and get a good job. I made money in the nineties, but who didn't? I never really felt it was part of a long-term plan. It was just what needed to be done right then. Amy has never eaten a sautéed shrimp without knowing exactly how it fit into her long-term plan for life."

"Amy told me you want children."

"That's one of the things we agreed about when we first met, long before we decided to get married. We each have our own reasons. I was adopted. I have a wonderful family. Sometimes I wonder what my life might have been like if I hadn't been adopted by them. I can't see anyone giving me a better life than the parents I had. I want to be able to give that sort of life, or maybe even a better one, to my children. And Amy had a rough childhood, so she felt the same, but for other reasons."

"Amy had a rough childhood? In Short Hills, New Jersey?"

"Well, I'm sure she's told you that her father died when she was little, and her mother remarried." Drew looked at Maggie as though she should know something else. "She and her stepfather had some issues."

Funny. Amy had never talked about her stepfather.

"Anyway, we both want children. But so far we haven't had any luck. Amy always wants to do things the right way. You know her. She's the sort who would never substitute margarine for butter in a recipe."

"Like your beautiful nursery upstairs. Perfect."

"Exactly. No baby, but a perfect nursery. That was one of Amy's long-term plans. My mother always said that we should wait, that it was bad luck to buy infant things before you had a baby. She didn't buy anything for me even though she knew she was going to adopt. She and Dad have a great story about stopping on the way home from the hospital where they picked me up and buying a crib." Drew smiled. "Babies don't care what kind of crib they sleep in. They care that someone holds them when they cry, and feeds them when they're hungry, and changes their diapers when they need it. But Amy didn't see it that way. She wanted everything to be just the way she'd always dreamed it." Drew sighed. "So here we are, in the perfect state, in the perfect house, with the perfect nursery."

For the perfect baby, thought Maggie.

"And now Amy even says she hears a baby crying in the house. She talks so much about it I even thought I heard it one night."

"Drew, I heard it too. The night before last."

Drew got up abruptly. "Then she's got us all going crazy." He looked at the wall clock. "It's six. We might as well get on with the day. I'm going to take a shower and then drive to the hardware store. Will said we could use some crowbars, and I don't have any. Why would I have needed a crowbar in New York City?" Drew shook his head. "The Waymouth hardware store opens at seven, so I'll get there and home before Will arrives at eight or eight-thirty. I'd better get some more vacuum cleaner bags too. If we're going to take up the linoleum and pull down part of a wall, there's going to be a lot of dust and dirt."

"For sure. I'll finish my cola, and claim the shower after you."

"Amy usually sleeps until eight or so. Why don't I bring back some doughnuts and sausage and we'll have breakfast then. If Will arrives, there'll be plenty for him too."

"Sounds good." Maggie sat and sipped her cola as she listened to Drew's footsteps going upstairs. There were always two sides to a story, two sides to a marriage. What was really happening in this one? Maggie shook her head, as though to get her thoughts in order. It was none of her business what was happening inside this marriage. Unless it affected someone else.

Why did she keep thinking of Crystal, that beautiful young girl whose body had been lying in a field not far from this house? This house that everyone agreed was perfect. Except for a few little problems. The paint. The roof. The phone calls. The fire. And now—the death. How had Crystal died? Would they learn that today?

Maggie shivered. Thank goodness it was going to be a beautiful day. The sun's warmth would be welcome. She finished her diet cola and decided to try for a short nap before her shower.

The next sound she heard was Amy's voice. "Maggie! Maggie! Come quickly!"

Maggie shook her head. Seven-fifteen. She had drifted into a deeper sleep than she had planned.

"Maggie, please! Wake up!" Her door swung open. Amy's sleep-tangled hair was around her face, and she was still wearing her nightgown. "Didn't you hear the crash? There's been an accident down at the curve below the house. I can't see the car, but I can see the end of one tree that's down. I called 911, and they're coming. But someone should at least stand and make sure no other cars zoom around that corner right now!"

Maggie was already throwing on a light sweater and climbing into jeans. "Drew went to the hardware store."

"How do you know that?"

"Five-thirty coffee and cola break in the kitchen."

Amy's expression was one of open doubt.

"I didn't seduce the man, Amy. He drank coffee; I drank cola. We didn't even share a beverage. I couldn't sleep after all the phone calls."

"Sorry. The phone calls were awful."

"Why aren't you dressed?"

Amy looked down at herself in recognition. "Right. I need to get dressed."

Maggie shook her head. "I'll go ahead and make sure no power lines are down. Stop cars." She ran downstairs.

Outside on the lawn her leather sandals slipped on the damp morning grass. The Douglas home was on top of a steep hill; the grading to the road was almost ninety degrees at the corner. She wouldn't attempt it. She ran to the end of the driveway and turned down the hill toward the curve in the road. She saw the car almost immediately. Clearly it had headed down the hill and not made the turn; it had hit a tree instead.

Clearly it was Drew's Jeep.

Chapter 13

—⁓—

*A Fair Chauffeur, 1900 lithograph by Howard
Chandler Christy (1872–1952). Published by
Charles Scribner's Sons, New York, 1906.
Woman behind the wheel of early open
automobile, with man seated beside her.
Christy created "The Christy Girl" for leading
publications of his day and during the 1920s
painted portraits of world celebrities. From his
folio* The American Girl. *7 x 9.5 inches.
Price: $65.*

The ambulance and the police car got there almost
simultaneously with Maggie. By the time Amy
arrived the road had been blocked off, a tow truck
called, and the ambulance team was maneuvering
Drew onto a backboard. The Jeep had hit the tree
and its body was folded back toward the driver's
seat.

Amy hovered, wringing her hands, as she tried to
stay out of the crew's way. "I'm fine, honey," Drew
called softly, and clearly with some effort. "Don't
worry."

"You're not fine. Just stay quiet and let us do the work," said the big woman pushing a board under Drew's buttocks.

"We meet again." It was Deputy Colby, the same officer who had been at the Porters' home two nights before and had given Maggie and Amy a ride home. "Any idea about what happened?"

"Drew was going to the hardware store." Maggie looked at the situation. "And, clearly, for some reason he didn't make the corner." She paused. "He couldn't have been going very fast. He had just driven out of the driveway." She pointed up the hill perhaps twenty-five feet.

"He doesn't seem to have used his brakes at all." Deputy Colby looked at the pavement.

There were no skid marks.

"He was lucky to hit that tree, actually. If he hadn't, he might have ended up in the river."

Maggie shuddered. Good thing Amy hadn't heard that. The medical team had Drew almost all the way out of the Jeep now. He was pale, and one leg was at a funny angle, but he was conscious.

"Are you in pain?" Amy asked, following alongside the stretcher.

"Sure am," answered Drew. "Strangest thing. I put my foot on the brakes and the pedal went all the way to the floor. Nothing happened. Nothing. The Jeep was fine yesterday."

"I'll have a body shop check out the brakes," Deputy Colby assured him. "Do you want to go with your husband in the ambulance, ma'am?"

"Yes, please." Amy was already climbing in.

"Where are you going?" Maggie asked as they started closing the doors. "I'll meet you there."

"Rocky Shore," answered the woman as the door slammed in Maggie's face. A tow truck was making its way down the hill.

"I'll leave a message later about the car. Their insurance company will need to know where it is." Deputy Colby made another note. "Do you know how to get to the hospital?"

"I have a friend coming." Maggie checked her watch. "Anytime now. He'll know."

"Good."

"Have they found out how Crystal Porter died? The girl they found yesterday afternoon?"

"I know who she is. Not too many people get murdered around here."

"Murdered!" Maggie stepped back. She had assumed something freakish had killed Crystal. A weak heart. An unintentional drug overdose. A snake bite.

Not murder.

"Kind of hard to hit yourself on the head," said Deputy Colby. "Can't give you any more details, of course, but sure didn't look like an accident or sui-cide. Medical examiner's office has the body. They may know more later today." He looked at her. "You folks are all from New York, right?"

"Amy and Drew are from New York. I'm from New Jersey."

"Wherever. You don't plan on going back there in the immediate future, right?"

"What?" Maggie stopped for a minute. Of

course. A girl had been murdered on Amy and Drew's land. They were all suspects.

"No one's going anywhere, Officer. Except to the hospital."

"Good. Because Detective Strait from the state police will probably be looking to talk with you all later today, once we get a couple of other issues ironed out." Maggie could hear a car horn honking on the other side of the curve. The deputy had closed the road, and someone wanted to travel it.

"We'll be here," Maggie assured him. "Or at the hospital. No flights to Brazil on the agenda."

He looked at her sideways. "Was that a joke, lady?"

She nodded.

"Just checking. 'Cause it wasn't funny. This isn't New York City. People don't get murdered every day in the state of Maine. Here we take murder seriously."

Chapter 14

___◦◦◦___

Osprey (or Fishing Hawk) Egg, *lithograph from* Nests and Eggs of British Birds *by the Reverend F. O. Morris, London, 1879. One large white egg, speckled with irregular brown marks. 6.75 x 10 inches. Price: $55.*

Maggie sat on the porch steps waiting for Will, another glass of diet cola in her hand. She probably drank too much of this stuff. A minor vice.

The morning mists were beginning to rise. The scene looked like a slighter softer and grayer version of a Monet painting. Herring gulls were circling; perhaps one of the lobstermen had just finished checking his traps. There was the loud hum of a boat on the river, and an occasional car drove by on the road below, but the sound of chickadees in the apple tree was louder than any other noise right now. Queen Anne's lace in the high grasses bordered the lawn. Goldenrod was beginning to bloom.

A perfect August morning in Maine.

The ambulance had left. The tow truck had

removed Drew's car. The deputy had made a very obvious point of writing down the license numbers of both Amy's and Maggie's cars before he had left.

Today Drew and Will had planned to take up the cracked kitchen linoleum and try to remove the wall Aunt Nettie swore was in front of the original kitchen fireplace. Maggie had privately thought of taking off for an hour or two to check out an antiquarian-book store she'd seen in Waymouth. Her trip to Maine was to have been one for relaxing, and adding to the inventory. Not for murders and accidents. Not to speak of ghosts and phone calls in the night.

Will should be here anytime now. She ran a hand through her hair. Had she even taken the time to brush it this morning? Probably not. Her hands automatically smoothed the long, wavy strands and began braiding them. She needed to get to the hospital to see if there was anything she could do for Drew or Amy. Why wasn't Will here?

A sudden flush of anger hit her. Why wasn't he here when she needed him? He hadn't been there when Michael had been in an accident. There had been no one to help when she had gotten that call, when she had taken Michael's things to the hospital. She alone had heard that Michael's leg was healing. His leg was healing, but a stroke had killed him.

This was crazy. She hadn't even known Will when Michael had had his accident eight months ago. It had nothing to do with today. Or with Drew. Michael had crashed his car because he'd had a stroke. Drew couldn't have had a stroke. She was stressing out, between the past two days and little sleep. Was it only four days ago she'd been doing an antiques show in Provincetown and sharing a glass of sherry with Gussie? She hadn't even sorted through her cash box since then, or sent customers' checks to her bank. She needed to do that. Today, if possible.

Why did Drew's brakes fail?

Will's RV came around the curve and turned into the driveway. Last night he must have been driving his aunt's car. Will always carried his inventory in his portable motel, just in case. Just as Maggie's van was filled with cartons and portfolios. Antiques dealers! Insurance companies hated them: inventory values changed with the seasons, and even those with shops were constantly transporting valuable stock to and from antiques shows. Antiques dealers were not reckless drivers. One accident could not only total their vehicle, it could eliminate their business inventory.

She walked toward the RV. "Good morning! Do you know where Rocky Shore Hospital is?"

"Are you sick?"

"Drew was in a car accident about half an hour ago. The ambulance took him and Amy to Rocky Shore. I said we'd meet them there."

"How bad?"

"He was talking. His leg didn't look good."

"So you saw him. Where was the accident?"

"At the corner." Maggie pointed. "The one you just came around."

"He must have been going too fast and missed the curve. That's a bad corner. Where had he been so early in the morning?"

"He wasn't coming home. He was on his way to the hardware store to get a crowbar."

Will frowned. "How could he crash if he was on his way out? He would have just put on the gas to get the car started!"

"He said his brakes wouldn't work."

"Get in. We're taking a drive." Will drove carefully along the twists and turns that took the road along the river. "Maggie Summer, you're an amazing woman. Whenever I'm with you, things seem to happen. Those murders at the fair last spring. And now a dead girl and an accident."

"Not just a dead girl."

"Not *just* a dead girl?"

"The deputy who came to check out the accident said Crystal was murdered."

"Shit." Will swerved the motor home slightly as his mind momentarily left the road. "What else did he say to cheer our day?"

"Not much. Except that Amy and Drew and I are all suspects, since she was found on their property."

Will shook his head. "A few years back I imagine some folks in town wished her mother, Rachel, had disappeared. But not Crystal."

"There are crazy people in the world, and sometimes they hurt people." Maggie hesitated. "What did everyone have against Rachel?" Rachel seemed so quiet, so matronly; how could someone like that have provoked anger?

Will read her mind. "Remember? I told you. Rachel didn't always look or act the way she does now. She was, shall we say, very popular with a lot of young men when she wasn't too much older than Crystal."

Maggie nodded. "So she was popular. The young fellows in town were competing for her?"

"Not exactly. Her favors were pretty liberally distributed." Will grimaced. "She was an embarrassment to the family."

"Well, I guess Rachel calmed down."

"After she got pregnant with Crystal. She lived at home with her folks at first. They weren't really happy about that, but they didn't kick her out. Then her grandmother died and must have left her enough money to buy the house that she and Crystal live in. She works over at the library, you know. Never got a degree or anything, but she knows the books better than anyone."

"And her social life toned down?"

"Way down. She didn't go out with anyone for years, that I heard of. Until Johnny Brent. When you saw her yesterday at the auction, didn't she say something about Johnny?"

"That he'd asked her to help out."

"That I don't know about. Walter English owns the auction gallery so far as I know. Has for years. Inherited it from his dad, who was also an auctioneer."

"Is there anyone in Waymouth or Madoc whose family hasn't been here for generations?"

Will grinned. "Not many. Keeps things cozy."

Maggie was quiet as they drove through Waymouth, and down Route 1. "Poor Rachel. Then she didn't have anyone but Crystal. She was so upset when Amy and I were there the other night."

"You and Amy visited them?"

"Crystal hadn't come home on time, so Amy thought it would be a good idea for the two of us to follow the path from Amy's house to Crystal's, to see if she'd sprained her ankle or something. We didn't see her." Had Crystal been lying in that field, so close by, when they had taken that walk up to her house on Egret Point? Maggie shuddered slightly. If only they had looked in the other field.

"I wonder when she died."

"Deputy Colby didn't share that with me."

"We're here." Will pulled into a long driveway that ended in a circular drive in front of a low sand-stone building. "You get out and check the emergency room. I'll park this monster in the lot and meet you there."

Maggie nodded. Signs to the emergency room pointed to the left.

Amy was sitting on an orange plastic chair, holding a white Styrofoam cup. "Maggie! I'm so glad you're here."

"Will drove me. He's parking his RV. How's Drew?"

"They're doing full-body X rays. The doctors

think his head hit the side window and got a few bruises. He might have a slight concussion, but the major damage is to his right leg and foot. Exactly what is broken and how badly they don't know yet." Amy brought the cup to her lips and then, realizing it was empty, crumpled it and tossed it neatly into a nearby wastebasket.

"How are you doing?"

"I'm okay. For someone who had a body found in their back field last night and their husband injured in an automobile accident this morning, I'd say I'm doing pretty well."

Maggie smiled. "I'd agree." She hesitated. Should she tell Amy that Crystal had been murdered? There was no reason to disturb her further just now. She'd have to know later, but by then at least she'd have some idea about Drew's condition.

Will joined them a few minutes later, and Amy repeated what she knew about Drew. "It looks as though I'm going to be here for most of the day," she added. "And I'm doing all right. They have a coffee shop nearby, and I have my cell phone with me. Why don't you two go antiquing? I'd just as soon stay here quietly. You can give me your cell phone number, Will. If anything happens, or when I need a ride home, I'll call you."

Maggie and Will looked at each other. "Maybe we could just do a few shops in Waymouth," Maggie said. "What do you think, Will?"

"For sure I don't think this is the day to take your kitchen apart, Amy." He looked at Maggie. "I suspect you'd like to see the antiquarian-book store."

Maggie nodded. "I'd hoped to."

"Then the two of you go. I'm fine, and they seem to be taking good care of Drew. After the last twenty-four hours, what else bad can happen?"

Chapter 15

———— ✺ ————

Behind the Scenes—How Stage Effects Are Produced. *Unusual 1875 wood engraving showing "behind the scenes" theatrical work, including men producing "Shooting Thunder Bolts," "Stormy Winds," and "A Shower of Rain." 8.75 x 11.75 inches. Price: $55.*

Maggie and Will spent the rest of the morning avoiding talk of the Brewer family, or Crystal, or even Drew's accident.

"That's five shops, and no buys for either of us," said Will as they left a small, red barn painted with a big ANTIQUES! CHEAP! sign. "But we haven't exactly been in shops featuring superlative pieces."

"Most of the stuff we've seen falls more into the 'collectible' or 'vintage' category," agreed Maggie.

"I'd say most of it falls more into the 'used junk' category," said Will.

"Only when junk is spelled *j-u-n-q-u-e,* of course."

"Of course."

"But you never know where we might find some-

thing. And we're looking for such different things."
Maggie climbed up into passenger seat of the RV.
"Although that last place was a total waste of time.
Who told that guy that two-year-old *Time* maga-
zines and bottles of sea glass were antiques?"

"Probably the same person who crocheted those
pot holders in the shape of lighthouses. I'm surprised you didn't snap up a whole pile to give to fellow professors for Christmas gifts."

"I was tempted. But I managed to squelch the
impulse," Maggie answered. "What about that
Victorian house I remember seeing not far from Cut
'n' Curl? Didn't it have an ANTIQUES MALL sign on
it?"

"That's one of Walter English's side operations."

"The auctioneer?"

"Right. Lots of dealers are his customers, of
course, so several years ago he got the idea of making money on both sides of the balance sheet."

"So he auctions goods to dealers, they put the
items in his mall, and he takes a percentage of the
sales?"

"That's it. And, of course, he has someone there
to answer questions about disposing of a collection
or a special item. He even runs his 'free appraisal
days' out of the mall."

Maggie shook her head. "In New Jersey there
are antiques malls. But most of them are co-ops.
Each dealer has his or her own area, almost like a
small shop. In addition to paying rent for their
space they volunteer to work in the mall one day
every week or two. That way customers always

have a few dealers on hand who can talk about the merchandise. And it saves the cost of sales staff."

"Have you ever taken space in a mall?"

"No. I've thought about it. But the co-op places would be hard for me because I have a regular job during the week and am off doing shows a lot of weekends. And prints are hard to display in cases. You?"

"I just started last winter. I use two malls. One in Buffalo, near home, and one in Westchester, where I share a booth with another dealer. I travel back and forth in New York State often enough that I can replenish the inventories in both places, or switch them around. I pay extra not to volunteer in the malls since I need to be free to travel to shows. Malls are a lot more convenient than having to be at a shop all the time, and less stressful than doing shows every weekend. I do almost thirty shows a year as it is. But now that I'm trying to make a living at antiques I needed to check out all possibilities for sales. The only major sales outlet I haven't tried yet is eBay."

"I haven't gone that route yet myself. But I know two dealers who've stopped doing shows and closed their shops and just sell on the Internet now. Let me know if the malls turn out to be good sales outlets for you."

"I'm monitoring them pretty closely. There are times this business is exhausting. But I got tired of teaching and never having enough time for the antiques. Somewhere there must be a middle line."

"I enjoy teaching, so I don't mind limiting the

antiques to the dozen or so shows I do each year. And I do a little mail order to old customers, and the usual 'by appointment' sales. I have several New Jersey and New York decorators who've discovered my prints and become a good source of income. If I can keep what they're looking for in stock!"

"What's the big trend in decorator prints this year?"

"Botanicals and fruit are always popular. Birds are a favorite. And I can always sell prints of eggs. They fit in both traditional and modern decors. And at the moment cows are out; butterflies are in."

"And, I suppose, hunting prints for the gentleman's study."

"The gun lobby has changed that a bit. Hunting and fishing prints used to be popular. Then hunting became less popular; fly-fishing was the popular sport. Recently I've noticed that although fish still do sell, prints of golf and baseball are more popular than those of fishing. But it varies by the year. And, I suspect, by the area of the country. Golfing prints, especially those done by Arthur Burdett Frost, are in demand. Lots of people golf, and Frost lived in Convent Station, New Jersey, from 1880 until 1907, so some people in Jersey collect his work because it has a local connection. When I do New York shows, though, people could care less about golf. They're looking for prints of dogs or cats. Or tigers, if they went to Princeton! Everyone has their angles. I have one customer who is collecting A. B. Frost prints just because the artist was a distant cousin of the poet Robert Frost."

"It's the same regional differences as with my kitchen and fireplace equipment. In the city I sell Victorian fireplace sets, or large brass pans or kettles that people use for display, or as a base for flower arrangements. In the country people are looking for trammels or iron pots or trivets to hang in or near their fireplaces. Sometimes their hearths are authentic; someone is restoring an old house, like Amy and Drew. Or sometimes the home includes the twentieth-century equivalent of 'an authentic colonial' fireplace. But my best sales are to collectors. I know one man who has three walls in his house covered with match safes, those fireproof boxes that used to hang near fireplaces or stoves to hold matches."

"That sounds decorative. They were usually made of iron or tin, right? Or brass?"

"At first. But by the end of the nineteenth century some were made of redware or another sort of pottery, or even china."

"When did people start using matches?"

"Around 1830. They were called lucifers, then. They looked pretty much like modern matches; the heads were made of phosphorous, brimstone, powdered chalk, and glue, and they burst into flame when they were pulled across sandpaper. In fact, they lit so easily that the first match holders, or match safes, all had fireproof covers. Then, in 1856, safety matches were invented. They would only light when rubbed against special chemically treated paper."

"So match safes that have covers were made before, say, 1860?"

"Some were made after that. But if a match holder doesn't have a cover, then you know it's from the second half of the nineteenth century or later."

"I have a match safe. It's iron, has a lid, and has strawberries on it."

"And what have you done with your match safe, Dr. Summer?"

"I keep matches in it, of course! It's hanging in my kitchen, near my drawer of candles."

Will grinned. "So the print lady has a match safe she uses for matches!"

"Well, I've never seen your home, but I'd bet it has a few prints in it!"

Will hesitated. "My wife decorated the house. And, yes, there are prints hanging in it."

Maggie gave herself an invisible slap. Why ask a question that would remind Will of his wife? Once earlier that summer he had said his wife's death had been difficult for him, and after that he had not mentioned her. After a moment she said, "Shall we try the mall?"

"Fine with me. I'm surprised we haven't heard from Amy yet. I hope Drew's leg isn't worse than they thought."

"Hospitals are sometimes slow. And, of course, he could even end up needing surgery." Maggie hesitated. "Let's do the antiques mall, and then head back to the hospital and check in with her."

The large Victorian home was complete with

wraparound porch, double doors, and at least three stories, not including the cupola. Maggie had a moment of house envy before she reminded herself of basic Victorian housing realities. Heating bills. No insulation. No air-conditioning. Roofing bills. Decorating costs. No wonder this beautiful house was being used commercially; at least this way it would support itself. Will held one of the stained-glass-paneled doors open for her. The front hall was high-ceilinged and held two Victorian oak coat stands, complete with mirrors. The rest of the hallway was covered with paintings and prints from floor to ceiling. Maggie did a fast assessment. Nothing too spectacular, and not a good place to display any of them; the walls were too high for customers to be able to see some of the paintings, and the hallway was too dark to show off anything well. Authentic Victorian decorating; not good marketing.

"May I help you?" A small, balding man rose from a 1930s oak desk in what had once been the front parlor. "Looking for anything in particular?"

"Thank you, no," answered Will. "We'd just like to browse." It was always a debate whether to ask for what you were really looking for, and risk doubling the price on it, or to wander, and possibly miss something that had been held back until a customer specifically asked for it. Maggie smiled to herself. She usually did what Will was doing. Especially in an antiquarian-book shop, where the owner might be less than anxious to sell to someone he knew was a print dealer. Print dealers might purchase a book and then take it apart. Destruction of a book was a sin in the eyes of most book dealers.

Will stopped to look at some early cookware hanging on a wall in the kitchen, while Maggie indicated she was going to check the upstairs. Seven large bedrooms were on the second floor. A large affluent family had owned this house. No doubt the third floor would consist of much smaller rooms for the help, and, possibly, a nursery. As on the first floor, prints and paintings were on the walls, but most of the prints were twentieth-century reproductions. Some were in authentic Victorian frames. She wondered if it was ever pointed out to customers that the frame was older than the print. She suspected not. Caveat emptor. The oil paintings and watercolors were generally unsigned and undistinguished. It was August, after all. Tourists and dealers had been checking this mall daily since early spring.

The white-painted stairs squeaked as she climbed the curving flight to the third floor. The oak stair rail went all the way up, which was a nice touch, but the house had no air-conditioning, and she suspected no windows were open. The temperature rose a degree or two with every step.

She turned to her left and entered the first open room. It displayed linens and quilts and Victorian clothing. Not her thing, although a nice variation to the other merchandise. Mostly furniture was displayed, covered with the clutter of china figurines, pieces of silver, pottery, frames, and the miscellaneous tabletop items that dealers called smalls. The second room was similar, with one wall covered with pencil drawings by someone whose work she immediately labeled "amateurish; not interesting enough to be called folk art." She just glanced in the other rooms. Their contents were similar.

Maggie headed downstairs toward Will. As she left the second floor, she heard voices. Maybe Will had found something of interest? No; that wasn't his voice.

"How much more stuff is there like this?"

"Enough. I can't say."

"And you're sure you don't want to put it up at auction?" She recognized Walter English's voice from yesterday's auction.

Maggie smiled. Someone had no doubt brought in some items to be appraised, and the auctioneer was trying to convince him to auction them off. It wasn't a coincidence that usually it was auctioneers who offered "free appraisal" days. After everyone and their cousin Suzie had started watching *Antiques Roadshow* on television, half the population was convinced they had a secret treasure hidden somewhere in their attic or garage, if not in their living room. Unfortunately most family heirlooms were just that: heirlooms to family members, with little value to others.

"I'm sure. But is it valuable?"

"As I said. Very unusual. I would have to check my reference books, but I think there are such a limited number that they are cataloged and numbered. Finding one that is not cataloged would be unusual. Are you sure you have more?"

"I can get more." The other man's voice also sounded familiar.

"Then I'd strongly suggest you put them in a secure location. And if you should decide to auction them off, I would be more than happy to assist you."

Her curiosity got the better of her. She walked down the hall past the pantry, trying to follow the voices. Walter English was in the former dining room, as she suspected, but she was too late to see whoever had been speaking with him, and whatever he had brought. As she entered the dining room, she heard the front door shut.

"May I help you?" said English.

"I was just looking for my friend," Maggie said, and turned back toward the kitchen. The auctioneer obviously did not recognize her from yesterday's auction, which was not surprising. In addition to the regular attendees, at this time of year probably one or two hundred summer visitors were at each auction.

"If your friend is Will Brewer, he went out to the barn to look at the tools there."

"Thank you." And, of course, everyone in town seemed to know Will. Small-town living had its advantages and disadvantages. She walked through the kitchen and out the back door, heading for the barn.

"You found me!" Will straightened up from several boxes of tools he was examining on a carpenter's bench.

"If you wanted to hide, you didn't try hard

enough. Walter English tipped me off that you'd be out here."

"Caught again. He came in while I was still in the kitchen and said they'd gotten some new things in back here that I might be interested in. He was right. I'm going to ask how much he'll take for this carton."

Maggie nodded. Old tools were not something that fascinated her, although she had seen some beautiful handmade teak levels and brass-handled planes. She peeked into the box. It was half-full of various sizes of clamps.

"Did you happen to see someone just leaving the house? I overheard an interesting conversation."

"I've been here for the last ten minutes or so. I can't even see the front of the house. What did you hear?"

"It sounded as though someone had brought in a valuable item to be appraised and implied there were more where it had come from. Walter English was trying to get him to agree to auction them off. I was just curious as to what the man had brought in."

"I have no idea. It could have been anything." Will hoisted the carton onto his shoulder. "I'm going to go talk with Walter."

"It was stuffy in the house. If it's all right with you, I'll stay outside and imagine what the gardens must have looked like a hundred years ago."

"Fine. I'll meet you at my carriage in a few minutes."

They exchanged grins and Will headed for the house as Maggie walked slowly up the driveway and admired the sunflowers bordering the fence. She couldn't get her mind off the conversation she'd heard. Who was the man talking to Walter English? Why was the voice so familiar?

The sunflowers were looking straight up. She checked her watch. Sure enough; it was close to noon.

Chapter 16

—❧—

The Human Skeleton, *steel engraving, by Henry Winkles, 1857, from* Iconographic Encyclopedia. *Shows three complete posed skeletons—front, back, and walking—and details of some joints.* 9.5 x 11.5 *inches. Price: $75.*

Amy was still sitting outside the emergency room when Will and Maggie arrived, but she was smiling. "Drew's going to be fine. Two small bones in his foot were broken, and one in his leg. The doctor put a pin in the leg, and he'll be wearing a leg and foot cast for at least a month, but after the pharmacy here at the hospital fills a couple of prescriptions, we can take him home. Your timing is great; he'll be released within the next half hour."

"Doesn't sound as though he'll be having an easy time, though," said Will.

"No driving, because it's his right leg, and he'll have to use crutches for a while. The doctor suggested he avoid steps for at least a few days. Maybe you two could help me move a bed downstairs for him? We have a single bed in the corner of his study."

"Sure thing. With three of us it shouldn't be a problem."

"How are you doing, Amy? You got so little sleep last night, and now this." Amy was pale, and with no makeup and her hair limp, she looked waiflike.

"I'm tired, no doubt. I'm just glad the accident wasn't worse. I'll be relieved to get Drew home and then collapse. But you're both on vacation! Drew's accident should not be your problem. Did you find any great antiques this morning?"

"We stopped at several shops, but this time of the season they've been pretty well picked over. We didn't get as far as the antiquarian-book shop. We did visit that Victorian house Walter English has turned into an antiques mall. Great house, but no great bargains except for a box of tools Will bought."

"Did you look for my corner cabinet?"

"I did, and not a one. But there are a lot of antiques shops left."

Amy and Maggie were both glad of Will's help when they wheeled Drew out. Drew was not an enormous man, but with the crutches and the cast he was awkward. Amy and Maggie followed along as Will helped Drew, who was also feeling the effects of the pain medication, into the back of the RV so his leg could stretch out. Despite the pills, Drew winced at every bump they hit on the way home. They were all relieved when Will slowly drove around the corner where the accident had occurred that morning, and into the driveway. Amy went ahead to open the door and Maggie went up the steps directly to the porch. One of the chaises there would be perfect for Drew to sit in so he could keep his leg and foot up.

The porch curved from the side of the house around to the front. As Maggie walked quickly toward the side facing the river, where the chaises were, she almost ran into a man bending down at a window that opened from the porch into the living room. "Who—?" She started to say, as the man turned around. It was Tom Colby, the neighbor and Civil War reenactor. "I'm sorry; you startled me! And I didn't recognize you out of uniform." Maggie smiled. "May I help you?" What was Tom Colby doing here?

Drew, struggling with his crutches, and Will were right behind her. Drew sat down heavily on one of the chaises, and Will helped him move his foot up. Amy came out the side door and covered Drew's leg with a shawl. "I don't think I'm going to need this in the middle of the day in August. I'm not an old lady," said Drew. "Tom! What are you doing here?"

Tom had backed up a couple of steps. "I heard about your accident this morning. Rough luck. I just came to check and see if I could do anything to help."

Maggie looked at Tom. What had he really been doing on the porch? After he left, she was going to check the locks on the windows. But Amy and Drew didn't seem to find his presence surprising.

Maybe he stopped in a lot. He did live just next
door.

"I'm fine. Lucky, I guess. Just broke a couple of
bones."

"Looks like you'll be laid up for a while."

Drew winced. "Yeah. It does."

"Maybe I could bring over those Civil War books
I was going to loan you. This would be a good time
for you to get caught up with your reading."

"Thanks, Tom," said Amy. "But I think today
Drew should just rest. He'd appreciate a visit more
tomorrow." She walked with Tom to the end of the
porch where steps led down into the yard. "Those
books are a good idea. Drew has been wanting to
read them."

"I'll stop in around noon tomorrow, then," said
Tom. "Drew, sounds as though your wife is taking
good care of you."

"The best," answered Drew, who had not
stopped Amy's dismissal of Tom.

Tom waved and walked off toward the path in
back of the ell that led to his house. The path near
where Crystal's body had been found.

"I'll find us something for lunch," Maggie said.
"We should eat." Amy nodded and looked relieved
that Maggie was taking over for a few minutes. She
sat down next to Drew.

Maggie scrounged quickly through the kitchen
and came up with bread and canned salmon for
sandwiches. Will joined her and they added potato
chips and raw carrot and zucchini slices to the
plates. Someone pounded on the back door.

"Mrs. Douglas?" asked the state trooper who stood in the doorway as Maggie went to the door.

"No; I'm her friend. I'll get her."

"May I come in? I'd like to speak with Mr. Douglas too, if he is home."

"They're both on the porch." Maggie led the trooper through the hall and living room. "Amy, Drew? There's someone here to see you."

Will followed in a minute with the sandwiches and cans of cola and iced tea.

"You folks've been having some problems, I understand," the trooper said.

No one said anything. Problems? He could have meant anything. Phone calls? Fires? Murders? Accidents? Maggie felt she'd lived a lifetime in the past four days.

"I'm Drew Douglas. I'd get up, but you can see I have a bit of a problem." Drew grinned ruefully. "I had an accident this morning."

"So I heard," noted Detective Strait.

"This is my wife, Amy. We've lived here for almost five months now."

"I'm Amy's friend Maggie Summer. I'm visiting from New Jersey. And this is—" Maggie turned toward Will.

"Will Brewer. I know." Detective Strait shook Will's hand. "How're you doing, Will? Haven't seen you this summer."

"Fine, Nick; I'm fine. Only been here a couple of weeks."

"Staying with Nettie, as usual?"

"Same as usual."

Detective Strait nodded. "And these folks are friends of yours?"

Maggie wasn't sure whether the tone of the phrasing meant he was expressing amazement at Will's choice of company or looking for an endorsement.

"I've known Maggie for a while," Will replied evenly. "Amy and Drew are friends of hers, and they seem like fine people."

"Glad to hear it." Detective Strait checked an earlier page in his notebook and then looked back at them all. "Frankly, folks, I'm a little concerned about your area of the world. You're new to these parts. Madoc is a pretty quiet place, as I'm sure you've noticed. We haven't got a lot of people moving in and out. But we've got nothing against folks from away. Just want you both to understand that."

Amy and Drew exchanged glances. Maggie waited for the *but* in Detective Strait's little speech. It wasn't long in coming.

"But since you've been here, this property seems to have attracted a lot of attention." He looked down at his notes again and counted out the issues. "First, there were some telephone calls at strange hours that seemed to be a problem. Second, there was a fire of unexplained origin. Third, and certainly most seriously, a young girl's body was found on your property yesterday." He looked up from his list again. "You folks might not have heard yet, but Miss Porter's death has been ruled a homicide."

Amy gasped softly, and Drew sat up as far as he

could. Maggie was glad she hadn't mentioned that earlier.

"And then this morning, you, Mr. Douglas, were involved in an accident."

"But that isn't the same thing. People are sometimes in car accidents. That's nothing like a murder." Drew looked as though he'd been accused himself.

"The deputy who responded to the 911 call this morning said your brakes hadn't worked well when you went around the corner."

"That's right. I know I put on the brakes, but the car kept going."

"Deputy Colby had your car towed, as you know, and he asked the mechanic to check out your brakes, Mr. Douglas." Detective Strait looked directly at Drew. "The rubber hose leading to the back brakes on your Jeep had been cut very neatly."

"No!" Amy jumped up. "I can't take this place anymore! We wanted to move to a quiet, beautiful place, to start a new life, and to have a family. This whole move has turned into a nightmare! We should never have left New York!"

"Nice, safe, quiet place, that New York City," agreed Detective Strait. "And if you ever want to move back there, why, that would be your choice. But as long as you folks are here, then I think we'd better think real seriously about what's been happening."

"We have no enemies," said Drew slowly. His face, already pale from exhaustion and pain, was now even whiter. "We don't even know very many people here.

We've met Tom and Shirley, next door, and Amy met Rachel Porter at the library and arranged for Crystal to come and help us out this summer. Rachel also helped us to find Brent Construction, and Giles and Brian Leary have been doing some work on the house. But we've hardly had time to meet anyone else. Maggie, who's known Amy since they went to college together, is the first guest we've had since we moved in, and we were pleased to meet her friend Will. And last night he brought his aunt for dinner."

"You brought Nettie over here?" Detective Strait grinned at Will, as though they were sharing a private joke. "Must have been an interesting evening."

"It went just fine," answered Will, almost as though the two of them were talking about a totally different subject from everyone else. "She told Amy and Drew a little about the history of the house. She's glad some young people are going to fix it up and raise their family here. Like folks did in earlier days."

As in the eighteenth and nineteenth centuries? Maggie thought. She wondered suddenly whether Detective Strait was part of the Brewer family somehow too. Everyone else seemed to be.

The detective turned back to Amy and Drew. "So, first of all, you're sure you don't know anyone in town except for the few people you just mentioned, and you don't have any enemies."

"No!" said Amy vehemently. "We just bought a house and are minding our own business."

"And what would that business be?" inquired the officer. "Just for the record, you understand."

"In New York I worked in advertising and Drew was a stockbroker. We haven't decided yet what we're going to do here."

"So you're both unemployed." Detective Strait made another note and turned the page in his notebook. "And you bought this big house, and you're having work done on it."

"That's right." Drew's fist tightened. "Do you want to see our tax return, or our bank balances?"

"Not just now, anyway. But thank you for offering. I'll just assume you folks have a little income from your investments." The detective looked up at them innocently. "Would that be right?"

"Yes," said Amy.

Will's face twitched a little, and Maggie too realized that Amy and Drew had just confirmed what everyone in Madoc had probably already deduced: they were rich out-of-staters who didn't need to work for a living. She could visualize the Douglases' roof repair bill rising as word got out.

"So, you folks have no enemies in Maine. Do you have any enemies in New York? Anyone who might have followed you here? I've heard some folks in New York take things pretty serious."

"No one followed us from New York! We're just normal, quiet people!" said Amy. "And our life in New York was normal—quiet—no problems! Crazy things only seem to happen to us in this town! It isn't our fault! We haven't done anything."

"And what do you suppose Crystal Porter did, to get herself killed like that?" Detective Strait said quietly.

"I don't know. She was just a young girl. I liked her. We talked about New York." Amy burst into tears. "Why is all this happening?"

"Nick, can you tell us what happened to Crystal?" said Will quietly.

"I wish I knew, Will. Someone hit her pretty hard on the head and the medical examiner figures she fell and then lay out in that field for a while and bled to death." He paused. "Rachel was pretty upset when we told her. She was especially upset when we told her Crystal was pregnant."

Chapter 17

—❧—

The Young Mother, *hand-colored lithograph
by N. Currier, c. 1850. (In 1857 Nathaniel
Currier partnered with his brother-in-law,
James Merritt Ives, and the firm of Currier &
Ives was created and then prospered.) Woman
standing and holding baby, while toddler
holding spaniel sits in chair beside her. Draped
background. 8.5 x 12.5 inches. Price: $125.*

Will left shortly after Detective Strait, promising to
take Maggie out to dinner later that day. Amy and
Drew looked relieved, Maggie couldn't help
but notice. They were exhausted and needed some
time to themselves. Right now it was best for everyone if she was a houseguest who stayed out of the
way.

Maggie yawned. Those telephone calls last night
had kept her awake too. She headed for her bedroom to take a short nap.

But although her body clearly wanted to rest,
Maggie's mind was too active. And confused. As
she lay, floating between the sleep her body craved

and the awareness of her brain, her thoughts wandered from murders to babies; from fires to accidents; from broken legs to broken windows. She must remember to check the locks on the porch windows that opened into the living room. She must remember . . .

Amy woke her at six-thirty to say Will had called; he'd made a seven-thirty reservation at a restaurant in Edgecomb, just down the coast. Maggie nodded and headed for a hot bath. Lavender soap and one of those plastic sponges woke her up. She chose a long Indian cotton skirt and a long-sleeved blouse and pinned a favorite rhinestone *M* to her collar. A student she had advised had given it to her at graduation several years ago. She brushed her hair hard. That nap had helped.

Will had changed to slacks and sports jacket and a shirt that particular shade of blue that brought out the color of his eyes. Maggie wondered if he had selected it or whether his wife had done that. She had died eight years ago. It was crazy to be jealous of someone who was dead.

Like Crystal.

Maggie concentrated on smiling, and relaxing, and was secretly glad that Will had borrowed Aunt Nettie's compact car again. It was a little less conspicuous than driving the RV everywhere, and it was definitely easier to park.

Their table at the Sheepscot River Inn overlooked the water, and they arrived in plenty of time to enjoy a spectacular orange and pink sunset reflected in the river. The Soave was dry, just as Maggie liked it, and there was even a pianist playing softly in the background and a small candle on the table.

She raised her glass to him. "This is lovely. Just what I needed tonight."

"I thought of including Aunt Nettie, but she shooed me out the door."

"She's a special lady. I can see why you come back every summer. There really is no other place like the coast of Maine."

"It isn't hurried, like the Cape, and the commercialized parts are almost caricatures of Maine, as though the state is quietly making fun of itself."

"And, even more, making fun of all us out-of-staters."

"I've thought sometimes of moving here. Having New York State plates on the car has always been a matter of some embarrassment. Maybe I'll do it after I prove to myself that I can make a reasonable living off antiques. For now I'll keep my house near Buffalo, and my teaching contacts. Just in case."

"It's always good to have a fallback position," agreed Maggie. "I've always lived in New Jersey. Grew up there, went to school there, and now I teach there. I love that it's close to both New York and Philadelphia. But since Michael died, I've begun to think of other possibilities. In lots of areas." Maggie took a mental deep breath. Was she ready to share this with Will? How well did she really know him? "Amy and I were talking the other night, before everything seemed to get even crazier than it already was. She and Drew want to have a family. That's one reason they moved here. They thought Maine would be a good place for children to grow up."

"No doubt. Some schools are better than others, but that's true in every state. And the closeness to the land—the seacoast, or the mountains, for those who prefer winter sports—is more a part of everyday life than it is in most parts of suburban New York or New Jersey." Will sipped his wine.

"Talking with Amy made me think about children too," Maggie said. "I think; no, I know. I'd like to be a mother."

Will looked at her curiously. "Is that a proposition?"

Maggie backed off. "No! I didn't mean it that way! It's just that Michael and I always assumed we'd have children, but we were both so busy, and we just never sat down and decided that 'this is the right time.' And now I'm thirty-eight years old and . . ."

"Your biological clock is ticking."

"I guess that's it. But that makes it sound so simplistic. What I really feel is emotional. I want to have a child to read books to, and take to museums, and teach to ride a bicycle and . . ."

Will had moved his chair away from the table and was leaning back slightly. "I'm not sure why you're telling me all this, Maggie. I like kids. Hell, I was a teacher for eighteen years. A pretty good teacher, I think. But now I want other things in my life."

Maggie's mood fell. Will certainly had a right to his feelings. And their relationship was new. He lived in Buffalo and traveled a lot. She lived in New Jersey. They were two separate people. Why should his not wanting children have any effect on her?

"It's great that you want to be a mother. I'm happy for you." It was Will's turn to look out over the river. "My wife wanted children too. I wasn't sure. I wasn't as supportive as I should have been when she got pregnant."

"I didn't know you had a child, Will."

"I don't. She had an ectopic pregnancy. She didn't want to bother anyone when she started having pains. She thought everything would be all right." Will said the words mechanically, as though he'd pressed a button and the words just spit out. "She bled to death, Maggie. The baby died and she bled to death. I wasn't even there. I was away, doing an antiques show in Ohio. She had to call a neighbor to take her to the hospital."

"Oh, Will. I'm so sorry." She had hoped to share a special thought, a personal hope, with Will. Instead, she had opened a painful part of his past. "I didn't know. I didn't mean to remind you of such a sad time."

They sat silently, facing their own thoughts.

"Maggie, I wish you the best of luck in whatever you decide to do. But children are something for other people. Not for me." Will picked up the menu. "Now, shall we relax a little and discuss something important, like what we're going to order for dinner?"

Sharing a large platter of mussels steamed in white wine with garlic and herbs helped them both relax a bit. By the time Will's stuffed haddock and Maggie's shrimp scampi had arrived, they had finished more than half the bottle of wine, and the earlier conversation had been pushed to the side.

"Will, I've only been in Maine a few days, but an awful lot has been happening. You know this area; you know these people. Maybe I'm being ultrasensitive, but it almost seemed to me that your friend Detective Strait was warning Amy and Drew today."

"He was. Mainers don't take too kindly to people from away who arrive and want to change things."

"All Amy and Drew wanted to do was buy a house, fix it up, and live here in peace."

"Probably so. But even before they arrived their coming was upsetting to people who felt that house should have stayed in the Brewer family." Will raised his hand as he saw Maggie open her mouth to protest. "I know. Charlotte hadn't the money or didn't see the need to keep the house in as good condition as she might have. And it certainly wasn't Amy's or Drew's fault that Charlotte left the house to Lizzie instead of to Shirley, or that Lizzie sold it. But, nevertheless, they arrived at a time when nerves were on edge."

"And Crystal . . ."

"And Crystal. That's a whole horrible situation that probably has nothing to do with Amy or Drew or the house, but, of course, since her body was found there, it makes the situation even more awkward."

"Could someone be trying to get Amy and Drew to leave?"

"It's possible. The telephone calls, the fire. When Drew and I see if we can expose the old fireplace, I want to take a look at where that fire started. And then there are the brakes on Drew's car. Even Crystal's body being found on their property. It could all have been staged to scare them off."

"But Crystal was killed! And Drew could have been! I can understand someone in the family being upset by their living in the family home. But murder? Attempted murder? And Crystal was part of the Brewer family! You said she was a distant cousin of yours."

"A branch the family wasn't too fond of, but, yes, family. I agree. The phone calls, maybe. The fire? I want to check that out. But Crystal's murder and the accident were beyond the possibility of chance or annoyance." Will hesitated. "I know they're your friends, Maggie. But have Amy and Drew had any problems recently?"

"Problems like being murderers? Like cutting the brake lines on Drew's car? Will, no. That's impossible." Maggie took a sip of her wine and thought for a moment. "This move has been difficult for both of them. More difficult than I think either of them wants to admit."

"For example?"

"Amy's been really scared by the phone calls and the accidents in the house. And she told me Drew is drinking more than he used to. When you were there last night, he seemed all right, but the day before he definitely was drinking too much."

"Is that new behavior?"

"I don't know. I've known Amy for years, but I haven't seen her much recently. I'd only met Drew twice before I arrived this week." She paused, not sure this was the right time to bring up the subject of children again. "They both told me they want to have children. But Amy hasn't been able to get pregnant, and that's putting pressure on both of them. Will, they have a room on the second floor of the house decorated like a perfect nursery. It even has a canopied crib and shelves of stuffed animals."

"Maybe she was pregnant and something happened, and they were left with all the baby things."

Maggie shook her head. "Not based on what she told me. She said Drew gave her the crib as a wedding present."

Will leaned back and whistled a little. "Weird. And some pressure. Most couples don't even begin to buy baby things until the second trimester. Just in case."

Maggie nodded. "I agree. It's very strange. I thought maybe they were planning to adopt, but Amy told me Drew wouldn't consider any child other than one biologically his own. He was adopted as a baby and feels really strongly about genetic ties. But Amy has shelves of books on adoption in her study." Maggie didn't mention that some of them were now sitting on the floor next to her bed, and that she planned to look at them later that night.

"That's sad, but it certainly doesn't explain anything that's been happening. You know, there have always been stories about that house. When I was a little boy, my father told me there was hidden treasure in the house, and hidden secrets."

"Your aunt Nettie told me at Cut 'n' Curl that a woman with a baby walked the halls there."

"Oh, yes. The ghosts. I've heard that too, but I've never met anyone who's seen them."

"You have now."

"You?"

"I'm not crazy, Will. And I haven't seen the woman in white. But I did hear the baby cry. It woke me up two nights ago. Amy came running in. She heard it too."

"You know that's impossible."

"Maybe. But it happened." No matter how she tried to change the conversation, they kept getting back to babies. And neither of them had mentioned that other baby. Maggie plunged ahead. "Detective Strait said Crystal was pregnant."

"Yes. That news will get around town faster than the news of her death. Everyone will revisit Rachel's teenage years. And wonder."

"The father of the baby could be her killer.

Maybe they argued; maybe he wanted her to have an abortion, and she refused. Or she wanted him to marry her." Maggie couldn't help thinking of Drew. Was it possible? Maggie wanted very much to know that there were other potential fathers for Crystal's baby.

"I assume the police will talk with a lot of people, but I'll check around. Being a member of the family means I might hear something that isn't common knowledge."

"Would you, Will? I think your detective friend is looking at Amy and Drew as possible suspects. And the sooner other suspects are identified, the better for them."

"I'll see what I can do. In fact, I think maybe I'll stop in to see the Learys tonight, after I drop you back in Madoc."

"The Learys who are working on the roof?"

"The same. Giles and Mary are my cousins. Of course, Maggie." He grinned at her incredulous expression. "I told you Aunt Nettie had a sister who married Silas Leary. In any case, they may have some ideas. And Brian was the one who found Crystal, wasn't he?"

"Yes. And they were good friends. They had a date planned for the night she was killed." Maggie looked up. "He could be the father of her baby, Will. He knew her well, and he was clearly upset about her death. Maybe he's the one responsible."

"For her pregnancy? Or her murder?" Will finished his wine. "I'll drop in and see how my cousins are doing, Maggie. But I can't believe a kid like

Brian would kill his cousin." He paused a moment. "Maybe sleep with her. But not kill her. Brewers don't do that sort of thing."

"Well, someone did." Brian seemed like a sweet kid. But someone killed Crystal, and she hoped against hope, for Amy's sake, that the person responsible wasn't Drew.

Chapter 18

———— ❦ ————

Pierrette. *French pantine, or paper marionette.*
Pierette is the female partner of French pan-
tomime character Pierrot, both stylized figures
introduced at the Théâtre des Funambules by
Jean Gaspard Deburau in the early nineteenth
century. Original uncut sheet. 11.5 x 15
inches. Price: $75.

Maggie had gotten back to Madoc before ten, but
Amy and Drew had left the door open and were
already asleep. It had been a rough day. Maggie
walked softly through the dining room to avoid the
living room, where they had put a bed for Drew.
The door to Amy's room was closed, but there were
lights on in the hall and on the table next to
Maggie's bed.

In New Jersey she would have been turning the
air-conditioning to high. Here, the soft river
breeze coming through the partially open window smelled slightly of pine and salt. A perfect
night for sleeping.

But after the nap she'd taken this afternoon

Maggie wasn't tired. The dinner with Will had been unsettling. He was the first man she'd allowed herself to be interested in since Michael's death, and a part of her had hoped that somehow he would be perfect. A perfect man would have embraced the possibility of children. But Will's past headed him in another direction.

It was unrealistic, she told herself, for one person to echo her every interest. She and Michael had been married for fourteen years, and they certainly hadn't agreed on everything. Why should she even fantasize that there was someone who would want exactly what she wanted, at the same point in their lives?

She picked up the pile of pictures of waiting children she had left by her bed the day before. They were still waiting. Babies, yes. But it was the older children whose faces she found most compelling. Faces that looked out from different worlds, asking for love. For a chance. A possibility. Dark faces; light faces. Faces born in Asia, Latin America, Africa, eastern Europe, and here in the United States. Sibling groups who didn't want to be separated. Children unlucky enough to be born imperfect.

Was she really ready to make that kind of commitment? A lifetime commitment to someone she had never met? But wasn't that what every mother did, before her child was born?

Maggie put down the sheaf of papers and picked up the books on adoption she had selected in Amy's study. She glanced through some chapter headings:

"Finding Your Child"; "The Honeymoon Period"; "Early Childhood Trauma Disorder"; "Raising an Interracial Family"; "The School and the Adopted Child"; "The Adopted Adolescent"; "When Your Child Wants to Search."

Even the topics were intimidating. She put that book down and picked up the book on open adoption. What was that? As she started reading, she realized there were whole worlds of relationships she'd been unaware of. She had thought adoption was a contract in which one or both biological parents relinquished their parental rights and their child was adopted by another couple. Or by a single parent. The adoptive parents and child knew nothing, or little, about the biological parents, and the biological parents had no way of knowing what had happened to their child. Open adoption was totally different. In these adoptions, the biological parents, or mother, often actually chose the adoptive parents. And the biological and adoptive parents not only met, but agreed to stay in touch, so the child would grow up knowing both sets of parents.

Whew! Maggie lay back on the pillows she'd piled up. How would that work in reality? Were both sets of parents so unselfish and loving that they could accept each other? Could they avoid jealousy? What if the child played one set of parents against the other? What would the child even call each of his or her two mothers?

Maybe it would be the best of all possible worlds. But if it didn't work . . . Her professorial side wanted to see studies on how the two types of adoption turned out, twenty or twenty-five years later. At least in open adoption there would be no fantasies about biological parents; no people like Drew who grew up longing to meet a genetic relative.

Maggie picked up the third book. It was a how-to on the actual adoption process. She read about ten pages before realizing that she had read one paragraph three times.

She hoped there would be no telephone calls during this night.

She hoped there would be no more bad news.

Chapter 19

—⁓—

Group of Snapdragons—Antirrhinum vars.
*1893 British lithograph by Cassell and
Company; included in* Cassell's Popular
Gardening. *Print is in two perfectly matched
pieces; divided where it was originally bound
in book. 8.75 x 11.75 inches. Price: $85.*

Drew was still sleeping, drugged by his pain medication, as Maggie and Amy sat at the kitchen table
planning the day.

"I should stop in to see Rachel," Amy said
slowly. "It will be a difficult visit, but it's the right
thing to do."

Maggie nodded. "Maybe you could get her some
flowers, or a platter of cookies."

"Flowers! Yes. And would you go with me? I feel
awkward about going, but even more awkward
about not going. It would help to have someone
with me."

"Of course I'll go with you." Maggie wondered
what their reception would be. Crystal's body had
been found on Amy's property; she had disap-

peared while walking home from here. At least part of Rachel's mind could hold Amy and Drew accountable. "It might even be better if I were with you. In case Rachel . . ."

"In case she holds me responsible. I know, Maggie. I could hardly sleep last night thinking about it. Wondering who would have wanted Crystal dead. She was so young and innocent, in so many ways. She had so many dreams."

"Let's make that visit this morning. Maybe there is something else Rachel could think of that we could help with."

"Since Drew has to stay quiet for a while, maybe later today would be a good time for you to show us some of your prints."

"You said you especially wanted to see the Winslow Homers and the N. C. Wyeths, right?"

"Yes. And maybe some of the Thomas Nast prints you mentioned. I was thinking about something for the nursery. He did some Santa Claus engravings, didn't he?"

"He was the first person to picture Santa as we think of him today, round and jolly with a full beard. Some historians feel his Santa Clauses were self-portraits, except that Santa had a white beard, and Nast a dark one."

"I thought Clement Moore's poem ''Twas the Night Before Christmas' was the first description of Santa as round and jolly."

"It described St. Nicholas in words, but, of course, didn't actually picture him. Nast took Moore's ideas, added some details of his own, and created the American Santa Claus. His engravings were printed in the year-end issues of *Harper's Weekly*. In most of them Nast's home in Morristown, New Jersey, was the setting, and his children were his models. If you had a full collection of Nast Christmas prints, you could see his children growing up, year by year."

"Are there any prints with babies?"

Amy certainly hadn't lost her focus on infants despite everything that had been happening. "One shows Santa bending over a baby's crib. I'll pull them all out later so you can take a look."

"That should be fun! And very different from the last couple of days. Drew will like seeing them too, especially the Civil War prints."

Civil War. Maggie suddenly thought of Tom, the Civil War reenactor she was sure had been trying to open the window on the porch yesterday.

"With all of the problems you and Drew have had here, Amy, do you have any kind of security system? Locks on the windows? Anything?"

"In Madoc, Maine? You have to be kidding!" Amy looked at her. "And you're not. No, we have no security system. Most of the windows have the original 'locks': nails in the sides of the window frames on the inside. You have to press the nail head in to raise the window or it won't move. It's actually a pretty safe system." She looked down at the bandage she still wore on her arm. "But the nails have disappeared from some of the window frames— after all, it's been over two hundred years!—and some of the nails have been painted over, so the windows won't go up at all. That's what I was coping with when that window collapsed on me the other day and broke."

"Have you thought about getting a better system?"

"To keep the ghosts in? We haven't had any problems with break-ins, and securing the windows wouldn't help with the telephone calls. I haven't heard about anyone near here even talking about such a thing. What would anyone break in for? We haven't got anything terribly valuable. This isn't New York."

"At least there were no phone calls last night. Or I didn't hear any."

"Oh!" Amy jumped up. "I forgot to turn the ringer back on! Drew and I decided to turn it off last night." She switched the ringer on the kitchen phone to "on." "I'd better go see if there are any messages."

Maggie stretched and walked around the kitchen. Outside, she could see the grayness of lingering fog softening and blurring the trees and lawn. This would be the time for ghosts, she thought. Fog put the world halfway between light and darkness. And there was a lot of fog on the coast of Maine.

Amy came back, carrying her pocketbook this time. "I listened to the messages. Two hang-ups, but they might have been telemarketers."

Sure.

"Drew had a call from someone at his old office, so I left a note next to his bed. And Will called you, bright and early this morning. He said he had to go out, but he'd call back later. Something about a visit last night."

Maggie nodded. "After he dropped me off he was going to stop in to see the Learys. Just to see how Brian was doing."

"A good idea. He's a thoughtful man, Maggie. I like him."

Maggie wondered briefly if she could share Will's feelings about children with Amy. But this wasn't the time for girl talk. Besides, she wasn't comfortable talking about parenthood yet. Especially with Amy. "I haven't seen Brian or his father working on the roof recently."

"Drew told them to take the week off. I'm sure their boss has found something for them to do, but we just didn't think it would be good for Brian to come back here so quickly. Crystal was his friend."

"It's hard to believe she was pregnant."

"It must have been early. She certainly didn't show."

"She must have been so scared. Only eighteen."

"Maybe she had a plan. Some eighteen-year-olds think they have the world all figured out." Amy paused. "Or maybe the father of the baby had a plan."

"Which she might or might not have agreed with." Does Amy have any idea about Drew and Crystal? Maggie wondered. Could I possibly have been mistaken in what I saw? No; she was quite sure about what had been happening in that bedroom. Should she tell the police? None of the answers were ones she wanted to act on.

They were both silent for a few moments.

"Let's go and get those flowers. There's a florist's shop in Waymouth. Then we'll go and see Rachel. I don't know what we can say that will mean anything. But I'll feel better after we've done it."

They choose a large bouquet of white marigolds and delphiniums and baby's breath with a few daisies. The grouping looked young and innocent. Crystal had at least been young.

Other neighbors must have had the same thought; several cars were in the Porters' driveway.

"I'm nervous. Here I am, the neighbor from away who owns the home where Crystal was killed, and all of these cars probably belong to family and longtime friends." Amy sat for a moment.

"We don't have to stay long. Just pay our respects," Maggie said quietly. "If you don't go, then someone will question that too. And you did get to know Crystal well this summer." Or at least you thought you knew Crystal well, she added to herself.

They didn't need to knock on the door; Shirley Steele opened it. She looked Amy and Maggie up and down and then said loudly, in the direction of the rest of the house. "It's so nice of you to come. And you've brought flowers."

Rachel came out from the kitchen. She wore no makeup, and her hair was combed, but the part wasn't straight. Her face was pale and swollen, and her faded-gray flowered dress was crushed and hung loosely. She'd aged years in the few days since they had seen her.

Amy handed her the bouquet. "Drew and I are

so sorry, Rachel. We wanted you to know that. And if there is anything we can do . . ."

Rachel nodded. "Nothing that can be done now. Except find whoever killed my little girl and make him pay."

They followed Rachel to the kitchen, where another woman took the flowers and filled a glass vase with water.

"Would you like something to eat?" Rachel gestured to the room. Besides Shirley there were two little girls, her twin daughters, Sorrel and Sage, Maggie immediately thought, and another woman. The table and the counters were covered with food. Two baked-bean casseroles, a plate of chocolate chip cookies, and another of brownies; a bowl of potato salad; a ham; a large plate of cranberry muffins; a blueberry pie and a lemon meringue pie. Theirs were the only flowers. Clearly sympathy in Madoc was said through the stomach. "Everyone has been so kind to bring food."

Except for the out-of-staters who hadn't expressed their feelings with the currency of the realm. But the flowers did look lovely. Shirley set the vase in the center of the loaded table, where her two girls were taking full advantage of the chocolate chip cookies.

"You took the biggest cookie." One of the twins pushed the other one slightly.

"You took two before that." The second push was a little stronger, and the girl moved to the other side of the table and stuck out a tongue covered with chocolate chip cookie crumbs.

"No, thank you," said Amy. "We just wanted to tell you how sorry we were."

"Sorry is as sorry does." Rachel sat down in a rocking chair, which had been set so its occupant could watch a small TV in the corner of the room. A large box of tissues was on the floor next to her chair. "Since you're here, and I know you mean well, you might as well look in Crystal's room and take the books you loaned her. I don't want anything about New York in my house any longer. All those dreams in her head helped to get her killed. I'm certain about that. Just thinking about New York did it. She didn't even have to go there."

Amy looked a little surprised. "Of course; I'll be happy to take them."

"Her room's just down the hall." Rachel hesitated. "The police were there already. It's messed up. But I'm not ready to cope with it yet." She started to cry. Shirley put a hand on her shoulder and gave her another tissue.

Maggie and Amy moved down the hallway lined with framed photographs of a pretty blonde baby, a beautiful toddler, a cute little girl, and a smiling teenager. Crystal's life. And Rachel's.

It was obvious which room was Crystal's. It had probably not been immaculate before the police searched it. But their presence had not helped.

The contents of bookshelves had been dumped on the unmade bed. Piles of boxes holding embroidery floss, children's games, Barbie dolls, and school papers were spread across the floor. They had most likely been in the closet, which was now open. Crystal's wardrobe seemed to have consisted mainly of jeans and T-shirts and wool sweaters; two pairs of three-inch heels had been kicked into the corner. Open bureau drawers exposed an assortment of flannel nightgowns and cotton underwear.

"What were the police looking for?" whispered Amy.

"Drugs? A diary?"

"A diary!"

"Lots of teenaged girls keep one. It might have told them who the father of her baby was. Or who might have been angry with her."

No wonder Rachel had been upset about "New York." Travel posters of the Empire State Building, the Statue of Liberty, and Central Park were taped to the walls, along with magazine pages of young models. Supermarket makeup covered the top of the bureau.

Amy looked through the books on the bed. "I loaned her a couple of photograph books of New York. That's all. And I said she could take any magazines Drew and I had finished with." A stack of *New York* magazines was on the floor near the window.

Maggie glanced at them. This year's, and addressed to Mr. and Mrs. Drew Douglas. "Maybe you should take these. Rachel obviously doesn't want them here."

Amy hesitated. "All right. I've found my two books."

Maggie picked up the stack of magazines. Most

of them were *New York*s, but she also saw two copies of *Adoption Today,* and on the bottom, several issues of *Baby Care*. She checked quickly. *Baby Care* had not been addressed to Amy and Drew. So Crystal had been researching possibilities in several directions. Rachel didn't need to see those other magazines. Her grief was strong enough. She didn't need to know what Crystal had been thinking. And, Maggie justified to herself, the adoption magazines had been Amy's.

Back in the kitchen the women sat quietly. Tears still ran down Rachel's face. The woman Maggie hadn't met came over to them. "I'm Mary Leary, Giles's wife. He's been working on your house this summer. It was very nice of you to stop in, but I think Rachel needs to be quiet now."

Amy nodded. "I only found two books and a few magazines that had been Drew's and mine. She wanted me to take them."

"Then you do that. The police have been through everything, and she's still in shock, of course." Mary glanced at the books and magazines Amy and Maggie were holding. "She had so many dreams, didn't she?" A tear started down her cheek.

"We'll be going now," said Maggie, moving Amy toward the door. "If anyone thinks of something we can do to help, please do call."

"We will." Mary paused. "I was sorry to hear about your husband too, Mrs. Douglas. There have been a lot of accidents at that corner."

Amy nodded. "Thank you. He'll be all right."

They all thought of Crystal. She wouldn't be all

right. Ever. Maggie wondered how Rachel would be too. No husband, no other children. Despite having neighbors and friends, she must feel very alone. Being a single mother mustn't be easy even in the best of circumstances. And these were the worst.

They headed home in silence. Amy said finally, "Rachel might not really have wanted me there, but I'm glad I went."

Maggie nodded. "It was the right thing to do. But I'm sure she connects you and Drew with Crystal's death. She couldn't help but do that."

"Crystal was so fascinated with New York. She asked me questions about everything from the subways to the Statue of Liberty. There were days she drove me crazy! 'Does everyone eat bagels for breakfast in New York?' 'Do people really get shot in the subways?' 'Is Macy's really the biggest store in the world?' 'Are there famous people everywhere?' 'Have you ever been to Tiffany's?' Some days it felt obsessive!"

"She was a teenager. She was dreaming. Doing her own kind of research."

"She thought Drew and I had led glamorous lives in the city. I once found her looking in my closet, and then she asked me how many evening dresses I had."

Maggie smiled. "You had a few, I'd guess."

"Three, I think. I had her put them in an old wardrobe in the attic space. There isn't much call for them in Madoc."

"Nor in the New Jersey community where I live,

except when there are special events at the college. And even in New York you can go to the opera dressed like Lauren Bacall or dressed in jeans."

"With most people wearing whatever they've worn all day to the office, in any case. I think Crystal had watched a lot of movies made in the 1940s and 1950s."

"No doubt. And there are certainly a lot of sides to New York."

"She just wanted to be grown-up, to move away from Madoc. To live a life more glamorous than making blueberry pies or helping me unpack boxes." Amy dabbed at her eyes. "Getting pregnant must have blown all of those dreams into fantasies. Do you think she would have stayed here and had the baby? Or had an abortion?"

Maggie decided not to bring up that Crystal had obviously borrowed some magazines on adoption too. One more alternative. Whatever decision she would have made was going to influence the rest of her life in some way. "And who knows what the father of the baby had in mind. If anything."

"A teenage boy confronted with that kind of reality usually runs like crazy. Or denies. Or blames."

Amy too had been pregnant as a teenager. Maggie touched her own abdomen. How would it feel to know you were carrying a child? To know you were responsible for another life? Whatever your decision was, it had to change the way you looked at the world.

And the way the world looked at you.

The back door was open when they arrived at the house. Drew must be awake. They heard another man's voice as they walked in.

"Tom! How nice of you to come over." Amy looked around the kitchen and started piling dirty coffee cups in the sink. "You and Drew must have had coffee and"—looking at the crumbs still on the table—"doughnuts."

"Yup. I just stopped in to see how he was doing."

"I'm all right, I guess," said Drew, standing awkwardly in the doorway with his crutches. "The throbbing isn't as bad now, but I'm not exactly ready to run a marathon."

"Nor should you even be standing." Amy went over and herded him back to the living room, where clothing and bedding were strewn in various directions. "Why don't you sit on the couch and put your leg up, as the doctor said? I'll straighten the room. You don't want to trip on anything."

"Tom got here just when I was waking up," Drew continued, sitting heavily on the couch. "He went upstairs and got me a clean shirt too. And a pair of shorts."

Of course Drew wouldn't be able to wear his jeans or even sweatpants; they wouldn't fit over his cast. Luckily, this was August. The shirt Tom had found him was dark green, embroidered in orange with a corporate logo of some sort suitable for a golf course in Short Hills. The shorts were a purple and yellow plaid. Maggie wasn't sure precisely where they would be suitable. But at least Drew was dressed and seemed comfortable enough.

"You're going to sleep downstairs for a while, then?" Tom said.

"I'm not supposed to try steps for at least a few days. Pretty boring, but I'm supposed to stay off my foot and leg. I'm already getting restless. Amy, maybe you could go to the library and pick up some books for me."

"Sounds like a possibility," said Amy. "Maggie agreed to show us her Homer and Wyeth prints later today too. We have the whole day in front of us." The telephone interrupted her. It was Will.

Maggie could hear the smile behind his voice. She imagined him sipping coffee in Aunt Nettie's kitchen, with a row of white and purple African violets in bloom on the windowsill behind him. "Good morning! Sorry I missed your call earlier. Drew turned off the ringer so everyone could get a good night's sleep."

"I had an interesting visit last night with Giles and Mary Leary. And Brian. I'd like to tell you about it."

"Here I am. Listening."

"I know. But telling you isn't so easy just now."

Maggie suddenly realized that her vision of African violets might be a fantasy, but Aunt Nettie's presence probably wasn't.

"Would you like to stop in here? Or maybe I could meet you somewhere. Amy may go to the library." Maggie hesitated. "Rachel isn't the only person who works at the Waymouth Library, is she?"

"I don't think so."

"Because she's at home this morning. Amy and I made a condolence call. In fact, Mary Leary was there too. And Shirley and her twins."

"The whole gang, eh? Any lynchings?"

"No. But I think we broke local tradition by bringing flowers instead of food."

"An unforgivable sin. Why don't I come over there this afternoon? We can take a short walk. And I'd like to check out that area in the ell where Drew said the fire started."

"That would be fine with me. Hold on one moment." Maggie held her hand lightly over the receiver. "Amy, could Will stop in this afternoon?"

"Tell him he has to bring his own crowbar if he wants to do anything with that wall! I never did get to the hardware store," Drew called back. "Does he like Homer prints too?"

"I heard that," Will said. "Tell Drew I have a couple of crowbars, but at this point I think we should wait a few days before disrupting his home. What was that about Homer?"

"Amy and Drew wanted me to show them my Winslow Homer wood engravings this afternoon."

"Sounds good to me. Have you ever gotten to that antiquarian-book store?"

"Not yet."

"Then why don't we meet there about one; I promised a friend in Buffalo I'd keep my eyes open for some New York State history books, and you can look over the dealer's stock while I'm bothering him with obscure requests. It would also give us a few minutes to talk before we go back to Amy and Drew's."

A few minutes to talk. What had Will learned that he wouldn't say in front of Amy and Drew? Or Aunt Nettie? Maggie wasn't sure she wanted to know.

Chapter 20

Vaccinium macrocarpon: American Cranberry,
*chromolithograph published by Prang, Boston,
1878. Shows plant, including root and cut-
away of fruit. Information from book* (The
Native Flowers and Ferns of the United States
in their Botanical, Horticultural, and Popular
Aspects, *by Thomas Meehan*) *in which this
plate was found includes natural habitat of
cranberries, poetry written about them, and
details about the cranes that are attracted to
them. Information attached. Few nineteenth-
century renderings of the American cranberry
exist. 7 x 10 inches. Price: $70.*

Maggie had already perused the Medical and
Children's shelves at Books Older Than U when
Will came up behind her. He reached around and
hugged her, including the two books she was holding. She leaned back against him and, for a moment,
felt safe, and far from Crystal and babies and car
crashes and the challenges of relationships. A hug
from a large man was reassuring in a primal way.

"Found anything good?" The voice in her ear was just lascivious enough to imply something more than a book worth purchasing.

Maggie stood up straight and turned around. "You, sir, have a slightly dirty mind."

"Only slightly? What have I done wrong this morning?"

Maggie held up one of the books. "An Arthur Rackham. *Peter Pan in Kensington Garden.* One of my favorites, and I'm almost out of stock of these illustrations."

Will peeked over her shoulder at a picture of a baby sitting up in a tree discussing life with a crow of approximately the same size. At the base of the tree, two lifelike mice (except that they were wearing blue-polka-dotted ties and blue-and-white-striped socks with their shoes) were listening in. "Nice. And what a sense of humor." He pointed at one mouse that was using a miniature shoehorn. "But the colors are so muted and the details so tiny! Do people buy prints like those to frame and hang?"

"They do. Often. Rackham is one of the few early-twentieth-century illustrators I carry. His work is unmistakable. No one else drew fairies and ghosts and small woodland creatures and elves the way Arthur Rackham could. My personal favorites are his series of mermaid illustrations for *Undine.* They're very art nouveau and very hard to find. Rackham has become much more popular during the past fifteen years. You used to be able to pick up a book like this for around twenty dollars. This one is a third edition and reasonably priced at one hun-

dred and twenty-five dollars. I've seen first editions
for three hundred dollars or more in New York or
New Jersey. *Undine* had a small printing and would
go for several times that. And a friend in England
tells me Rackham prices in America are considered
bargains. In the U.K., prices for the books he illustrated have gone through the roof. The only thing
you have to be careful about is that Rackham's
work has been reprinted within the last twenty
years. Some print dealers might be tempted to sell
those reproductions as originals."

"Not you."

"Not me. I guarantee the dates on my prints. But
some of the later-twentieth-century reproductions
were done well. I wouldn't buy any loose Rackham
prints myself. I prefer finding the original book.
Then I know for sure what the date is."

"So you've found something already. Need more
time?"

"I haven't even checked the shelves of natural
history!" Maggie turned back and then added, "I
saw some shelves of modern secondhand paperbacks in the front. Would you see if there are any
suspense or mystery novels there that Drew might
like? He's already getting bored."

Maggie headed for the Natural History section,
where she most often found books with color
plates. She overheard Will asking the owner for several history books.

Most of the shelves she scanned quickly. The
bindings were obviously twentieth century, which
meant the illustrations were too recent for her—and,

most likely, were photographs. She didn't carry photographs, not even early ones. That required knowledge that she had found neither the time nor the interest to acquire. But prices of daguerreotypes and early photographs were skyrocketing. She'd already missed out on any dealer's window of opportunity. All she knew were the basics: the earlier the better; the more identifiable the subjects, the better; men in uniforms, especially Civil War uniforms, were good; Native Americans and African-Americans from the mid–nineteenth century were good; animals and children were good. The chance of getting any real bargains on early photographs was rare today.

Her hand stopped on a set of four leather-bound books titled *Flowers and Ferns* by Meehan. She opened one of the volumes carefully. It was beautifully bound, but a number of the illustrations had come loose. Not good for a book dealer; not bad for a print dealer. Although she would hate to hurt these bindings.

The cover page listed the actual title as *The Native Flowers and Ferns of the United States in Their Botanical, Horticultural, and Popular Aspects.* So far so good. She hadn't heard of this book. Most of the ferns she had were from the British Cassell's series and were beautifully lithographed, but they were European. American customers wanted American subjects. Prang was the publisher of these volumes. Maggie's smile widened. Prang, located in Boston, was an outstanding American printer of chromolithographs. Chromolithography had been perfected in Germany and Switzerland, but Prang had come close to reaching that perfection. The technique was time-consuming and expensive and was used for a window of perhaps thirty years. She checked the date: 1878. For an American chromolithograph, that was early. She looked carefully through the pages, which had some foxing, the yellowish brown discoloration that meant the book had at some time been exposed to dampness. For the book's age the foxing wasn't bad. Some customers saw foxing as a distinguished sign of age, much as an elderly gentleman would not be embarrassed by fine lines on his face. But a dealer also had to keep in mind that some customers would reject a print with any foxing. Some of these chromos were beautiful; others would not be salable.

Maggie started paging through the four volumes to get an estimate of how many of these prints would sell well. She would then divide that number into the dealers' price for the set of books and make her decision as to whether it would be a good purchase for her.

Remember, Maggie, she said to herself, you still have to remove these and mat them. And they'll have to be matted individually because the chromos fill the pages to different degrees. No measuring one print and then cutting three dozen mats to match. These books would consume hours of time before she could get them close to a customer.

There were 45 to 50 chromos in each book; perhaps 190 total. But some were badly foxed; some of those that were loose had torn edges. And some of the subjects would sell much faster than others.

Customers wanted big, bright flowers for their walls, not tiny, delicate ones. She hesitated again. This collection showed the plants' roots. That would turn off some buyers, although someone truly interested in botany would consider it a plus.

Unfortunately, not that many botanists were looking for nineteenth-century prints.

The dealer was asking $1,000 for the four-volume set. She did the math in her head: 180 prints, but perhaps only half of those would sell well. So— 90. A little over $10 a plate. She looked through the second and third books again. She could probably get $60 a plate for the better plates. But not for all. A good profit, but not a guaranteed one. And first she'd have to do all that matting.

Let's say that after matting she could make an average of $40 a print. Optimistic. She'd then have to sell twenty-five flowers or ferns to get her initial investment back.

Maggie put the books back on the shelves. It was a nice printing. She hadn't seen it before; no doubt it was a limited edition.

But she already had the Cassell's ferns, which were slightly larger, and brighter, and therefore more salable even though they were European.

And she didn't relish the idea of hours of matting these particular prints. The leather bindings were beautiful. Maybe this dealer would find someone who would value the whole package. She hoped so, because it was a special set. But, no, not quite right for her.

Maybe she just wasn't in the right mood to

spend that much money. She had just bought the Wilson birds at the auction.

Will was at the front of the store sorting through a stack of used paperbacks. "This is a great collection of bestsellers for vacation reading. Only one dollar each. Bargains!"

Maggie agreed, and they chose ten books for Drew, and several each for themselves. Will had found one of the books on his friend's list: an early Washington Irving in acceptable condition for someone interested in the content, not the binding.

"Not a bad shop," said Maggie, as they left. "Maybe I should have bought those flowers and ferns."

"Stick to your initial instincts. My experience so far with you, Maggie, is that your instincts are usually right."

"I wish I had better instincts about what is happening with Amy and Drew."

"Let's put the books in our cars and go and sit over by the water." Will pointed at some large rocks comfortably situated so they had a full view of Waymouth Harbor. "I want to tell you about my visit with the Learys."

"Giles Leary is your second cousin? Third cousin?"

"Close enough. I've never been into genealogy that much. He and I are about the same age and spent a lot of summertimes together when we were growing up. 'Hanging out' the kids would call it now. We called it fishing and rowing and clam digging and perfecting our curveballs."

"A childhood from the dim, dark ages," Maggie said, smiling. "Before video games. So you and Giles go back a bit."

"That's why I felt comfortable stopping in. He's done all right over the years; hasn't made a fortune working for Johnny Brent, but he and Mary have a nice little house not far from Aunt Nettie's, and they have Brian."

"Brian was a close friend of Crystal Porter's from what I gathered."

"More than a close friend. Turns out I got there just in time last night to hear part of a major argument he and his dad were having."

"About Crystal?"

"And about who was the father of her child." Will hesitated a moment. "Brian said that he must be, but she hadn't told him she was pregnant. He was really furious at her. Kept saying he would have married her. He loved her. He would have taken care of her."

"Well, that explains the pregnancy." Maggie hoped it did. Crystal had been sleeping with Drew. And now Brian. Could there have been any other man involved? And was Brian really the father of her child? Crystal hadn't told him. Or maybe she didn't really know. "And his parents' reactions?"

"Mary was pretty quiet. She tried to calm both Brian and Giles. She said Crystal was gone; they should mourn her and do what they could to find her killer. Her pregnancy was water under the bridge, and Brian should just keep quiet about his role in her situation."

"They said all that with you there?"

"Well, part of it they said while I was still on the porch, ready to knock. Voices go right through screen doors. But I did knock, and Mary let me in. Everyone was pretty quiet for a few minutes, and then Brian went stomping off."

"Sounds like a teenager's reaction."

"Mary knows Giles and I are old friends. She got us some coffee and then excused herself. She looked pretty tired."

"And torn between her husband and son. Did you and Giles talk?"

"We said polite things for a while, and then we added some cognac to our coffee and talked about when we'd been young."

Maggie looked out to the harbor. A teenaged boy had just rounded the point downriver in a small, bright green speedboat and almost swamped two kayakers. Kids. Taking risks that could so easily get out of control.

"I found out what Giles's real problem was."

"Other than having a son who didn't practice safe sex and whose girlfriend was just murdered? That sounds real enough to me."

Will ignored her sarcasm. "Giles had told Brian time and time again to stay away from Crystal."

"Because she was trouble?"

"Because she might be Brian's sister."

Chapter 21

—◆—

The American Tar: Don't Give Up the Ship.
*Hand-colored lithograph of young, bearded
American sailor dressed in traditional white
pants, blue sea jacket, and middy, posed on a
blue sea chest with the American flag in the
background. (Tar, from tarpaulin, was a slang
expression for a sailor.) N. Currier, 1845.
(Pre–Currier & Ives partnership.) 11.14 x 8.8
inches; small folio. Price: $600.*

"Crystal was Brian's sister?" Maggie thought back
quickly. "You said Rachel hadn't told anyone who
the father of her baby was. So it was Giles?"

"He thought it might be. He hadn't told Brian
that, of course. He just told Brian that Crystal was
his cousin, which she was in any case, and he
should lighten up the relationship."

"And he didn't."

"I asked Giles if he was sure Crystal was his
daughter. He wasn't positive. But he thought there
was a good possibility."

"I remember you said several young men around

town were glad when Rachel didn't name anyone as Crystal's father. So it could have been someone else too."

"It could." Will looked at Maggie. "For example, it could have been me."

Maggie just sat.

Everyone had a past.

But sometimes it was easier not knowing about it. "You? You walked out on a pregnant girl knowing she might be having your baby?"

"I'm not proud of it, Maggie. I had just graduated from college, and my mind was on my future. I figured Rachel was the only one who knew for sure, and if she'd wanted my help after the baby was born, she would have said so. She never said anything."

"Did she say anything to Giles?"

"Nope. I asked him, and he said the same thing. That after Crystal was born he was waiting to be called on the whole situation. Rachel didn't open her mouth."

Maggie sat for a moment, trying to absorb this new information. Her own feelings about Will's actions were getting in the way of her logic. She must remain calm. She must think. "Rachel is the only one who really knows who Crystal's father is."

"If she did know for sure. There were several of us around that year. It might not have been Giles or me."

"Who else could it have been? For example?"

"Tom Colby."

"Who was also Rachel's cousin. Right?"

"Right."

"Do you think Rachel ever told Crystal who her father was?"

"I doubt it. If she had, I suspect Crystal would have told someone else or contacted her dad to say hi. I don't think she knew."

"Do you know if Rachel tried to break up Crystal and Brian?"

"Giles said she did. But it might just have been any mother trying to keep her daughter away from boys."

"The detective who came the other day, the one you knew?"

"Nick Strait."

Maggie looked at Will. "He's about your age, and Giles's. I suppose he's also a possible candidate for fatherhood?"

Will grimaced. "No, Maggie. Not everyone in the state of Maine. Just a few of us, that one summer."

"He said Rachel didn't know Crystal had been pregnant. But when Amy and I were in her room— Rachel asked Amy to take back some books Crystal had borrowed about New York—I saw magazines about baby care. And adoption. If her mother had seen those in her room, she would have at least suspected the pregnancy."

"What did you do with the magazines?"

"I took them with me. The adoption magazines were Amy's and I didn't want Rachel seeing the other magazines if she hadn't noticed them before."

"Rachel would have been plenty mad if she'd known Crystal was following in her footsteps."

"And if she thought there was even a possibility

that Brian and Crystal were brother and sister . . ."

"How angry can a mother get? How worried?"

"I don't know, Will. Upset enough to kill her own daughter?"

They both sat on the rocks in silence for a time. A lobsterman checked his traps nearby. A young couple jogged down the road. Two crows squawked a warning to a nearby chipmunk.

"Will, you told me a secret. I'm not happy to know it, but I am glad you trusted me enough to tell me." Maggie stared out at the river. The waves made by the small motorboat's wake were now lapping the shore. "I know something too that I haven't told anyone." She turned and looked at Will. "Crystal also slept with Drew Douglas. I don't know how often, but at least once."

"How did you find that out?"

"I saw them." Maggie avoided looking at Will.

"Did you tell Amy?"

"I couldn't. I just couldn't. And now Crystal's dead, and I'm not sure what I should do. But if the afternoon I saw them wasn't the only time, Brian might not be the father of Crystal's child."

Will reached over and took Maggie's hand. After a few minutes she took it back. "Will, we have to think. Who would have had a reason to kill Crystal? Her mother could have known she was pregnant and been so furious she did something unthinkable. Brian talks a good story now, but he wouldn't have been the first teenaged boy to turn on a pregnant girlfriend. Could Giles have known? Or maybe he was trying to break them up and got into an argument with Crystal. He was there working on Amy and Drew's home too." Maggie felt totally confused.

"And what if Crystal had threatened to tell Amy about her relationship with Drew?"

"Oh, Will. If Crystal was carrying Drew's child, how would Amy feel? She's been trying so hard to get pregnant. I can't tell her."

"Someone is pretty mad at Drew if they cut the brake lines on his car. Are you sure Amy didn't know about him and Crystal?"

"And what about the fire earlier, and the telephone calls? Maybe Brian suspected something and was getting back at Drew."

"If you start assigning blame for actions like those, you could even put Crystal on the list. Maybe she was jealous of Amy."

"You said Shirley Steele was pretty put out when Amy and Drew moved into the house. Maybe she's strongly suggesting they move on."

"Or Tom Colby thinks the Douglas house would be a great place for sister Shirley and her kids to go."

"Even if Drew and Amy left, that doesn't mean Shirley, or anyone in the family, would get the house."

"No."

They both sat in silence, knowing they were expected back at Amy and Drew's house soon. And that right now that was the last place either of them wanted to be.

Chapter 22

—❧—

Great Fire in Portland, Maine: Tents Among the Ruins, *and* Great Fire in Portland, Maine: Distributing Food to the Citizens at the Old City Hall. *Two wood engravings by Stanley Fox on the cover of* Harper's Weekly, *July 28, 1866, including the* HW *title art: "A Journal of Civilization," with an artist's palette, a telescope, a book, a globe, a pen, and a lyre. (The Portland fire was the result of mismanaged fireworks on the Fourth of July and destroyed about one-third of the city.) Full page, 11 x 16 inches. Price: $75.*

"You're finally here! I was beginning to worry." Amy met them out on the lawn. "I've been back from the library for over an hour now, and I thought our schedules were pretty well coordinated."

Amy and her schedules!

"I'll bet you found all sorts of bargains at that bookshop or just took off for some . . . personal time." Amy looked from Maggie to Will and then back again. "That's it! I'm sure! You just wanted some time on your own. Well, why not?"

"We found some books to add to Drew's reading list," said Maggie, handing Amy the bag of books. "And we each found a couple of the volumes we were looking for too, so it was a successful bookstore visit."

"Drew will have a vast selection, now," Amy agreed, looking into the bag. "Between what I found at the library and these, he may not even mind having to keep quiet for a while."

"How is he feeling?" asked Will.

"He's still a little dopey from the medication and the pain. And frustrated by the whole situation."

"Frustration sounds like a good sign. It's better than boredom," Will said. "Why don't I go in and say hello, he's probably feeling very left out with us talking here on the lawn."

"What's next on the list, Amy?" Maggie asked.

"We were going to look at your Homers. But Drew said Will was going to check out the old kitchen. They talked about it the other day. Drew's still concerned about the fire we had earlier this summer."

"I can understand that. Especially now. He wouldn't exactly be able to leap out of the house were there a problem."

"No."

"And how is your arm, by the way? We've been so focused on Drew's leg I forgot to ask."

Amy held her elbow out to display. "It's doing all right. Just takes time. And it's been less than a week."

"And a week ago I was still doing an antiques show in Provincetown. Which reminds me that later tonight I'd like to call Gussie. I promised I would."

"Whenever you'd like."

Drew and Will were deep in conversation in the living room. "Do you know when they stopped using it as the kitchen?"

"No. From what your aunt said, maybe as late as the early 1930s."

"And have you had the chimneys cleaned and inspected since you've been here?" Will was clearly quizzing Drew.

"There are two chimneys. The one over the ell, which would have gone to the old kitchen, we haven't had checked at all, other than Giles and Brian tarring around it when they were working on the new ell roof. The main house has five flues—one for each of the old fireplaces—all in one central chimney."

Maggie, listening, thought quickly. The old kitchen, living room, dining room, and the two master bedrooms. A classic colonial mansion.

"And have you had that chimney checked?" Will was pressing a point Maggie wasn't sure of.

"The flue that originally led to the dining room fireplace had been closed off whenever Charlotte put in central heating. We had the company that supplies our oil come and clean and check that one. It was dirty, but structurally okay. The guy who came took a fast look at the other flues. He said they'd need to be lined before we could safely use the fireplaces."

"And so you haven't."

"No. Of course not. We may be from the city, but we know an old frame building could go up quickly. That's why we were so concerned over the fire in the ell. Would you mind taking a look?"

"There are a couple of possibilities. You said the fire department couldn't locate the source of the fire."

"They said it wasn't electrical. The only electricity in that room is one lightbulb hanging from the ceiling. But some material burned. Luckily, it gave off a lot of smoke, and one of the first things we did when we moved in was install smoke detectors."

"Let me get the flashlight I have in my car. The room is in the center of the ell?"

"I'll meet you there," said Drew, pulling himself to his feet and standing on his crutches, despite Amy's glares. She and Maggie followed him out through the kitchen to the series of small rooms that in many New England homes connected the barn with the main part of the house. Ells were originally designed to make it easier to care for animals and get supplies into a house in bad weather.

Maggie smelled the lingering odor of smoke as soon as they stepped across a low threshold into the room, empty except for smoke marks on the walls and ceiling, and a spot about three by four feet where the pine floor had charred, and the center had burned through. That spot was close to the brick wall Aunt Nettie had mentioned. Maggie crouched down near the hole; there was earth just below it. "There's no basement under the ell?"

"No."

Maggie reached down and touched the ashes and dirt below the flooring. "It's damp!" she said, surprised. There had been no rain since she had been in Maine.

"The fire department guy said that was one of the things that saved the house. Along with our hearing the smoke detector, and Amy's calling 911 immediately while I used our kitchen fire extinguishers. There might be a spring under the ell. That would also explain why no one dug a basement here."

Will came in at the end of Drew's explanation. "That makes sense too when you look at this wall. Aunt Nettie said this was used as a kitchen in the 1830s. A kitchen then would need the same things a kitchen would need today: water, and a way to cook. She said there had been a stove in this room. A wood-burning iron stove would have been the height of modern kitchen appliances in the 1830s." Will got down on his hands and knees and crawled along the floor, looking at it closely. "I'd say this floor has been replaced at least once, maybe more often, since 1830. With the dampness underneath, probably it rotted out periodically. It wouldn't have been hard to replace. But because this isn't the original flooring, we can't see exactly where the stove was."

He stood up again. "But we know it had to be vented through a stovepipe to the chimney over this section of the ell, and the brick wall was a part of that." He opened each of several iron doors in the brick wall. "The compartment behind this door"— he pointed to the lowest one, which was almost on the floor—"probably was to store foodstuffs so they wouldn't freeze. Anything needing what we would think of as refrigeration would have been put in the cellar of the main house. I'll bet there are remnants of bins or storage containers there, right?"

Amy nodded.

"This door," Will continued, moving up the wall, "was probably for the stovepipe." He got out his flashlight and beamed it up into the space. "I can't tell for sure, but I'll bet this is a straight track to the chimney you haven't had checked, on the ell roof."

"What is this big depression in the bricks, lined with metal?" Amy asked. "It's big enough to bathe a baby in!"

"And might have been used for that. But, more likely, considering that personal cleanliness was not considered as vital in the 1830s as it is today, it was used to wash dishes or clothing. Today there are no entrances or exits for water, but I'd be willing to bet that at some point in the past there was a pump near here, to bring the water from that under-ground spring you mentioned into this room. The water would then be put in this container to warm it; the container would have been near the stove, remember, and on the same wall as the stovepipe. And there might have been an outside drain at some point. That could have been covered or torn out when the floor was replaced."

"That's interesting," said Drew. "You obviously know your old kitchens. But how could a fire have started?"

"The fire was here, right?" Will pointed at the hole in the floor.

"Yes."

"So the fire was pretty much where the old stove must have been."

"All right."

Will hesitated. "Now, I'm guessing. I haven't been up on your roof, and I haven't examined your chimney. But you said the fire was in material of some sort."

"At first I thought we might have left some cleaning cloths out here, while we were emptying these rooms." Drew hesitated. "There was some junk in the ell that we took to the dump. Wooden crates and cardboard boxes and hundreds of old bleach bottles and peanut butter jars."

"We assumed Charlotte was saving them to use for canning," added Amy.

"Most likely. Most women up here can vegetables in summer, and although Charlotte didn't do any preserving in her last years, she probably would have kept the supplies out of habit. But you decided no cloths had been left."

"We didn't think so. We told ourselves that somehow we must have left something here, though, or nothing would have ignited."

Will shook his head. "I can tell you're pretty careful people. I don't think you left any cleaning cloths here. I think someone put some cleaning solvent on some rags, perhaps wrapped the rags around a small child's bouncing ball that would keep everything moving, and dropped them down the chimney from the roof."

Amy went over to the brick wall. "But the iron

door was closed. The material wouldn't have gone anywhere."

"Wait a minute, Amy." Drew hobbled over to the site of the fire. "I think Will is right. The door was open that night. I remember one of the firemen closing it to stop any drafts from accelerating the fire."

"We always closed it," Amy pointed out. "I thought there'd be dust up there, and I didn't want it coming down into a room we'd just cleaned."

Will spoke slowly. "I think someone came into the house, opened that door, and then left. Then either the same person, or an accomplice, dropped the fiery cloth down the chimney, hoping it would start a blaze. You've been having roof work done, right?"

"All summer," said Amy. "Different parts of the roof, of course."

"So there have been ladders around."

Drew inhaled deeply. "Someone tried to burn the house down. And we were in it."

Will nodded. "I'm not an expert, but the possibility fits the circumstances."

"And that someone was able to get into the house without our knowing it."

Or with their knowledge, Maggie thought. The construction crew, Giles and Brian, had been in and out all summer. Tom Colby, from next door, seemed familiar with the house. Crystal had been there.

Of course, half of Madoc was familiar with the house. It was the Brewer house.

"Let's go back to the living room," Amy said.

"Drew should have his leg up. And I think we should all have a drink."

"Or two," added Drew.

Will and Maggie waited a minute before following them.

"You've really scared them. And me," said Maggie.

"But they need to know. And"—Will gently touched Maggie's cheek—"I'm not too thrilled you're staying here just now."

The touch wilted Maggie for a moment. She wished he would hold her and make all the problems connected with this house disappear, if only for a moment. But she was a realist. "I'm not going to be scared off, and neither are Drew nor Amy."

"Now the question is . . . did whoever set the fire have any connection to Crystal's death?"

Despite the August heat Maggie shivered slightly as they walked back through the ell to the kitchen, where she could already hear the tinkling of wineglasses. For once she wasn't interested in diet cola.

Chapter 23

———~———

The United States Arsenal at Augusta, Maine.
Wood engraving by Kilburn, published in
Gleason's Pictorial, 1857. *Shows arsenal,
American flag, and the Kennebec River entry
to the arsenal, including two small boats.*
6 x 6 inches. Price: $45.

Despite his words, Drew knew he shouldn't drink
while he was taking medication. "Someone may be
trying to get us, but I'm not going to make it that
easy for them," he joked.

The other three sipped a fragrant burgundy on
the porch, watched a lobsterman pull three of his
traps and check them as herring gulls followed in
expectation, and tried not to think too hard about
the possibility of someone's getting access to the
house. Access to Drew's car would not have been a
problem. It had just been parked in the driveway.
This was Madoc. It hadn't even been locked.

Maggie turned from the river scene to the ell.
"What is above the old kitchen room and the other
rooms in the ell? I just realized there is space there."

Amy answered, "Lots of space. That's the attic. Someday we might want to finish it off, but for now we've just started cleaning it out, especially where there were leaks. Some trunks and boxes are there, and we've put our winter clothes and Christmas ornaments in the corners we've cleaned. After living in New York City, having that much space for storage is a real luxury."

Will and Maggie looked at each other.

"What sorts of things are in the trunks and boxes?" Will asked.

"Papers, mostly. Some look like old captain's logs." Amy put up her hand to stop Will's words. "I know; they probably belong in your family. They shouldn't have been left here. But they were, and I had planned to check through them, just to see what we could learn about the people who lived in this house, and then donate them to the Waymouth Library. Their archives could use the local history information, and that would make the papers available to anyone who wanted to study them."

"An excellent plan, Amy," said Will. "I wasn't trying to interfere. In fact, that's what the family should have done years ago, since my guess is the heat and cold in that attic space haven't been kind to those papers."

"You're right. And there were several cartons of papers I just threw out, because mice or red squirrels had chewed them up, probably for nesting materials."

"But what fun to look through the things!" Maggie felt more relaxed now. Going through old boxes of what someone had once considered a treasure was a familiar and potentially exciting task. "Amy, would you mind awfully if Will and I took a look at the attic? Just in case there's something there you might not have noticed."

Amy hesitated.

"I promise! We won't touch anything without your permission."

"I was just thinking. Crystal helped me put some clothes and boxes up there to store, and we had to move some of the really horrendous stuff. There was a chair whose seat had totally mildewed from the rain dripping down, and whose wooden frame is water-stained and warped. And there was a box of old toys Crystal looked through one afternoon. I gave her a small carved boat that she particularly liked." Amy looked over at Drew, who was dozing a bit after his most recent dose of pain medication. "Why not? Come on. It will take our minds off other things."

"Wasn't one of the rumors about this house that there was treasure hidden in it?" said Maggie. "Seems to me I heard someone say so. Maybe Shirley."

"Unless Shirley thinks pickle jars filled with dust and dead flies are a treasure, or she really values stacks of green plastic blueberry baskets, I don't know what in the attic would meet the criterion of 'treasure.' But why not look? If you both don't mind getting a little dusty."

The attic space was as Amy had described it. Larger than Maggie had imagined, and, although she could see some parts had been cleaned out and the floor swept and new cartons stacked, most of it was still untouched.

"When we bought the house it was supposed to be empty. But at the last minute the Realtor said the owner hadn't had time to clean out this area." Amy shrugged her shoulders a bit. "We thought the same thing you did—maybe treasure! But that was before we started going through it. We haven't checked everything. And the papers should go to the library. But what is really needed up here, I'm afraid, is a direct slide to a Dumpster. We took several carloads of stuff to the dump, and Giles took a truckload for us one weekend. But we just haven't had time to get into a lot of this stuff. We had to clean out the rooms below here too, you know."

The attic was hot and stuffy. Will tried to open one of the low windows that lined the room but gave up. "They've been painted closed. Many times. They could be opened, but it would take a while."

"We just thought we'd leave them that way for now," Amy said. "At least in the winter we won't worry about too many breezes blowing through here. There is so much that has to be done in this house that the windows in the attic just didn't seem a priority."

"At some point you should do them, though," said Will. "There's very little ventilation in here. Not good for whatever you're storing, and . . ."

"Possibly a fire hazard," finished Amy. "You're right. But not this afternoon." She gave them a brief overview. "Crystal and I did try to organize this corner. There"—she pointed at a carton in a corner—"is the carton of toys. And there are the three trunks of papers I told you about."

Maggie walked toward them, totally entranced by the idea of trunks full of nineteenth-century papers, but Amy continued her tour. "We didn't get all the way back into that corner, but there are several boxes of old picture frames. And a lot of broken glass."

"Are any of the frames Victorian?" Maggie asked. "Gilt? Or Currier and Ives frames?"

"You can check that out for me. Just be careful not to cut your hands on all the broken glass." Amy glanced down at the bandage on her arm. "Crystal and I piled all the parts of chairs over there. It looks as though every time a straight chair was broken they stuck it up here. It's like a giant Lincoln Logs set. Maybe some of the pieces could be put together to form a full chair. But I don't know if any of the chairs would be worth the time. That pile over beyond the chairs is just old cardboard and boxes. Crystal and I thought we'd take them to the dump some afternoon." Amy paused a moment. "There's an old bureau in the corner, but it was under a leak, and it's so warped we couldn't open the drawers, so maybe your treasure is in there. The rest of the stuff"—she gestured at piles of broken electric fans and heaters, a large carton of moth-or-mouse-eaten yarn, a small collection of used marker buoys, some clam baskets, and an assortment of unidentifiable wooden and metal objects—"well, you're welcome to look through it." She grinned. "And don't forget to check all the boxes of birds' nests and eggs and dried seaweed and sea glass and shells. This place is full of treasures." She started sneezing. "And my allergies are another reason we didn't spend more time up here. I must be sensitive to dust. Would you mind checking this stuff on your own for a while?"

"No problem," said Maggie. "While we're up here, would you like us to fill some garbage bags or boxes with stuff like the old birds' nests? They're not going to help your allergies and should be disposed of."

"I'd love it!" She reached up on top of a wardrobe near the door and handed them a box of supermarket plastic garbage bags. "You see, I just happen to have some handy. Have fun, both of you. If you find any diamonds or emeralds, let me know. And—I'd prefer the emeralds. They're my birthstone!" Amy sneezed her way out of the attic and down the stairs.

"Wow." Will looked around. "And this is part of my family's heritage too. Maybe my great-grandfather sat on one of those chairs and broke it."

"If you're going to get sentimental, Will, that's fine. I suspect Amy might even let you take that broken chair as a souvenir. She was right; this place is really dusty and hot. I don't think we'll want to spend a lot of time here."

"But we certainly should check some things." Will lifted the wooden lid on one of the trunks. "It would be easier to go through the papers downstairs. The light would be better, the dust would be minimal, and they are going to the library anyway."

Maggie sadly agreed. "So we'll put those off for now."

"Why don't you check out the frames, and I'll look under some of these junk piles and make sure there's nothing of value that Amy and Crystal missed."

Maggie picked up one of the empty cartons and shook it to get at least some of the dust and dead insects out. "A garbage bag would be no good for glass, and I've been warned. I'll at least isolate the large pieces so they can safely go to the dump without harming anyone. There have been enough accidents around here already."

Will took a garbage bag. "My good deed will be disposing of some of these birds' nests and small pieces of driftwood." The attic beams were covered with rows of them. "Even if my great-grandfather collected them, I think their time is over." He reached up and took the nearest one down and dropped it in the plastic bag.

"Make sure to check for Amy's emeralds before you throw anything out, now!"

"This was my family's home, remember? I don't seem to remember any family jewels, missing or not missing. If there is treasure here, I don't think it's a bird's nest full of diamonds." Will reached up to take another one down and started coughing. "Although that would have been a good hiding place. I don't think these things have been touched in a hundred years."

"I was surprised at the box of toys. Everyone has

said there were only single women who've lived here for the last hundred years."

"Which means, of course, that those toys are definitely going to be checked out," Will agreed. "Although some of those ladies could have kept some toys around for nieces and nephews and cousins to play with when they visited. Being unmarried doesn't mean being a hermit."

"I certainly hope not," Maggie said quietly to herself. That was a nice thought. The unmarried ladies of the house keeping a box of toys for visiting children. She worked her way through to several cartons filled with frames. "This is going to take more than a couple of minutes."

"Not to worry. There are plenty of birds' nests here to keep me occupied." Will was happily working his way down the beams and already had half a garbage bag filled.

It was peaceful in the attic, and despite the heat, Maggie and Will worked comfortably together.

Within an hour they had two cartons of glass and five garbage bags of junk ready for the dump, and Maggie had chosen about a dozen frames that were worth saving. The box of toys had yielded some iron wagons and cars that had some value; several of them more than "some value" Maggie suspected, although she wasn't a dealer in toys. But she had been going to call Gussie sometime today anyway. She'd ask an expert.

Will found one small nineteenth-century iron fireplace set—"Probably originally used in one of the bedrooms!"—and had filled several Mason jars with sea glass. "In case Amy and Drew are the sort who like to display it in their windows. If not, it's all set for the dump."

They took one more look around and decided it was time to share their treasures with Amy and Drew.

No emeralds, but some progress had been made, and they'd found a few things that could be recycled into the house if Amy and Drew chose to do so.

"These picture frames are good ones?" Amy looked interested, if a bit doubtful.

"Definitely. You wanted some nineteenth-century prints. When we get to those, maybe we could match up some frames and pictures."

"It would be nice to hang some of the same picture frames that were originally in the house," Amy agreed. "But the gold on these frames is flaking off. They really don't look that good, Maggie."

"Gold leaf will solve that problem. An art store should have some, and I'm sure someone there can give you lots of advice on how to restore these. I've seen elaborate gilt frames rebuilt and restored, and none of these have major problems."

"And the wooden frames? They're so dingy."

"These three are oak, and this other one I think may be cherry. Liquid Gold is the solution."

"Gold?"

Maggie laughed. "You can get it at the supermarket. It's a very rich oil that you could put on these frames. Probably several times. It will almost erase the use and will put the moisture and richness back in the wood. Just make sure you put the frames on top of some heavy plastic before you put the Liquid Gold on them, because it seeps through anything porous and can make a major mess."

"And the toys?"

"If you don't mind, I'll ask Gussie about them tonight when I call her. She would know how valuable they are. It's up to you whether you keep them or sell them, but you should know what you have."

"I'd like to bring those trunks downstairs to one of the empty rooms in the ell. The light is better there, and Maggie knows paper more than I do. I'm curious because it's my family. But maybe we could all look through them. And at least two of those trunks could also do with some Liquid Gold and would make great coffee tables or blanket chests." Will looked ready to go back for the trunks that moment.

"Do you think the three of us could lift them?" Amy glanced at where Drew was sitting with his foot up.

"I think so," said Will. "If they turn out to be too heavy, we could move some of the papers to cartons and just bring those down."

Agreed, the three of them headed for the attic. The first trunk was embossed metal over wood, and lighter than they anticipated. But taking it downstairs was still a challenge. "There is no way this is simple," Maggie said, laughing. "If Will takes the bottom weight, then he has to walk backward, and we have less weight, but we have to practically bend double to get the stuff down."

"Maybe we could just bump the trunk down from step to step?" Amy asked hopefully.

"No way! That might damage the trunk, and we haven't had a chance to really check it out yet," said Will.

The second trunk was heavier because it was solid wood.

Before they moved the third trunk they all stood in the attic for a moment. "You guys did a great job in only an hour." Amy looked around and only sneezed once. "The birds' nests are down, and I hadn't been able to reach them. And so much of this other stuff is organized better. And I love the iron fireplace set you found, Will! It must have been hidden under that other metal stuff."

"Most of which really is junk," agreed Will. "But it will be fun to have the set back in one of the fireplaces when you have the chimneys cleaned out." He looked down at the trunk they were to move. "Did you say you and Crystal had moved these trunks before?"

"They were over by that outside wall, but there was some dampness there, so we pushed them to the center of the room."

"Have you moved them since then?"

"No; they've just sat here."

Will squatted down and smoothed his fingers over one of the boards in the floor.

"This board looks as though it's been moved recently. There's not as much dirt along the edges as there is near the other boards." They all got down on their hands and knees and looked. Will was right.

"Have you had any of the boards in this floor replaced?"

"No. A couple will need to be, but that's another thing far down our 'to do' list. We figured getting the roof fixed first was most important, since the boards in the floor were getting worse with the dampness. Once the roof was fixed, things would stabilize until we had time to fix them. Were we wrong?"

"You were right. But I think this board has been taken up. Recently."

Will got up and went over to the pile of rusted metal bookcases and pieces of metal and selected one aluminum strip that was thin but sturdy. "Might have been part of a clothes rack at some time," he commented. "Would you mind if I tried this on the loose board? If it's nailed down well, I won't force it. But it's a wide old pine board, and it looks pretty sturdy."

"Go ahead," said Amy. "But I don't know what you're going to find."

"I don't either," said Will. "But I'm curious. There is something different about this board. I want to find out what it is."

He took the piece of metal and slipped it into the crack between the board he was looking at and the next one. He had been right. It was an easy fit, and there was little dirt. Thick dust had settled between the other boards. Maggie and Amy were down on the floor watching as Will pried the board up with remarkably little effort.

"No nails," he said, examining the board. "Or

they were removed long ago. No new marks." He put the four-foot board next to what was now a hole in the floor.

The hole was a space perhaps eight inches deep and four and a half feet long, and it had been lined with a quilt. Many years ago, Maggie noted, as she reached out and touched the edge of the quilt. It was linsey-woolsey, and the soft fibers fell apart in her fingers. But what they were all looking at was what was on top of the quilt.

Five rifles.

"There is your treasure, Amy," Will said softly. "If those guns are what I think they are, they may not be emeralds, but they are definitely treasures."

Chapter 24

~

Eldorado Blackberry, *1892 lithograph, drawn by D. G. Passmore and included in the* Report of the Pomologist, U.S. Department of Agriculture. *One branch of blackberry bush, with fruit and leaves. 5.5 x 9 inches.* Price: $48.

They removed the guns carefully, so the metal would not be scratched. The stocks were walnut; Amy immediately thought a little oil would help. "You said there was an oil that would make the frames look better. Maybe it would help the wood on these rifles."

"Don't even think about it!" said Maggie. "I'm definitely not an expert on firearms. But I know enough to be able to give an educated guess as to what these are, and to know that the less we handle them the better. They are in extraordinary condition. They may never have been used."

They put them carefully next to each other on the living room coffee table so Drew could see them too.

He reached out and touched one, then withdrew his hand. "Watch out! These have angular bayonets. But most nineteenth-century rifles had some sort of bayonet attached. Why would these be so special?"

"Any rifle—any gun, for that matter—made in the nineteenth century was made for heavy and regular use. Like Will's cast-iron pots or brass trammels, they were tools, and they were made to last. They weren't for display. Their construction could mean life or death for someone. So it would be very unusual for a finely made rifle never to have been used. And, of course, that would make certain types of collectors value it very highly." Maggie looked carefully at the rifles. Could they be . . . She knew very little about firearms. But she did know about the Civil War. She looked at Will. "Is it time for me to get out those Winslow Homer prints?"

"I think it is." They smiled at each other, connecting with something to which Amy and Drew did not have a clue.

"Before we start going through prints, I think we should be thinking of dinner," said Drew. "Just because you all had wine early doesn't mean we need to eat at a sophisticated ten o'clock. This is Maine, where the evening news starts at five. And I'm getting hungry!"

Maggie glanced at her watch. It was almost six-thirty. She was hungry too, now that she thought about it.

"Do you folks like fried food?" asked Will. "Because there's a place in Waymouth where they specialize in it. And they do takeout."

Maggie smiled. "Totally evil, and totally delicious, if I'm thinking of the right place."

Will nodded.

"Will took me there the day of the auction preview." The day he told her about this being his family's home. And she'd asked him about ghosts. At least the ghosts hadn't made a visit in the past couple of days. Although she had heard that baby cry. Maggie realized she hadn't even thought about that today. There had been too many more immediate issues to concentrate on.

"Take-out fried food sounds like a wonderful idea. And we should really learn more about the local places to eat. Can we call and order ahead?" said Amy.

"Absolutely. And I'll even play delivery boy and pick up the dinner." Will headed toward the telephone. "That will give you time to get out the Homer prints, Maggie, before I get back."

"The man has a one-track mind," grumbled Maggie.

They decided to make it a buffet. Fried scallops, fried clams, fried haddock, fried shrimp, and onion rings, plus two salads, which they planned to combine. "We'll have more than enough," Will cautioned. "Their portions are generous. But they do make a great blueberry pie too."

As Will took off for Waymouth, Maggie headed for the Shadows inventory in her van to find the Homers. She might as well bring in the Wyeths too, since Amy and Drew had asked about them earlier in the week. It took a few minutes; her portfolios were lined up and tightly packed. Although she had only three portfolios of Homers, and one of Wyeths, she had to move two dozen other portfolios to get to the ones she wanted. Had it only been five days since she'd packed up the van after the Provincetown show? It seemed years. She hardly remembered what she'd sold at the show. As she moved portfolios out of the way, she saw the one labeled "Nast—Christmas." Amy had asked about one of those prints, possibly for the nursery. She pulled it out too and leaned it against the car next to the "Homer—Civil War" and "Homer—Other" portfolios. She still had to find the Wyeth and the "Small Homers" portfolios.

Amy was pleased: the timing was perfect. By the time Will had returned bearing tubs of fried seafood, Amy had set the table and Maggie had found the requested portfolios and put them in the living room.

The kitchen smelled irresistible. Only one thing would have made it even better. "Do you have any beer to go with all this fried food?"

"Maggie! No diet cola?" teased Amy.

Before Maggie could answer, Will pulled out two six-packs of Sam Adams. "Great minds, and so forth. I thought someone might be interested in beer."

"Perfect!"

They sat and ate the fried food with their fingers, saving the formality of knives and forks for their portions of the enormous salad that two orders had turned out to be. Dishes of fresh tartar sauce Amy had mixed up were soon almost finished. For the moment, words weren't important.

After dinner Drew settled himself back on the living room couch. "Now what's the connection you and Will obviously found between Winslow Homer and some guns in our attic?"

Maggie went over to the "Homer—Civil War" portfolio and leafed through the prints. She pulled out a matted wood engraving and handed it to Drew.

The print showed a young Union soldier sitting high in a tree, his rifle balanced on a branch, poised to shoot. "*'The Army of the Potomac—A Sharpshooter on Picket Duty'* I've seen this somewhere before."

"No doubt. Probably in your college survey-of-art course. But you're remembering the oil painting Homer did of this same scene. That oil painting was his first to be exhibited. After that, he did a wood engraving of the same scene. The painting is a classic depiction of innocence—the young man—and death—the rifle—and became so popular that the wood engraving is also one of Homer's best known."

"Which no doubt accounts for the seven-hundred-and-fifty-dollar price tag I see on it."

"True."

"I know enough about the Civil War to know a sharpshooter was a Union soldier whose job was to go ahead of the other troops and pick off the Confederate officers or any other specific men they felt would make a difference to the battle."

Maggie nodded. "Right. There were two sharpshooter regiments. And they used special rifles. Extremely accurate percussion, straight-breech models with double-set triggers. Although several major companies supplied rifles for the Union Army—the Army of the Potomac, as it was known at first—the most accurate were considered to be a special group of the 1859 model of the rifle manufactured by Christian Sharp."

Drew's interest was obviously piqued. "I always thought a sharpshooter was someone who could shoot sharply. As in 'look sharp!'"

"That's what most people think. But actually the Yankee sharpshooter regiments got their name from their Sharps rifles."

"Incredible." Drew looked from the wood engraving to the rifles on the table and back again. "And you think these rifles are the same as the one in the engraving?"

"I don't know for sure. But I've a friend in New Jersey who collects guns, and I've learned a little from him. No matter what these rifles are, they're mid–nineteenth century in mint condition, and that gives them value. But we know they're made by the Sharps Rifle Manufacturing Company in Hartford. It says so on the barrel. What really got me excited was that on the top of the barrel, near the breech, it says 'new model 1859.' I think that's the group of two thousand rifles that were issued in 1862 to Colonel Berdan's First and Second Regiments of sharpshooters." Maggie hesitated. "One thing I don't know: why the letters *J* and *T* are on the buttstocks of all five rifles."

"Would your friend know about the serial numbers?"

"I think he could look them up. There are books tracing the rifles. I once saw a list researched to the point of knowing which serial number had been issued to which Union soldier, and what happened to the soldier. But these guns are different. Because they look so new, they may never have been issued. Or"—Maggie hesitated—"I hate to accuse any of your ancestors, Will, but someone might have lightened the munitions supply a little."

"I know there were a couple of people in the family who fought in the Civil War. Tom would know their regiments. I'd never heard any of them were sharpshooters, but they might have been. There were members of Berdan's regiments from Maine."

"If these rifles are what you think they are; if their serial numbers agree they were some of the guns issued to Berdan's sharpshooters, then how much would they be worth?" Amy sat on the floor next to Drew's couch and held the wood engraving he'd handed to her.

"I don't know. Especially if these rifles were—liberated—during the Civil War and then hidden for some reason. They may be the only ones in this condition. There would be no comparables. We'd probably be talking in the thousands." Maggie hesitated. "But that isn't an estimate, and we haven't checked the serial numbers. You'd need a firearms expert to confirm my suspicions; someone who was an expert would also have a knowledge of current values."

"We understand," said Drew. "But obviously until we know for sure what these rifles are, and have decided what we're going to do with them, we need to get them out of sight and into some safe place."

"You're right. And that's one of the things that's bothering me," put in Maggie. "Will found these because we moved the trunks and he noticed that one of the boards in the attic floor was different. It had been moved before. Not long ago. If these rifles were hidden there after the Civil War and not disturbed until now, there would have been plenty of dust around that board, just as there was around the other boards upstairs. I think Will is right, and someone else found these before we did."

"Chances are it was pretty recently, then," said Amy. "Because that attic was totally crammed with boxes and cartons and broken furniture when we moved in. Those piles had been there for years."

"When did you and Crystal clear out the space in the middle of the attic and move the trunks?"

"About three weeks ago. It was just after we'd moved some of Drew's and my winter clothes, and those formal dresses I told you about, Maggie, into the old wardrobe in the attic. I noticed the dampness near the trunks and wanted to prevent any further damage to the papers, so Crystal and I spent the rest of that day, and the next one, cleaning out."

"That was about the middle of July," Drew said. "I remember taking several loads of the junk you found to the dump."

"So there were only one or two days when that space was empty: after you took the junk away, and before you moved the trunks."

"That sounds right."

Maggie hesitated. "Do you remember whether you moved the trunks before or after the fire?"

"It happened right about that time," Amy said slowly. "I remember thinking that, thank goodness, we had gotten a lot of stuff out of the attic before the fire, so at least that wouldn't have added to the flames."

"So whoever set the fire could have found the rifles," Drew said.

"It's possible. But if they did—and knew their value—then why wouldn't they have taken them?" Amy looked unconvinced.

"Maybe they didn't know the value. Maybe they didn't have time."

"Or maybe they did take one, to find out how valuable they were. And, if they were valuable, whoever found them planned to come back for the others."

"That sounds silly. Why not just take them all at once? Especially if the person set the fire. If the building had gone up, so would the rifles." Amy shook her head.

"Maybe because you and Drew found the fire much faster than anyone thought you would. Maybe there wasn't time," Maggie said.

"Wait a minute. I don't see how the fire and the rifles could really be connected. Will said maybe the fire could have been dropped down the chimney from the roof. That would mean someone climbed up a ladder to the roof, and then got down fast, so no one would see him. Before he might get caught in the fire." Amy was making a mental itinerary.

"But someone had to have been in the house before that to open the iron door to the flue."

"But those are separate levels. The iron door is on the first floor. The rifles were in the floor of the attic, which we saw this afternoon wasn't accessible through a window. Someone would have to have gone up the stairs, through a couple of empty rooms, and into the attic." Drew shrugged. "I think we're trying to connect events that just aren't related to each other."

Maggie thought a moment. "Maybe. But the timing is certainly close. Were Giles and Brian working on that part of the roof then?"

"They might have been," Drew said. "I don't remember. They were on the roof of the main house in the early part of July; there was a lot of rotten wood there to replace. But not as much as on the ell. They've been up on the ell roof since, well, it could be mid-July. They've just about finished."

"During the roofing there might have been a time when there would have been an opening from the roof to the attic."

"Giles and Brian wouldn't have left a hole in the roof even for one night," said Amy. "They've been so careful about everything."

"But they might have left part of the roof tarped for one night, especially if no bad weather was predicted. I've done that when I've been roofing," said Will. "Lots of people do."

"I can't believe Giles and Brian would have set a fire, or looked for rifles, though! It doesn't make sense," said Amy.

"There are a lot of things that don't make sense," Maggie said. "But for right now I think we'd better hide these rifles somewhere in the main house."

"If someone were checking to see their value and found out they were worth money, they would come back for the rest." Drew looked around the room. "Well, one thing we haven't had so far in this house is a burglar."

Maggie remembered Tom Colby, the Civil War reenactor, looking through the window. And something else clicked into place. But accusing anyone now would be pointless. Tom was Will's cousin, and Drew's friend. It might be nothing.

"Let's just put the rifles under our bed, upstairs," said Amy. "No one would look there, and they'll be safe until we have them checked out."

While Amy and Will put the rifles away, Maggie returned her print to the portfolio. "I'm weary," she said. "I'll admit it. This has definitely been a full day. And I do want to call Gussie tonight. Shall we call it an evening?"

"Make sure you ask her about the toys," said Amy.

"I will. And, if you'd like, I could try to reach my friend about the rifles."

"Would you try?" said Drew. "I'm curious."

"I wrote down the serial numbers and the identifying information," Maggie said. "I'll see if he's home. He may have an interesting story to tell us."

Chapter 25

Four Snakes, *German chromolithograph,*
c. 1870. Brown and yellow-marked snakes
(python, cobra, black snake, green snake)
coiling dramatically around fallen tree on the
ground. One snake holds a struggling frog in
its mouth. 10.5 x 14.5 inches. Price: $90.

Maggie closed the door of Amy's study. She sat in the brown leather executive desk chair and spun around. She wanted a few minutes to think.

She and Gussie, the owner of Aunt Augusta's Attic, an antiques business specializing in toys, had met at an antiques show and had been friends for ten years. Gussie was coping well with the effects of post-polio syndrome that were now keeping her closer to her home, and to her motorized wheelchair. Just last weekend they had both done the Provincetown Antique Show, Gussie assisted by her nephew Ben, and by the current man in her life, lawyer Jim Dryden. Talking with Gussie always helped Maggie put life in perspective. She could really use some perspective now.

Maggie shook her head slightly and began drawing circles on a pad of paper. She labeled the circles, remembering an old creativity exercise she'd learned years ago. Isolate the elements; then see where they interrelate. She labeled the circles with the strange happenings at or near the Douglas home.

Circle One: Amy had seen a ghost. Maggie forced herself to go on to the next circle.

Circle Two: Annoying telephone calls. Usually at night. That was verifiable; Maggie had heard them.

Circle Three: A fire without specific origin. Maggie thought about that one for a while. If Will's theory was right, then someone, or some people, were not only willing to risk hurting Amy and Drew, they were willing to risk hurting this house. Since this home meant so much to the Brewer family, that would seem to rule out a family member.

Circle Four: Crystal's murder. And Crystal's pregnancy. Were the two related? Maggie reached for an eraser and separated the two.

Circle Five: Crystal's pregnancy.

Circle Six: Brakes cut on Drew's car. That must have been done by someone specifically looking to injure, or even kill, Drew. And Amy, or even Maggie, might have been a passenger in that car.

Circle Seven: Possibly valuable rifles found in attic. Rifles, Maggie added, that might have been found by someone else before today. Were the rifles possibly the "treasure" that was rumored to be in this house?

That was it. Drew drank a little too much sometimes, and he and Amy wanted to have a child. Issues, perhaps, but not life-and-death issues.

No. One more thing.

Circle Eight: Members of Brewer family upset that home sold out of the family.

That would be Shirley Steele and Tom Colby, who lived next door. Other members of the family might have felt the sale wasn't appropriate, but they weren't advertising their feelings.

Maggie carefully made the circles darker, thinking about each one.

There were overlaps. Crystal was a member of the Brewer family. The telephone calls were harassment and might be connected to someone unhappy about the Douglases buying this house, but they weren't violent.

Cutting the brakes on the car and setting a fire were violent acts, but acts of someone who was still at a distance, relatively impersonal.

Crystal's murder was violent and very personal. Her pregnancy was very personal.

And the Brewer family relationships could include issues mixed with her pregnancy. But who had known she was pregnant? Maggie had heard of no one who said, "I knew Crystal was pregnant. She told me." Her mother might have guessed; Brian was sorry he hadn't known. At least that's what he said. Crystal, of course, must have known, although Maggie had read all too often about girls who didn't figure out that they were pregnant until it was too late.

Too late for what? Good prenatal care? An abortion? An early wedding? Any of the above. It was definitely too late for Crystal. And the magazines in Crystal's room pointed to her knowing she was pregnant. Or at least thinking about pregnancy.

Maggie picked up the telephone. It was after eleven, but Gussie usually read late. She needed to talk to someone far away from Madoc, Maine. Someone who could help her make sense of all this.

Gussie answered on the first ring.

Maggie could feel herself relaxing, just hearing Gussie's voice. "I'm fine, Gussie. And guess who else is here? Will Brewer!" Gussie had met Will when they'd all done the Rensselaer Antiques Fair over Memorial Day weekend.

"Turns out his relatives used to own the house Amy and Drew bought. Gussie, there is a lot going on here. But, first, before I forget, this afternoon Will and I went through some of the things in the attic of this house. Generally, a lot of junk. But there was one box of toys."

"Yes?" Gussie's voice had brightened from friendly to alert.

"I'm no expert, but some of them look good. Most of them are iron: a miniature woodstove with iron pots, an elephant-shaped bank, several cars. No dolls. One pretty ragged early teddy bear. A board game; I didn't check to see whether all the pieces were there. A pack of cards, ditto. And a couple of what look like lead British soldiers. In any case, I don't know what Amy will decide to do with the stuff, but I wondered if you could give me a fast telephone appraisal."

"Based on what you've said, not really. Sounds

like most of those things would be from about 1890 to 1915. Iron toys, especially iron vehicles, are good. Banks are good. But condition is critical. If they have any of the original paint, that gives them more value. The more paint, the more value."

"What if someone stuffed the miniature woodstove with toothpicks instead of kindling?"

Gussie laughed. "Well, the toys were played with! That says good things about the family in the house, but not for the value of the toys. The teddy bear could be the highest-valued antique you mentioned. If it really is a period teddy bear, say 1910 to 1920, then it could be worth several hundred dollars even in pretty crummy condition. Mint teddy bears are getting thousands at auction now."

"So what should I tell Amy?"

"Tell her to keep anything she really likes. It would be nice to have the toys stay where they were played with and loved. But if she doesn't want something, either take it to a local auctioneer for an appraisal and auction it off, or send me pictures and I'll make her an offer. Although I'm not sure any of those things are really for me. Condition is the key."

"I know." That was true of all antiques. And Gussie was particular about only buying toys in near-mint condition for her business.

"So. That wasn't hard. Now what else is happening? Amy was so upset when she called you!"

"It's complicated, Gussie. There's a lot going on." Maggie looked down at the circles she'd drawn on the pad in front of her. "I'm having trouble sorting it all out. Knowing which details are the important ones."

It took at least fifteen minutes just to explain the basics of what had happened.

"Maggie, now, tell me the truth. Are you in any danger?"

"I don't think so. Unless, of course, someone sets another fire. But I'm not so sure about Amy and Drew. I have to believe that someone wants them to leave. That may have to do with keeping the Brewer house in the family, or it may have to do with just getting rid of people from away. I don't know. Crystal was the one murdered, and she didn't own this house. In fact, she was part of the family that has owned it. That's why I'm so confused. I can't decide which details are important and which are not. And I'm worried about Amy and Drew." Maggie paused. "And one more thing, Gussie, and it may be important."

"Yes?"

Maggie lowered her voice, just in case Amy or Drew was still awake. "Drew and Crystal were sleeping together."

A pause. "Are you absolutely sure about that?"

"I saw them."

"Maggie, you have to tell someone. If you don't, it might be withholding evidence."

"I really don't think Drew killed Crystal, though. And it would be so awful to tell Amy. She's already feeling her marriage is unstable because she can't get pregnant."

"Maybe she's right to feel that not all is well.

Wouldn't you have wanted to know, if Amy had found out something like that about Michael?"

Maggie thought. "I don't know, Gussie. I just don't know."

"Think about it, Maggie. If you don't tell Amy, then at least talk to Drew. See what he says."

"That sounds like blackmail."

"Give him a chance to tell Amy himself. If she has to find out, and I think she does, then it would be best if he did the telling."

Chapter 26

The Fog Warning, *1893 lithograph of Winslow Homer oil on canvas completed in 1885; one of three Homer oils depicting North Atlantic fishermen displayed at the World's Columbian Exposition in Chicago in 1893. Lithograph published as result of that exhibition. Man in fishing gear rowing a dory filled with halibut in a rough sea as fog rolls in, obscuring his view of the vessel he must return to. 7.5 x 10.25 inches. Price: $210.*

Sleeping was difficult. Maggie tried to think of what she would say about Drew's relationship to Crystal. And to whom she would say it. By morning she was still weary and had come to no satisfactory conclusions.

As Amy scrambled eggs, Maggie made toast from anadama bread and shared Gussie's comments about the toys. Drew paid more attention to the morning's *Portland Press Herald* then to Maggie. "The only mention of Crystal's murder is a small article on page twelve saying the investigation is ongoing."

"I had hoped they would solve it quickly. How horrible for Rachel to have to live through days of waiting to find out who killed her daughter." Amy put some butter and raspberry jam on the table next to the plate of toast.

"Not to speak of no one's being able to settle in to getting any work done. When will Giles and Brian be finishing the roof, did they say?" Drew folded the newspaper and put it down on the table.

"They should be back next Monday. Remember, you gave them the week off." Amy divided the eggs three ways and Maggie poured herself a diet cola to start the day as Amy and Drew sipped coffee.

"I'd like to take those toys over to Walter English to appraise, as Gussie suggested," said Amy. "I really don't want to keep any of them, except maybe the little woodstove. That's cute, and decorative. But I want our baby to have all new toys, bright and shiny. Who knows what germs old toys might carry?"

"That's fine with me. One more carton out of the attic, and a little extra money would be a help now. Fixing this house is costing a lot more than we'd thought, and we've only started." Drew put his cup down next to the newspaper. "It would be nice if the house would contribute a little to its own upkeep."

They all thought of the rifles under the bed upstairs.

"We knew when we moved here that it wouldn't be easy," said Amy.

"But we had no clue it would be this involved

and expensive," said Drew. "Between your infertility treatments and the stock market decline, funding this move has not been simple."

A knock on the door interrupted that thought. Maybe it's Will, Maggie hoped.

It wasn't Will. It was Detective Strait, and his visit was not a social call. Will had helped smooth things the last time Strait had been here. There was no help now.

"Mr. and Mrs. Douglas, Ms. Summer. Sorry to disturb your breakfast, but I need to ask you all a few more questions."

"We'll help in whatever way we can," said Drew.

"It appears that Crystal was assaulted between three and four in the afternoon. None of you remembered when she left this house, but, considering where her body was found, she probably encountered her killer shortly after leaving here. I need you all to think back about what you were doing that afternoon."

"Brian and Giles Leary were here, too," said Amy.

"I've already talked with them. They say they left a little early that afternoon to pick up new supplies. Their story checks out. They were at the hardware store in Waymouth between three and three-thirty that afternoon."

"They could have stopped back here, to drop off whatever they'd bought."

"Could have, but didn't. They went over to help Mrs. Leary set up tables for a church supper."

A church supper, thought Maggie. Pretty good

alibi. No wonder the detective was here. She, Drew, and Amy were apparently the only people on the premises when someone hit Amy on the head.

"What about a hitchhiker, or a biker, or someone just wandering through the area?" Drew asked.

"I've checked with everyone who lives in this neighborhood, and no outsider was seen. Although Crystal had been sexually active, there were no signs of sexual assault, so the sex was most likely consensual. And she carried no valuables. So we have no motive. Let's just go over the time frame again. Ms. Summer, you had just arrived in Madoc the day before."

"That's right."

"Had you any contact with or knowledge of the deceased young woman before you arrived?"

"I live in New Jersey and haven't even visited Maine for years. I hadn't heard of Crystal until I arrived here and Amy introduced her."

"And what did Mrs. Douglas say?"

"She just said, 'Crystal, this is Maggie, a college friend of mine. Maggie, Crystal's helping me with some things in the house this summer.'"

"So you assumed she was a maid of some sort?"

"Not a maid exactly. A teenager earning some extra dollars. She was working in the kitchen when I saw her. But she and Amy—Mrs. Douglas— seemed to have an informal, friendly relationship. I didn't think much about it."

"And when did you next see Ms. Porter?"

"Not until the next day."

"In the morning?"

"No. She wasn't here, or at least I didn't see her, at breakfast time. I left the house and went to an auction preview, and then had lunch with a friend."

"That friend being?"

"Will Brewer."

"And when you returned from your lunch?"

Ouch. Maggie couldn't see a way out of this. Even Gussie would not have anticipated a detective's cross-examination being the way she'd tell Drew and Amy what she knew. "I walked in the house. The kitchen door was unlocked."

"And where were Mr. and Mrs. Douglas and Crystal?"

"I assumed Amy wasn't home; her car wasn't in the driveway. There was no one in the kitchen."

"And?"

"I went upstairs to my room to lie down. I hadn't slept well the night before."

"Did you see Mr. Douglas or Ms. Porter anywhere?"

Amy was sipping her coffee. Drew was listening closely. Did he have any idea of what she'd seen? Had he heard her steps on the stairs? "Yes. I saw them."

"Where were they?"

"In the master bedroom."

"And what were they doing in the master bedroom?"

Maggie hesitated a moment and then knew she had to say it. "They were having sex."

Chapter 27

Fulmar Petrel, adult and young, *1826 hand-colored engraving by Prideaux John Selby (1788–1867), British painter and member of the Royal Society of Edinburgh, who painted natural history subjects. Birds on rocks by sea; icebergs in distance. 15.5 x 22 inches. Price: $975.*

Will stood outside the door, a grin on his face and a crowbar in his hand. "Morning, Maggie. Hope I'm not too early. Drew and I thought we'd do some work on the kitchen this morning." Detective Strait appeared behind Maggie.

"Will, I need to question Mr. and Mrs. Douglas about some details connected with Crystal Porter's murder. I think, Ms. Summer, that I won't have any other questions for you just now. But don't go too far away."

Maggie walked out into the yard as Will put the crowbar down by the door.

"What was happening in there? You look as pale as one of those ghosts Amy says she's seen."

Maggie took Will's arm and headed him farther out into the yard, where they couldn't be overheard. "I may just have told your friend Nick Strait something that would give Amy or Drew a motive to kill Crystal."

"You told him Drew and Crystal were sleeping together."

"He was asking me moment by moment when I'd seen Crystal, and I couldn't lie. Will, it was horrible."

Will put his arms around Maggie. She leaned into him, wishing everything in life were as simple as this moment. She wished they could stand that way forever.

Will broke the embrace. "You had to tell the truth, Maggie. You did the right thing."

"But I should have let Drew or Amy or both of them know ahead of time. To blurt it out in front of a detective! How can I face them again? I just want to get in my van and drive to Timbuktu."

"Last time I checked there was an ocean between us and Timbuktu. Besides, I think I heard Nick asking you to stick around."

"He did."

"Do you really believe Amy or Drew killed Crystal?"

"I can't think that! But your friend Nick sounded as though he was out of suspects. He's looking for someone who had a motive."

"And you gave each of them one."

"Right! Amy could be jealous; Drew could be covering an affair."

They both looked back at the house.

"I suspect there are some very interesting conversations going on in there right now."

"Oh, Will. This is horrible."

"What Drew did was horrible." Will's voice was no longer gentle. "How could he possibly justify taking advantage of a young girl who was working in his own home? There is no way he didn't know that what he was doing was wrong. And now Crystal is dead. I don't know whether that's his fault, Maggie, but Drew ought to be punished in some way no matter what. He did an unforgivable thing." Will's anger was real.

Was he thinking that Drew could have been sleeping with his daughter? Maggie pushed some hair out of her face and wished she could as easily push this whole situation far, far away. They walked several steps farther away from the house, looking over the road toward the river. The water was a brilliant blue and wind was blowing the tops of the waves into small whitecaps. How could life be so complicated and still so beautiful? "What can we do?"

"We can think about something else. Were you able to get in touch with your friend who might know about those rifles?"

"Yes. The serial numbers match. Assuming that no one went to the trouble not only to reproduce rifles and serial numbers, but also to hide them in old material in the attic of an old house, those five rifles were among the two thousand purchased by the Army of the Potomac and issued to Colonel

Hiram Berdan's First and Second Regiments of United States sharpshooters in 1862. But it turned out that serial numbers aren't always as easy to document as I'd thought. The key is that the rifles have *JT* stamped on their buttstocks. That meant John Taylor, the army inspector for that period, had checked them. Other initials would mean one of his civilian employees had checked them. John Taylor personally inspected those key two thousand rifles."

Will inhaled. "So they're as valuable as we suspected?"

"My friend wouldn't even guess at a figure. Auctions are unpredictable, and they'd have to be authenticated by an expert in antique American firearms first. But they definitely are valuable rifles. The mystery is how they got into this attic."

"Not a mystery, Maggie. I asked Aunt Nettie about it last night. She said three Brewer men fought in the Civil War. Two came back. One was a sharpshooter."

"But how could he bring back weapons in unused condition . . ."

"We'll probably never know. And I'm not sure I want to know, considering that it is an ancestor of mine who did the deed, and knowing the Union shortage of Sharps rifles."

"What did Aunt Nettie think?"

"She was embarrassed for the family, of course. Said she hoped Amy and Drew wouldn't publicize the find. Although whether they go to Walter English Auctions in Waymouth, or to Sotheby's in

New York, this sort of find is going to be covered at least by the antiques press and the Civil War publications, and quite possibly by the mainstream media. Hidden rifles like those pictured in a famous Winslow Homer painting: it's too good a story to be ignored."

Maggie nodded. "You're right. And I assume Amy and Drew will want to sell the rifles, so I'm sorry for your family, Will."

"All families have parts of their history they'd like to forget. The Brewers will survive. The real mystery is who else knows about the rifles."

"You really think someone was there and found them before we did, don't you?"

"The more I thought about it last night, the more I was sure."

Maggie walked a few more steps. "I think I know how we could find out, Will. But with everything that's happening here now, I'd like to wait. We've hidden the rifles. There are so many other issues that seem more important." She looked back toward the house in time to see Detective Strait driving away.

"At least he didn't take either of your friends away in handcuffs, Maggie."

"How can you joke about something like that?"

Will looked down at her. "I know Nick Strait. I wasn't joking."

Chapter 28

❧

The American Tar: "Don't Give Up the Ship,"
1845 hand-colored lithograph by N. Currier.
Classic image of American sailor in short navy
wool jacket and middy shirt with scarf, seated
on sea chest; cannon, American flag, and
sailing vessel in background. Captain James
Lawrence's dying words to the crew of his
ship, captured by the British in 1813, became
the rallying cry of the U.S. Navy. 8.8 x 11.14
inches. Price: $400.

Will and Maggie walked slowly back toward the
house. Neither of them was in a hurry to see Amy
or Drew.

"Will! I'm glad you came," Amy greeted them,
as they walked into the kitchen. "You're just in
time to join us for a cup of coffee."

"Morning, Will," Drew added. "Another beautiful day."

Will and Maggie exchanged glances. Where was
the hysteria and anger they had imagined they'd
find here?

"A cup of coffee would be great," said Will cautiously. "Maggie was just telling me that she'd reached her friend who knows firearms."

"And?" asked Drew.

"He thinks yours sound legitimate. But without seeing them he couldn't be absolutely positive."

"Great!" said Drew. "Maybe we just paid for the roof and could have some plastering done inside."

"And new wallpaper for another bedroom," added Amy, as she handed Will his coffee. "You don't take sugar, right?"

"Just milk, thank you." He accepted the cup and poured some milk from the pitcher on the table. "But to handle the rifles the right way you'll need to have them authenticated. If I were you, I'd call Sotheby's in New York, tell them the story, and ask if they would handle them. They have experts on call in all areas, and the publicity they could generate would be good for the sale price."

"I'll have to go back to the city in a couple of weeks. Maybe I could take one down," said Drew.

"Check with your airline. I don't think anyone would be enthused about your flying with a rifle, even one from the nineteenth century, and you wouldn't want one damaged in checked luggage."

"I'll call Sotheby's and ask them what they'd suggest."

"Good idea."

Maggie sipped some cola she'd left at her place and reached for a piece of toast. Wasn't anyone going to say anything about what had happened? This was almost worse than being thrown out of the house. Amy was always in control, but Drew too? Maybe they didn't think Maggie would have shared what she knew with Will, and they were just waiting until he left to let her know what they felt. Maybe she should pack her suitcase now.

"I brought my crowbar over this morning. In case you decide we should go ahead and try to uncover your hearth and fireplace." Will hesitated. "I know this might not be the best time, but I would love to help. And I'll only be in Maine a few more days."

Maggie looked at him. She was sure he'd said he'd be in Maine another ten days to two weeks.

"I had planned to stay longer, but last night I got a call asking if I'd replace a dealer in a Rochester show next week. It's a show I've been wanting to get into, so I couldn't say no."

Amy beamed. "Then let's go for it! I'm dying to know what's under the linoleum and behind that wall, and you know more about what we'll be getting involved with than anyone. I'd like to have you here when we make the grand attempt."

"I'm afraid I won't be as much help to you as I'd hoped, though." Drew grimaced at his leg. "The pain isn't as bad today, but this cast is pretty limiting."

"Maggie and I can pull down plaster," said Amy. "Be a great way to get out anger and aggression!"

Maggie winced, but Amy didn't look at her.

"Besides the crowbar, we could use any long chisels you might have, or screwdrivers, and hammers," suggested Will. "We're going to make a mess. Do you have a small vacuum cleaner? Probably we should close off the rest of the house so the dirt stays in the kitchen. Some duct tape and several garbage bags would do that if we tape them over the door frame."

Maggie looked around. "Before we do anything, we need to clean up this kitchen and get any food far away from the dust."

"The refrigerator," agreed Amy. "Let's put anything open, even the boxes of crackers or cereal in the cabinets, into the refrigerator."

"All our hammers, chisels, and screwdrivers are on the workbench in the barn," Drew said.

"I'll find them." Will headed out toward the barn.

By the time Will had returned the women had cleared away the food. Amy had moved a vase full of dried flowers to the dining room. "Can you imagine what these flowers would look like covered in plaster dust?"

They pulled Amy's office chair from her study for Drew, and he propped his leg on one of the kitchen chairs.

Will examined the floor and wall, tapping it, measuring, then checking both the wall and floor with a level. "The level was a ridiculous idea," he said. "Everything in a house this age is uneven."

Drew agreed. "Half our furniture has at least two of its legs propped up by little pieces of wood."

"Or paperback books, for now," said Amy. "And every time the wind blows hard across the river my lipsticks roll off the dresser."

"More little blocks of wood," said Will. "And don't do it by eye. Use a level. It's the only way you can really see just how different in height the boards in the floor are. This house has wonderful wide pine boards, but most weren't cut to precision thickness, and some have warped over the years. Not to speak of the general settling that happens in any structure. Or the buckling in the plaster." He ran his hand across the wall Aunt Nettie had said hid the fireplace. "This house was well made. And it has already lasted through two hundred Maine winters and summers and a move across the river. It will no doubt survive today's attempts to bring back the past."

Maggie watched as Will checked and measured one more time. Finally he said, "We should take up the linoleum first, because it went down last. We'll see how easily we can remove it before we decide whether we should do the whole room or just this corner."

They all seemed totally engrossed, thought Maggie. Was it possible that a detective had been here an hour before, questioning them about a murder and adultery? Where were the shouting, screams, tears, and recriminations? Instead, Will was handing a chisel and hammer to Amy. They were going to take up linoleum.

The seventy-year-old linoleum was brittle; so brittle it broke off easily in irregular chunks. Below it, seventy years of dust had settled through the seams and edges of the flooring. Amy, Will, and Maggie were down on their hands and knees. Amy and Maggie both wore latex gloves that Amy kept in her kitchen, and Amy had tied a silk scarf around her face, but she was still sneezing. Drew supplied the required tissues.

Below the linoleum and the dust were pine boards, as Will had predicted. They used their screwdrivers and chisels as gently as possible, sliding them beneath the linoleum with the help of a hammer when necessary, then raising the linoleum until it chipped off. The work went so well that they decided to finish the entire kitchen floor. That meant a break to move out the kitchen table and chairs, and a related decision to leave the linoleum as it was below the old appliances. "We can take up those pieces when we get new appliances," said Amy. "We have enough work already clearing the floor."

About every twenty minutes Amy would decide she had to breathe fresh air and would stand by the door for a moment, or work vacuum cleaner duty, trying to pull out some of the dust deeply embedded in the pine floor's grain.

"Just get as much dirt as you can," Will said. "When we take down that wall we're going to cover everything with plaster dust and soot, unless they totally closed off the flue in 1833 and it has stayed closed." Will stood up and stretched. "That is highly unlikely."

It was noon before they finished.

"I'm not sure this would be termed 'finished' by a contractor," said Maggie, laughing, as they all stood back to admire their handiwork and sipped from cans of bottled water or cola that had been in the refrigerator, safely out of reach of the dust.

"If Johnny Brent's crew said this was 'finished,' I think we'd have a little discussion about payment terms," said Amy.

What had been the linoleum was now tied up in nine heavy-duty garbage bags. Except for the pieces left under the refrigerator and stove, the 1930s flooring was gone. What was left was an unevenly colored pine floor. The floor had been vacuumed half a dozen times but the air was still colored with dust, and it was settling on everything.

"Just as we predicted," said Drew. "Thank goodness you put the food away."

"And I don't want to take any out right now," said Amy. "We need a break, and we need some lunch." She grinned as she looked at everyone. "And look at us! I was going to suggest we go out somewhere, or at least go and get something and bring it back, but we're all covered with dust." As if to confirm her point, Amy sneezed.

"Hello? Anyone home?"

"We're in the kitchen," yelled Drew in the general direction of the porch. Whoever had arrived was coming in that way.

"All right if I join you? Just thought I'd meander over with these Civil War books you wanted, and find out if you were resting." Tom Colby stood in the doorway and looked around the kitchen in surprise.

"Thanks. And you're welcome to join us. If you dare." Drew grinned. His black hair and eyebrows were now brown with dust.

Tom just stared. "Are you folks taking the house apart?"

"Just looks that way, Tom. We got rid of the old linoleum." Drew spun around on Amy's swivel chair. His leg dragged on the floor and created a small spray of dust in its wake.

"Yup. I figured that out," said Tom. "What're you goin' to do now? Take a group shower, or just hose everything down?"

"Sounds like two good ideas, Tom!" Amy tried to laugh, but started sneezing again.

"Actually, we were just trying to figure out how to get lunch without having to either take showers or get dust on the lunch."

"That's a problem," said Tom.

"We could just take bread and cold cuts out on the porch," suggested Amy, her voice emerging from the tissues she was holding near her face.

"Or one of us could shower and go back for some more of that fried food," said Maggie. "Although I'm not sure fried food twice in two days is optimal."

No one seemed too excited by either of those ideas.

"This is one of those moments I miss New York," said Drew. "Take-out places! Delivery!"

"We've got most everything New York has right here," said Tom with a quiet smile.

"How about pizza delivery? That's something I haven't heard of up here."

"Yup. We got it."

Amy looked at Tom. "From where? I don't remember seeing a pizzeria within ten miles!"

"No pizzeria. Just pizza. You call Annie Wilde. She'll do it up, and her boy, Clyde, he'll bring it to you."

"And where is this Annie Wilde's restaurant?"

"No restaurant. Just Annie's house. She's up on Heron Point. If someone were to call her, it'd probably take forty-five minutes for the pizza to arrive. She does 'em up to order, and that takes a bit of time."

They all exchanged glances. It was unanimous.

"Pizza!"

Chapter 29

———∽———

Untitled. Print of anonymous nineteenth-century woman. N. Currier hand-colored lithograph, 1846. Woman in simple off-the-shoulder dress; ribbons in dress and woman's eyes are blue; otherwise, print is black and white. 9 x 12.5 inches. Price: $95.

Tom voted himself a member of the demolition team as they sat on the porch breathing fresh salt breezes into their dusty lungs and devouring the best pizza Maggie had eaten in years.

"Annie makes her own tomato sauce of course, out of her garden, and the cheese is from Amos Dodge's farm over to Warren. Fresh vegetables from over to Skillins's garden stand. Pretty good stuff." Tom was obviously enjoying the appreciation of these folks from the big city who were amazed to find pizza this good four hundred miles north of New York. "You can find just about anything in the state of Maine, you know. You just got to know where to look."

Amy and Tom started talking about the very best

place to get home-baked Italian bread, while Will leaned over toward Maggie. "Pretty cool friends of yours, considering the circumstances. I thought I might have to run a rescue mission and find you a bed at Aunt Nettie's." He leered with a wink. "Course, that wouldn't be a problem except for Aunt Nettie, you understand."

"I have no clue what is happening," Maggie whispered back, hiding behind the pizza slice covered with fresh tomato and mushroom slices and Italian olives. "But we are making progress on the kitchen, if not on crime detecting."

"This is more my style anyway," Will said. "Antiques. Construction. History. Pizza. All areas I feel some sense of control over. Why is it that when I see you people seem to get themselves murdered?"

"You're exaggerating. No one was murdered the day we went to the exhibit at the Metropolitan," Maggie pointed out.

"True. Good point." Will's blue eyes twinkled as he looked down at Maggie's dust-covered hair and body. "Hope they've got a good deep well. We haven't even started on the wall, and look at us. Long showers are going to be in order later today."

"At least you and Tom will be on separate wells," said Maggie. Truth be told, she had about used up her energy for old-house improvements today. She would have enjoyed taking that shower right now and then settling back on this porch with a book. But the group consensus was definitely in favor of finding the old fireplace.

"If Aunt Nettie said it was there," Tom said for about the third time, "it must be there. Aunt Nettie knows this house and its history and the Brewer family better than anyone else. Be something if it really is behind that wall, and been there all these years. It would have been the fireplace used when the house was first built over on the island."

"Right, 1774," said Drew. "I wonder what condition the bricks will be in after all these years? They could have crumbled into nothing."

"Or be in pristine shape. No way to tell until we take that wall down." Will rose and made a minor attempt to wipe dust and pizza crumbs off his beard with a couple of paper napkins. "Pizza's gone, and I'm ready. Anyone care to join me?"

Amy had brought out paper plates and lunch was cleaned up quickly with the help of another garbage bag. By the time everyone had made some attempt to wash up, Will was standing in front of the wall with a chisel and hammer.

Amy had covered her nose again. The first gentle taps of the hammer brought down powdery plaster. And then more plaster. And more. Chunks fell easily, as the old mixture of powdered clams and oyster shells, water, and sand crumbled. After a few minutes Amy had to leave the room. The heavy dust filled the air. Tom happily joined Will at the wall, while Maggie chased after both of them with a whisk broom and dustpan, trying to get at least the larger pieces of plaster into garbage bags before the dust invaded the whole house.

Within minutes it was clear Aunt Nettie had

been right. The plaster coated thin strips of lath. Behind the lath was a brick wall.

Drew kept out of the way and joined Amy on the porch when he realized plaster dust was seeping into both the top and bottom of his cast. The doctor would probably not be thrilled.

Will handed Maggie a small saw and she started cutting away the lath. It was soon clear that one of the issues was how much plaster and lath to cut. They made a rough vertical line just beyond what might be the mantel: a smoke-stained, two-inch-deep board set into the middle of the wall. Above the mantel the fireplace flue tiered to the ceiling and beyond, but the brick wall continued in back of it. Below the mantel, plaster dust was only the beginning of the dirt problem. Over the roughly 170 years since the lath and plaster had closed up the fireplace, soot, dirt, and anything else that had come down the flue had piled up. Rain and snow had bonded the dirt and soot to some degree, but piles of that black mixture, chimney plaster, and the occasional bones of a dead bird or bat that had fallen down the chimney now poured out onto the kitchen floor.

"Stay away!" called Maggie, as Amy peeked her head around the corner. "You do have a fireplace here. The bricks are filthy, but in great condition, but there's a little problem with soot."

Amy ducked back out.

"You're going to have a terrific kitchen!" yelled Maggie after her. "Someday!"

Will and Maggie and Tom, now covered in layers

of brown dirt, gray plaster dust, and black soot, took turns trying to scoop up the debris, which kept coming.

"How far up in the chimney was this stuff piled?" asked Tom, shaking his head. "This is the dirt of the ages."

"Exactly," agreed Will, whose hair and beard and face were now blacker than the crows who were complaining about the lack of seeds at the feeder outside. "One hundred and seventy years of dirt. Even at one inch a year . . ."

"One hundred and seventy inches of this?" Tom shook his head, shaking some of the soot from his body. "It's going to be impossible to get all this stuff up. And it's sinking into the floor. They'll never get that floor clean again."

"It will have to be power scrubbed and then sanded," agreed Will. "Gently, because it's pine. But the floor we uncovered is a different color from the boards in the rest of the house in any case, so Amy and Drew will have to decide whether they'll stain them all to match, or be authentic and paint them all a dark color."

"Oh, they shouldn't paint these boards!" said Maggie.

"In the nineteenth century people did. Brown, mostly. And then put braided or hooked rugs or Oriental carpets on top of them. Helped keep the dust down and the breezes out."

Twenty-three garbage bags were now filled and ready for the dump. The last few were heavy enough that it took two of them to lift the bags and get them out of the kitchen and into the yard.

Finally the flow from the chimney was beginning to slow. Maggie held up a hand. "Stop! I hereby declare a major break! I have got to have something to drink to wash this stuff in my throat down, and Amy and Drew have to come in to see what we've found!"

"Thank you, lady!" Tom hesitated not a moment before putting down the garbage bag he was filling and leaning against the wall. "Is there any beer?"

"There was some yesterday," Will said. His black fingers left distinctive marks on the refrigerator door as he handed Maggie a diet cola and took out beers for Tom and himself.

If Will were a suspect in anything, those fingerprints would be great evidence, thought Maggie. This didn't seem the moment to say that out loud.

"Amy! Drew! Come look!"

Amy and Drew had been sitting on the porch, frustrated that they couldn't be more of the process. Amy had gotten a long sock and pulled it over Drew's cast to protect his foot from any more dirt. He limped in after her and Maggie pulled up a chair for him.

"Wow." Amy looked at the fireplace. It was intact, and real, and large enough to sit inside, should someone have wanted to crouch on top of the soot that was still sifting down like soft black snow flurries. "It's gorgeous!"

"It will be," agreed Will happily. "Once it's all cleaned up, and you furnish it with some great colonial kitchen copper and iron pots. And I think there is a real treasure back here. I wanted to wait until the owners of this estate were present to confirm, but I've kept my eye on a line in the back of the fireplace."

He reached in through the dirt and grime and pulled out a triangular-shaped piece of iron, thick with soot. "I was right! Whichever Brewer closed up this fireplace was either smart or lazy. And you're the beneficiaries."

Silence.

"See? It's the original crane!"

"Wow!" said Amy. "And it fit into the fireplace?"

"Absolutely. Blacksmiths made these beauties to order when someone was building a house. You never see them outside of their original locations because there would be no reason to take them. If this hadn't been left in the fireplace, you would have had to pay a blacksmith big bucks to make one that would fit, and, of course, it wouldn't have been authentic." Will looked at the dirty piece of triangular-shaped iron in his hand appraisingly. "A nice job too. Fine smithing." He smiled softly. "And one of my ancestors commissioned this piece, and my family ate food cooked in pots hung on this crane back in the 1780s and '90s."

Tom took it from Will, and they exchanged a glance. They were both Brewers. This was a Brewer fireplace. And they had uncovered it. It was a moment of shared pride.

"As soon as it's cleaned up, we must invite Aunt Nettie back to show her," said Amy.

"She'll be very pleased," Will said.

"Could anything else be in the fireplace besides the dirt?" asked Amy.

"A *lot* of dirt," said Maggie. "Incredible how much dirt."

"Well," Will said. "Sometimes there were hooks up in the chimney above the fireplace, where bacon or ham could be hung to cure. They would have been mortared in, so it's possible there might still be one."

Will got into the fireplace with a flashlight in his hand. His jeans would never be the same, Maggie thought. He bent over and then peered up the flue. "No hook. They either didn't have one, or took it out, or at some point it fell out." He turned the light slowly from one side of the chimney to the other. "But there is something up here." Carefully he reached, pushing his big body up the chimney opening.

I hope he doesn't get stuck, Maggie thought. Santa Claus he isn't. His beard was now black.

"There's a brick shelf." Will's voice echoed a bit. "Just a minute. Almost." He pulled himself out of the fireplace. In one hand was the flashlight; in the other, a wooden box a little bigger than a man's-shoe box. "Someone left this up there. Sometimes there were hiding places in these old kitchens. Or niches where they might put a ham to smoke. I've never heard of putting a wooden box in a chimney, though. It would have burned."

"Unless someone put it there just before they closed off the fireplace. They'd know there would be no fires then."

"True."

"Maybe the family put together a time capsule of items that were significant to them in, when was it? About 1833."

"Or maybe a woman in the family hid her jewelry here, or her silver."

"Or her love letters," put in Amy.

"And no one knew, and they sealed up the fireplace."

They all stood, looking at Will holding the box. It was filthy and, despite some of the soot falling off as Will moved it, certainly still an inch deep in dirt. He took his hand and wiped most of it away. "I suspect these aren't diamonds or, sorry, it was emeralds you desired, right, my lady Amy?"

She smiled at him and bowed in response.

"But whatever treasures this box contains are yours by right of ownership."

Nice touch, thought Maggie. Since Will and Tom were the two people in the room who had any claim other than possession to whatever might be in the box.

Will handed the box to Amy. She took it carefully and, kneeling in the dirt and plaster that still covered the floor, put it down. Her light brown eyes shone with excitement as she carefully located and then cleaned off a small tarnished brass latch. The box opened easily. Everyone leaned in to see what treasures it might contain.

Inside, wrapped in what might once have been a piece of blanket, was the skeleton of a baby.

Chapter 30

—❧—

The Praying Mantis, *E. J. Detmold illustration
for* Fabre's Book of Insects, *1921,* New York
(translation of Fabre's Souvenirs Entomolo-
giques). *Delicate pastel rendering of elegantly
posed mantis. Frame border. 6 x 7 inches.
Price: $65.*

"Oh, my God," Amy gasped. She pushed the box
away from her but still stared in horror. "My
God."

"It's a little coffin," Tom said quietly.

"But who is it?" Drew asked. "Why would anyone put a baby's body in a chimney flue?"

They were all silent. Maggie reached over and put
the cover back on the box. "Someone who was
scared. Someone who was hiding something.
Someone who was angry. There are so many reasons
why. And there are no reasons. We'll never know."

Amy started crying, a few tears slowly making
their way through the dust on her face. She started
sneezing again.

A heavy knock on the door brought them all

out of their thoughts. Tom was closest to the door.

"Tom! Didn't expect to find you here. Just had a few more questions to . . ." Detective Strait walked in the room. "What happened here?"

Maggie rubbed at her wrist to brush the soot off her watch. It was eight hours since the detective had left them this morning.

"We found the old fireplace," said Drew quietly.

"So I can see." Detective Strait walked closer to check out the details, his large shoes leaving deep footprints in the soot. "Even the hearth is still intact. Very impressive." He looked at them all. "And you did this all just today?"

Tom nodded. "I don't suppose," he said quietly, looking at the others in the room, "I don't suppose the police would be interested in a body we found?"

Detective Strait turned around quickly. "What did you say?"

"Nick, it's nothing," said Will. "Nothing in your department, anyway." Will picked up the box and carefully removed the cover and showed the contents to Nick.

"You found . . . that?"

"On a shelf inside the fireplace flue. It must have been there since the fireplace was closed up in about 1833."

"You're right. Out of my jurisdiction." Detective Strait reached out a finger toward the tiny skull, then pulled his hand back. "Will, you and Tom are Brewers. I'm assuming this child must be too. You'll be taking care of it?"

"I guess."

"I don't think it's necessary to report this officially. For the family's sake."

"We'll need to bury it, sure," said Tom. "Have a nice ceremony. Put it in the family plot up at the old cemetery at Spruce Point."

"The body is a baby. Not an 'it.'" said Maggie. "The child deserves a proper burial." Her mind was a whirr of dirt and grime and faces of unwanted children. Someone had loved this child enough to try to keep him safe. She shuddered slightly, not even wanting to voice the possibility that the baby had been alive when the box had been put in the fireplace. That would have made even less sense. The infant had died and for some reason had not been buried. Instead, he or she had been entombed in this house. Soot must have gotten into Maggie's eye. She found herself blinking, then tearing up.

Will took charge. "Nick, it's late. And"—he gestured toward the box—"there's been a death in the family. Is it critical that your questions be asked now? Because if they can wait until tomorrow, I think it would give us time to get cleaned up, and to notify the rest of the family."

Nick nodded and took off his hat in respect. "That'll be all right, Will. Questions can wait. Sorry about . . . what you found." He started toward the door. "But I will have to talk with you all tomorrow morning." He looked over at Tom. "You too, Tom. Just verifying some times and places."

"Tomorrow morning will be fine, Detective," said Amy. "Thank you for understanding."

"Tomorrow morning at eight."

"We'll all be here."

"Not Will. I don't need him. But the rest of you."
Detective Strait put his hat on and walked out
the door.

"What are we going to do now?" asked Drew.

"I am going to go home and talk with Aunt
Nettie and tell her what happened," said Will
calmly. Still in charge. "She's active in the church.
She'll know whom to call."

"I'll go home and tell Shirley, and then I'll call
the rest of the family," Tom said. "I need to get
cleaned up too."

"Tom, do you know the person to call at the
cemetery?" Will was already planning.

"Yup. I worked with the Spruce Point committee
last fall, cleaning up some graves."

"Let's do it quickly. Not too many people
involved. No press."

"Right. Just the family. That's what's right,"
Tom said.

"What . . . what should we do with . . . it . . .
now?" Drew hesitated, looking at Amy, who was
still crying quietly.

Maggie suddenly wanted to reach out, to claim
the child. She would keep the box in her room, even
for just the night. But it was Amy's house and Will's
relative. It was not her place to say. There were people to claim this child now. A family to be called.

"I'll take the child," said Will. "I'll take him to
Aunt Nettie." He held the box gently with both his
hands. "See what you can arrange for tomorrow
afternoon, Tom."

Chapter 31

~~~~~~~

Untitled. Wooden toy soldiers. From folio by Roberta Samsour titled Czechoslovakian Folk Toys, *printed in Prague, 1941. 8.5 x 10 inches. Price: $60.*

Will and Tom had taken the stacks of garbage bags out to the barn before they left. Amy and Maggie cleaned up the kitchen as well as they could.

Amy then announced that Maggie could not possibly stay in Maine one night longer unless she had eaten lobster. And the lobster at the co-op was the best: caught that day and steamed to order, with all the traditional accompaniments—steamed clams, potatoes, corn, blueberry pie, and salad.

"Sounds wonderful," said Maggie, although she would really have preferred going straight to bed. She dreaded being alone with Amy and Drew. Right now she was just too tired to deal with their anger about her telling Detective Strait she had seen Crystal and Drew together. And Amy must be feeling twice that anger . . . there would never be good circumstances under which to hear your husband had been unfaithful. Maggie knew that from personal experience. But surely these particular circumstances were among the worst.

"You'll love it!" Amy said. "A great view of the harbor at sunset, and all the boats. Just put on your old jeans and a T-shirt, since eating lobster is messy!"

"Messy" seemed an understatement to describe this entire week.

Maggie stood in her room, conscious that she'd leave a mark if she sat anywhere. She hoped Amy wouldn't take long in the shower. Her skin felt gritty with dirt; her fingernails were black; and her long hair was tangled and stiff. The joys of restoring an old house.

Despite the way the day had begun, what a lot they had accomplished. And how beautiful the old fireplace would look after the dirt had settled and the bricks were carefully scoured.

Although Maggie knew she would never look at the fireplace without thinking of the box that had been hidden within it. Why would someone put a baby's body in a fireplace? It was the sort of thing a young, unmarried mother might have done. A young woman like Crystal.

Detective Strait would be back in the morning. A killer was still out there.

And Will and Tom were planning a funeral for a child who had died perhaps 170 years ago. Maggie's thoughts blurred together. When would Crystal's funeral be? Had the medical examiner released her body yet?

"Maggie? Your turn in the bathroom!" Amy's tap on the door brought Maggie back to the moment. Everything would look clearer after a hot shower.

They ordered their lobsters, collected three bottles of Shipyard ale, and sat on the rough, weathered, gray picnic tables overlooking the harbor, waiting for their number to be called. "Just one bottle for me, since I'm driving, and one for you, Drew, so you can take that pain medication to help you sleep tonight. But Maggie can have all she wants!" Amy was organizing everyone, as usual. Still no talk about what had happened that morning.

Maggie looked out over the harbor. Did Amy think giving her permission to drink meant Maggie would down half a dozen ales? Amy did like people to do as she directed.

The sun was low, its reflection orange on the now dark blue waters of the harbor. A large sailboat was just coming into dock on the far side of the protected water. Several large cruisers were anchored closer by, along with an assortment of smaller vessels, and perhaps a dozen lobster boats. A young couple in a purple canoe paddled by the dock where Amy, Drew, and Maggie sat among tourists and locals, waiting for their lobsters. A herring gull perched on a railing, watching to see if he could scrounge his dinner. A large hand-painted sign next to him read, "Beware of gulls! Protect your food!" A mother chased a toddler away from the railing.

Amy was the one to break the silence. "Maggie, I know what you're thinking. About what you told the detective this morning. But it's all right. Truly. Drew and I have some issues . . ." Amy shot a side-long glance at Drew, who was looking out at the harbor and ignoring them both. "But we're going to be fine. Our marriage is too strong to be hurt by a little thing like adultery. Drew and I have the same goals, and working toward them together is what is keeping us together." She reached over and patted Drew's hand.

Maggie just looked at her. A little thing like adultery? It hadn't seemed like such a little thing when it had been her husband who was sleeping around. How could Amy say something like that?

"Just enjoy your lobster, and let's not talk about it again. We'll all just pretend it never happened."

No one else said anything. Perhaps there was too much to say to even begin. Amy stretched her shoulders and Maggie flexed her hands. She ached all over. Starting with her head.

"Thirteen!"

"Our number!" Amy and Maggie rose together to retrieve their dinners. Tonight thirteen was a lucky number; the lobsters were steamed to perfection, the clams were sweet, the corn and potatoes done just right. And all was served with plastic cups of melted butter, and piles of paper napkins. They happily dug in, and Maggie found she was hungrier than she had thought. She wished Will were with them.

But Will was planning a funeral.

By the time the ale and lobster and corn were gone and the blueberry pie had all but disappeared, they had all revived. "We still haven't looked at your prints, Maggie," Amy said. "Why don't we do that when we get home? I'm not ready for bed, and we seem to find other things to do during the day."

Wasn't that the truth.

Back at home Maggie pulled over the portfolios she had brought in from the car only yesterday. "I brought in the Winslow Homer wood engravings. This portfolio is full of his Civil War prints, done about the same time as his *Sharp-shooter*, which we looked at yesterday." Rifles, Maggie reminded herself. She needed to check something about rifles. There had been no time today. "The other portfolios are of subjects not related to the war. Most were published in *Harper's Weekly*, but some in other newspapers. He also did some smaller prints, for newspapers and book illustrations. I have those in a separate portfolio." She pointed at each of her bulging brown portfolios in turn. The portfolios were well used; the handles on one had torn off. Paper was heavy.

"What about those other portfolios?" asked Amy, pointing at the two other portfolios Maggie had brought in.

"One contains N. C. Wyeth's illustrations for Kenneth Roberts's *Trending into Maine*, that we mentioned the other day. And the other one has the Thomas Nast Christmas engravings we talked about." Maggie wasn't sure this was the time to mention that Amy had wanted to see the Nast picture of Santa Claus and a baby. But that was the one she remembered.

Amy remembered too. "Oh, please, let's look at the Nasts first. Christmas is such a happy time of year, and we could use some happiness today."

No argument there. Maggie got out the large portfolio and put a pile of matted wood engravings on the coffee table.

"You'll remember that the European St. Nicholas was rather a skinny fellow, with a long beard. No artist had depicted him as a round-faced, smiling Santa with a wide white beard until Thomas Nast. Nast actually was born in Germany, but he immigrated to New York with his family when he was six. When he was fifteen, he got his first job as an illustrator, working for *Leslie's Illustrated,* a popular newspaper. By the time he was twenty-two he was hired away by *Harper's Weekly* to be a Civil War correspondent."

"So he did the same sort of work Winslow Homer did?"

"They had the same employer and are the best known of the Civil War artists. But after the war they went in very different professional directions. Homer turned to painting and by 1874 was working full-time as an artist specializing in oils. Nast stayed with *Harper's Weekly.* Although his Christmas scenes were loved and are the most well known of this work today, Nast was famous in the nineteenth century as a searing political cartoonist. I did my doctoral thesis on his influence on New York politics from the late 1860s through the

1870s, especially the pressure his cartoons put on the New York City government, which eventually took down Boss Tweed. Among his other lasting contributions to American culture were symbolizing the Democratic party as a donkey, and the Republican party as an elephant, and picturing Uncle Sam. He was a real political power with a pen."

"Whew! But these"—Amy was looking through the prints Maggie had brought—"are just his Christmas prints."

"They're his most popular. I have some of his Civil War work and cartoons at home; I use the cartoons in one of my classes. Most people today are just interested in his Santas."

"They look familiar."

"Because they've been reprinted on everything from stickers to Christmas cards to coloring books."

Amy looked carefully, then handed the prints to Drew. "You know what strikes me as strange? In almost all of these Christmas pictures Nast has included toys that are symbols of war: drums, flags, toy soldiers, toy guns, bugles, and maybe I'm imagining, but even the wooden horse in one of these prints looks like the Trojan horse."

"Good catch! Why he did that I don't know; certainly those were popular boys' toys of the Civil War period, which is when he started drawing the Santas. And Nast was a great one for symbols," Maggie said. Amy looked over Drew's shoulder as he carefully examined the pile.

"Here's one in color! I thought they'd all be in black and white, like the Homers."

"They all were originally in black and white. But over the years some people have hand-colored the engravings. Those Victorian ladies who liked to color prints were much more apt to color Santas than they were to color Homers. Although I do occasionally see one of Homer's engravings that someone has colored."

"Are they worth more if they're colored, or if they're as they were originally meant to be?"

"Value is in the eyes of the beholder. Purists would never accept a colored print, but some collectors like the colored ones. It really is personal choice. And," Maggie added, "the skill of whoever hand-colored the engraving. I've seen some coloring that is much too bright, or just not in appropriate colors for the period. I wouldn't buy prints poorly colored, and I don't think my customers would want them. Hand-coloring, no matter when it was done, needs to be done well."

"Are you implying that some people are hand-coloring old prints today?" Amy looked up in amazement.

"I'm afraid so. No one needs to worry about the coloring on Currier and Ives prints, or on early botanicals or other natural history prints. Those prints were hand-colored as part of the production process before they were sold or bound into folios or books. The ones that people color today are engravings, like Nast's, that were in mid-nineteenth-century newspapers. Or occasionally steel engravings from earlier books. I would certainly never endorse coloring an old engraving. But some customers do like the Nasts colored. Maybe because all the reprints you see today, all those postcards and Christmas cards, are in color. People expect Nast's originals to be in color too."

"So none of his original engravings are colored?"

"Not the ones that appeared in *Harper's Weekly*. In the 1880s and 1890s some of his Santa Clauses were reproduced as lithographs and printed as children's books by McLaughlin Brothers, in Boston. Those lithographs are well done. And they are in color."

"I love the one of the little girl talking to Santa on the old telephone," said Amy. "And the patriotic Santa, with the flag in back of him and the children."

Maggie looked over her shoulder. "Those were Nast's own five children."

"And this one." Amy smiled. "This is the one you told me about. Oh, look, Drew. Wouldn't this look wonderful in the nursery?"

Maggie watched as Amy and Drew looked at a large print of a chubby baby sleeping peacefully in a crib. A sprig of holly lay on his blanket, and Santa Claus was smiling at him through the bars of the crib. It was titled *Another Stocking to Fill*. After all that had happened today . . . how could they still be focused on filling that perfect room upstairs?

Drew leaned over and kissed Amy on the forehead. "I think you've made a sale, Maggie. Although I really like the telephone one too."

"It would look wonderful if we could find an old wall telephone set to hang near it, wouldn't it?" Amy said.

"Well, when we do, then we'll call Maggie," said Drew. "For now, one Santa Claus in the house is enough. But I would like to see those Civil War Winslow Homers."

Maggie packed up her Nasts, leaving out the print Amy and Drew had liked. They were still buying pictures for the nursery? But she certainly wouldn't turn down a sale. And the $350 price had been right on the mat.

Maggie pulled out the Civil War Winslow Homers. "You've already seen the most famous of his Civil War engravings, *The Sharp-shooter*. Most of Homer's war engravings are based on events behind the lines: men lining up at the sutler's tent to buy supplies, the surgeon with wounded men, soldiers opening boxes for Christmas, soldiers playing football." As she spoke, Maggie handed them the prints she was describing.

"Football! I wouldn't have thought of that as a Civil War print!"

"Actually, football was developed as a sport by soldiers during the war. It wasn't an intercollegiate sport until 1869," said Maggie. "As far as I know, Homer's engraving of football in 1865 is the first one anyone did of that sport. In addition to his 'behind the lines' engravings, Homer did two other sorts of Civil War prints. There are two battle scenes." Maggie took them out and placed them side by side: *The War for the Union, 1862—A Cavalry Charge* and *The War for the Union, 1862—A Bayonet Charge*.

"Wow," said Drew, looking at them closely. "These are wonderful! Is the bayonet charge the Twentieth Maine's famous charge at Gettysburg?"

"No; that didn't happen until a year later. Both of Homer's prints were done as public relations for the Union side, to show the folks at home how well their forces were doing. Neither of the scenes is based on a specific battle. But they are realistic."

Amy pointed at the rifles pictured in *A Bayonet Charge*. "Are those the rifles we have, Drew?"

He looked closely. "Some might be. It's hard to tell."

"The battle scenes are wonderful, but I don't think I'd want them in the living room," said Amy.

"That's good, dear, because they're going in my study," replied Drew. "Put those in the pile with the Nast Santa and the baby, Maggie."

"What about the non–Civil War wood engravings?" Amy looked over at the other large portfolio they hadn't opened.

"There are some that would be especially appropriate for Maine." Maggie bent down and flipped through them quickly. "Here's one of my favorites: *August in the Country—The Seashore*. It's an early one, so not technically as strong as some of the later ones, but it's delightful." The print showed fully dressed women and children on the beach. An elegantly attired gentleman was trying (unsuccessfully) to scare the ladies by waving a lobster at them, while a plump little boy was angrily trying to remove a crab from his finger.

"You're right. I love that one. See the woman sketching on the dune?" Amy put that one aside.

"There are other beach scenes." Maggie pulled out *High Tide* and *Low Tide*. "This makes a good pair. And here's one that's hard to find because it wasn't published in *Harper's Weekly*—it was published in *Every Saturday*, which didn't have as wide a circulation. But I love it. It's called *A Winter-Morning: Shoveling Out*."

The print showed a small New England house with snow almost up to its roofline. Two men were digging a path through the deep snow with heavy wooden shovels, while a woman threw crusts and crumbs to some birds.

"I like that one too," said Amy. "Are there any maritime engravings? I always think of Homer as an artist of the sea."

"He didn't move to Maine and do his studies of the sea until after he had finished with his wood-engraving period," said Maggie. "Only three of his works from this period are at sea. *At Sea—Signaling a Passenger Steamer* is dark. I know it's a storm, but I don't care for it as much as some of his others. There is also *The Approach of the British Pirate Ship* Alabama, which focuses on the people on the ship, not on the sea. And *Homeward Bound*, showing the deck of a sailing vessel. He did that one on his way home from Paris, where he'd been studying for a few months."

"Yes," Drew and Amy said together.

Drew added, "Definitely that one. You can feel the spray, it's so realistic! I love the slanted deck and the elegant passengers."

"Now, before you decide, you should know about Winslow Homer's Gloucester Series," said Maggie. "Those are—next to *Snap-the-Whip*—his most popular wood engravings. Unfortunately I don't have all of them in stock. As soon as I get them, they sell. I even have a waiting list for *Dad's Coming*. That one shows a boy sitting on a beached dory. His mother and little sister stand near him, and they're all looking out to sea. *Gloucester Harbor,* shows a scene like the one we saw at dinner tonight: several boys in two skiffs, rowing through a harbor with two sailboats in back of them."

"Which do you have?"

"I have *Sea-Side Sketches: A Clambake*, and *Ship-Building, Gloucester Harbor.*" Maggie put them next to each other on the table.

"I understand these are the most popular, and I do like them, but I really like the winter scene and the one on the ship better," said Drew. "What do you think?" He looked at Amy.

She nodded. "I agree. I do want some Homers for the house, and those seem just right. For different rooms, I think. And you still want *A Cavalry Charge* and *A Bayonet Charge* for your study?"

"Definitely. And if I ever do become a history teacher, they would be wonderful for a Maine classroom, even if Joshua Chamberlain's victory was a year later."

"So write us up a bill, Maggie. I don't even want to look at the rest. You've just sold a Nast and four Homers."

As Amy went into her study to find her checkbook, Maggie put the unwanted prints back in her portfolios. Wow! Those purchases just paid for her trip to Maine, and then some: $325 each for the two battle scenes; $375 for *Homeward Bound,* plus $300 for *Shoveling Out.* Plus the $350 Nast. A total of $1,675.

"I'll give you guys ten percent off, and even it off, since you're friends," Maggie said, as she added it up. "That would bring the total to an even fifteen hundred dollars. You have some wonderful selections here. They'll look perfect on your walls. They look well matted in black or off-white, and I like gold frames, but that's your choice. Just make sure whoever does your framing mats them in acid-free boards. Most framers know to do that, but it never hurts to remind them. That will prevent any deterioration. And antireflective glass would be a protection too, if you're going to hang them anywhere near direct sunlight."

"What a day!" Amy wrote out the check and handed it to Maggie. "I've just about had it. And that detective fellow said he'd be coming at eight in the morning, didn't he?"

"He did. And then I think we'll have a funeral to attend in the afternoon." Drew pulled himself up on his crutches.

By the time Maggie crawled under the two light blankets she needed on this August night she was exhausted. But after fifteen minutes of tossing and turning she realized her body was tired, but her mind was still working. She switched on the lamp next to her bed and looked at the pile of adoption books and pictures on her floor. She picked up one book, thinking she might read for a while, but then her mind started on a path she didn't like following.

She didn't like it at all.

Chapter 32

---~S~---

Scene in Dearborn Street When the Fire
Reached the Tremont House, *hand-colored
wood engraving of the Great Chicago Fire,
1871. From* History of the Great Fire. *8.5 x
10.5 inches. Price: $65.*

Morning did not dawn bright or early. Madoc was
faded by heavy billows of fog blowing across the
river. It was not a morning to rise early, and no one
did. Maggie had hardly started sipping her diet
cola, the coffeepot was still dripping, and Amy
hadn't even started her "to do" list for the day
when Detective Strait arrived.

"I'd like to talk with each of you separately," he
said. "You do realize you are all suspects in the
murder of Crystal Porter. And I am also trying to
establish a motive for the brakes on Mr. Douglas's
car being cut."

"You can't believe Maggie or I would do that to
Drew!" Amy said. "What possible reason would
either of us have to hurt him! And, besides, either
or both of us could easily have been in that car."

"That's why I need to talk with both of you, ma'am. Separately."

"You can talk with me first. Amy and Drew haven't even had their coffee yet," said Maggie. "Is the porch private enough?"

"That would be fine."

"Ms. Summer, how long have you known the Douglases?"

"I've known Amy since college. We were roommates. That was about sixteen years ago."

"And you've kept closely in touch with her since then?"

"We talk on the phone every few months, and perhaps once or twice a year we get together. Amy lived in New York City, and I live in New Jersey."

"And Mr. Douglas?"

"I met him once when I saw Amy in New York, and then at their wedding three years ago. I hadn't seen him since then until this week."

"As far as you can tell, as a close friend of Mrs. Douglas, do she and Mr. Douglas have a happy marriage?"

Maggie hesitated.

"In your opinion."

"They decided to move to Maine, and to start a new life. To have a family. Change is stressful. It puts pressure on a relationship."

"You sense stress in their relationship."

Did adultery fall under the heading of "stress"?

"I think they care a great deal about each other and are planning their future together. But, yes, there have been a lot of stresses in their lives recently—the move, their wanting to have a family, the fire, the phone calls—and now, of course, Crystal's murder." Maggie looked out toward the river. The pine trees were silhouetted in the fog like the ferns Victorian ladies pressed into their memory books.

"Did you talk with Crystal Porter while you were here?"

"Just to say 'hello,' and 'nice to meet you.'"

"How did she seem to you? Was she angry? Relaxed? Anxious?"

Maggie thought. "I didn't pay much attention. She seemed comfortable with Amy. On the afternoon I arrived, Amy told her she could go home early, and she said no, that she'd wait because Brian Leary was going to give her a ride home."

Detective Strait made some notes. "That was the day before the murder."

"The day before she disappeared. Yes."

"And could you tell me more about the circumstances in which you saw her on the day of the murder?"

She knew he'd want to go over that again, but Maggie hated the whole situation. "I had been out. When I drove in, I noticed Amy's car was not here, but Drew's was. I knocked on the back door but no one answered. It was unlocked, so I just walked in. I didn't see anyone. I decided to go to my room and lie down for a half hour or so." Maggie hesitated and then forged ahead. "As I was walking up the front steps, I heard noises."

"Voices?"

"More like sounds. I could see from the stairs that

the door to the master bedroom was open. I thought Amy and Drew were in there and walked softly, so they wouldn't be disturbed or embarrassed."

"You walked by the open door."

"Yes."

"And you looked in?"

Maggie blushed. "Yes."

"And what did you see?"

"I saw Crystal's clothes on the floor, and Drew and Crystal on the bed. They were—making love." *Making love* wasn't the phrase Maggie wanted to use, but it was the one she was most comfortable saying to a detective.

"What did you do?"

"I was surprised. Shocked. I didn't want them to see me. I walked as quietly as I could to my room and closed the door."

"And what did you hear after that?"

"I didn't hear anything until Amy knocked on my door."

"And when was that?"

"Perhaps half an hour later."

"And she came into your room?"

"Yes. She was very relaxed. She said she'd been shopping and now had some paperwork to do; she'd be in her study for the next thirty minutes or so, and then maybe we could go for a walk." Maggie didn't mention that Amy had appeared to want her to stay in her room. Not yet. And Amy hadn't said that specifically.

"Did she say anything about her husband? Or about Crystal Porter?"

"She didn't mention either of them." Amazingly enough, Maggie added to herself.

"And did you tell your old college friend what you had seen while she was grocery shopping?"

"No. I didn't want to upset her, and I really didn't know what to say. I didn't say anything."

"And the last time you saw Crystal was when she was in the master bedroom with Mr. Douglas."

"Yes."

"Did you stay in your room for the thirty minutes?"

"Closer to forty. I wanted Amy to have the quiet time she needed."

"And when you came downstairs, where was Mr. Douglas?"

"I didn't see him. I assumed he was in his study, or on the porch."

"But you don't know for sure where he was."

"No."

"And Mrs. Douglas?"

"She was in her study. She put away her paperwork and we went for a walk."

"And from that point on you were with Mrs. Douglas?"

Maggie thought carefully. "We went for a walk. When we got home, we joined Drew on the porch. We had some wine. After a while Amy went into the kitchen to start dinner, and the telephone rang. It was Mrs. Porter. Crystal hadn't come home. Amy was concerned. She suggested to Mrs. Porter that she'd walk up to their house to see if perhaps Crystal had fallen on the way."

"And you went with her?"

"Yes."

"Which way did you take?"

Maggie got up and walked to the end of the porch. She pointed past the driveway, toward the field she and Amy had crossed. "Across that field, and then through a woods."

"You didn't go into the field in back of the barn; the field between this house and Tom Colby's house, next door."

"No." That was the field where Crystal's body had been found.

"Why did you go the way you did?"

"Amy said that was the way Crystal usually walked home."

"Was it a clear path?"

"No. Not until we reached the wooded area."

"And you didn't walk back."

"Deputy Colby gave us a ride back home. He was at the Porters'. Rachel Porter was very worried about Crystal."

"Can you think of anything else that might be helpful for me to know, Ms. Summer?"

Maggie hesitated. "Tom Colby and Will Brewer are arranging a funeral for the child whose bones we found yesterday. I think it will be this afternoon. Will you be there?"

Detective Strait looked at her. "Should I be?"

"I think that might be a good idea," Maggie said softly, but intensely. "I think you should be there with the family."

"Are you sure you have nothing else to tell me?

There is obviously something you're not saying."

"Because I'm not absolutely sure. And because it would be difficult to say."

"You're not withholding evidence."

"I don't have any evidence. But I might find something out between now and this afternoon."

Detective Strait looked at her. "Will Brewer told me you helped solve two murders down in New York State earlier this summer. You wouldn't be having any ideas of interfering with an official investigation, would you?"

"Certainly not, Detective." Maggie smiled her most beguiling smile. She hoped. "But if by chance I should find out something that would help you, then I'd like to know you'll be close this afternoon."

"At the funeral."

"Yes."

"Will also said you were a stubborn woman."

"Did he?" Then the detective and Will must have talked for a few minutes about her. That was flattering. She hoped.

"Can I trust you not to do anything stupid? And to tell me if you should—by chance—find out something?"

"Of course, Detective. You're in charge."

Of course . . .

Chapter 33

❧

A Maine Sea Captain's Daughter, *lithograph
by N. C. Wyeth for Kenneth Roberts's*
Trending into Maine, *1938. Portrait of a
Victorian woman sipping tea by a window
overlooking a Maine seaport. The woman is
said to have been based on a portrait of
Kenneth Roberts's grandmother. 5.5 x 7.5
inches. Price: $60.*

Maggie and Detective Strait looked at each other,
both of them determined.

"Withholding evidence is a crime," he said.

"A woman's intuition isn't evidence, wouldn't
you agree?" Maggie stood up. "There are no facts I
haven't told you."

"Ms. Summer, be careful. A girl was murdered,
there's been a suspicious accident, and there was a
fire that might have been arson. I don't need to deal
with any more bodies."

"And I certainly wouldn't want you to. You'll be
at the burial this afternoon?"

He nodded. "I will."

They returned to the kitchen just as Amy was putting down the telephone. "Will called, Maggie. The burial is to be at two, and Aunt Nettie has invited all of us to her home afterwards for tea or sherry."

"I'm glad Tom and Will were able to arrange it. Will everyone in the family be able to come?"

"I didn't ask specifically, but it sounded that way."

Maggie nodded slightly. "I need to do a couple of errands this morning. Detective, are you through questioning me for the moment?"

"Yes. But I need to talk with Mr. and Mrs. Douglas."

"Then I'll excuse myself. Amy, I'll be back later this morning, in plenty of time to change for the cemetery."

"All right. Where are you going?"

"I saw something at one of the antiques shops Will and I visited the other day that I'd like to look at again. That's all." And that might indeed be all, Maggie thought to herself, as she walked through the fog-dampened grass. Her well-used blue van looked even more faded than usual in the gray of the morning. The fog was beginning to lift, but as she looked back at the house, it was still shrouded in wisps of gray.

She arrived at the Victorian house where Walter English sold antiques before it had opened.

As she paced restlessly up and down the narrow street, she wondered, Was she right even to ask questions? What if she was wrong? Would she get innocent people in trouble? Should she get involved? But then she thought of Amy, and of Drew, and of the child they might have someday. And of the child whose bones had been hidden in the fireplace. The child who would finally be put to rest this afternoon.

Generations of Brewers had lived in that proud white house on a hill in Madoc, Maine. Their descendants still watched the tides rise and fall on the Madoc River and buried their dead in the same cemetery.

This was a different world from the one she had grown up in, the world of suburbia where everyone came from somewhere else and was on their way somewhere farther still. The world in which her parents had lived and died. The world that most of her students had grown up in, and in which she and Michael had chosen to make their home. The high schools where she lived prepared 96 percent of their graduates to leave home, attend college, and find careers elsewhere. Their homes were, by and large, clean and painted and furnished comfortably. Their bookcases were filled. Their grass was cut. And the names of the homeowners changed from year to year. She and Michael had owned their home for twelve years, and they were the only people—she was the only person, Maggie corrected herself—who had lived on their block that long.

Here, someone who had lived here only twelve years was a newcomer. If you had not been born here to someone who had been born here you would always be "from away." The air was fresh;

the street she paced this quiet morning seemed peaceful. But Amy and Drew had not found peace here.

Was it Maine? Or had they brought the unrest with them?

She needed to find out.

For herself, and for Amy. Whatever was happening had to stop.

After Walter English arrived to unlock the door, Maggie gave him a few minutes. For better or worse, she thought ironically, as she entered the antiques mall. She needed some answers.

Chapter 34

—✺—

*Kilmarnock Weeping Willow, Roch
Lithograph Company, Rochester, New York,
1895. One in a series of lithographs of
American trees. During the nineteenth century
weeping willows were often planted in or near
graveyards, and their presence (in life or in art)
was symbolic of death and grieving. 5.75 x 7.5
inches. Price: $48.*

The Douglas house was quiet when Maggie returned. She had gotten one answer. She just needed to put the rest of it together.

She took the portfolios she had left in the living room, checked a few details, and then returned them to her van.

Drew was on the porch. "Did you get your errands done?" he asked.

"Yes. I did." Maggie hesitated. But it wasn't quite time. "Where's Amy?"

"She went next door to ask Shirley what people would be wearing this afternoon, and to make sure we'd be welcome. She suddenly had the feeling that since we weren't Brewers, perhaps we wouldn't be wanted."

"Will called here this morning, so I think he would have said something if we hadn't been. The child was found on your property, after all."

"Yes." Drew looked out over the river. "The fog's risen. Funny. When we lived in New York, I never paid attention to weather except to check whether to wear a raincoat or a topcoat. Here every day seems to define itself by the weather." He smiled at Maggie. "I like it."

"I'm going to go and get dressed," Maggie said. "And I have some papers of Amy's I want to gather and return to her." Upstairs, she once again looked through the piles of pictures of children waiting for homes.

Then she put on the only dark clothes she had brought: a navy blue linen skirt and a matching top she had packed as an extra outfit to wear at the antiques show, or perhaps to wear out to dinner in Maine. She had navy sandals too. She took her large canvas bag and tucked one of Amy's books into it. She would return that one later.

The other books and papers she carried downstairs and put on Amy's desk. Everything was as Amy had left it. Neat. In piles. Waiting for Amy to get to the next column on her "to do" list.

All there was to do now was wait.

By two that afternoon the fog had completely lifted. The sun reflected brightly off the polished surfaces of the newer granite or marble headstones in the cemetery. The older, rougher stones were of various sizes and shapes. As she and Amy joined the small group of people walking toward the back of the cemetery, Maggie noticed one white marble headstone topped by a carved lamb. A child's grave, Maggie knew immediately. Probably from about 1870. She would have liked to have spent more time here. There were stories everywhere. The man buried next to three consecutive wives, and his five children who had died as infants. The family of seven who had all died within one week. Epidemic? Fire? Maggie longed to know. She hoped someone knew. These were people who had lived in Maine and had died here. Had watched the sunsets and gauged the heaviness of the fog; had loved and hated and learned and forgotten. And, now, perhaps had been forgotten.

Having a family to remember them, even centuries later, was important. There was a deep truth and continuity to this place that she had not felt in more pristine suburban cemeteries.

She and Amy walked slowly, so Drew could keep up on his crutches. Looking ahead, she saw Will's strong shoulders bend slightly as Aunt Nettie held on to his arm with one hand and balanced herself on her cane with her other. Shirley had Sorrel and Sage with her, dressed in identical red dresses. Red wasn't usual for a funeral, but this wasn't a usual funeral, and children shouldn't have to wear black, Maggie agreed. Tom Colby was there, in his uniform, complete with rifle. She smiled. Why not? Although it was likely that this child had been born and died before the Civil War. Giles and Mary

Leary were there too, with Brian, whose navy suit jacket was a little short for his arms. And, to her surprise, Rachel Porter was here. Here to mourn another child, before hers had been buried. There were one or two other people she didn't know; one of them must be the minister. And, there, to the side, was Detective Strait. He had come. He raised his hand slightly in greeting when he saw her. She nodded back.

There were no paved or even graveled paths in this cemetery. They all made their way slowly over the uneven grass, around the stones that were set in irregular patterns. Some were upright; some were on the ground. There were a few monuments of size, but most stones were modest, listing only a name and dates. The closer they got to the back of the cemetery, the oldest part, the more stones were carved with the name Brewer. This was the family burial ground and clearly had been so for over two hundred years. The dates told the stories. Would Will choose to be buried here, among his ancestors? Maggie wondered. Were his parents here, or had they been buried near Buffalo, where they had lived?

Those ahead had stopped. A small hole had been dug near a Brewer who had died in 1840. Good, thought Maggie. Perhaps whoever was buried here would have known this child.

A slim young man began saying a prayer. Maggie couldn't concentrate. She crossed the fingers held demurely in front of her. Did she have the right to do what she was planning? But, on the other hand, did she have the right not to?

The minister ended a short reading. Maggie started as Tom Colby fired a salute over the grave. Then Sorrel and Sage each went forward and dropped daisies on top of the tiny coffin. Did they understand that this was a child being buried? A child who had lived and died many, many years before they had even been born? They must understand something, Maggie thought. The box was so small. Then Rachel went forward and also dropped a flower: a white rose. Rachel was crying. So was Amy. Maggie's eyes were damp. She put her arm around Amy and hugged her briefly as they all turned and walked slowly back through the graveyard to their cars. It had been a short ceremony, but it had been appropriate. How many of these people were thinking that someday this would be their place too? Maggie had never thought about where she would be buried. Michael had been buried in a plot in Ohio near his parents. She would not be buried there.

Will's hand on her shoulder brought her back to the moment.

"You got my message? You're all coming back to Aunt Nettie's?"

"Yes." Maggie looked up at him. Will was a man who knew his roots. She wondered what it felt like to have a place to come home to. A place you'd returned to every summer since you were born. A place you were known; a place you belonged.

"Is Amy all right?"

No one else Maggie could see was crying. "She'll be all right. It's been a difficult week. She's probably just reacting to it all."

Will nodded. "Follow the other cars; everyone is coming. We'd be disappointed if you didn't come."

"We'll be there. And I hope you don't mind, but I asked Detective Strait to join us."

Will stopped and looked at her. He knew her too well. "You found out something."

"I have some ideas."

"This is my family, Maggie. We've lost Crystal this week, and now this baby."

It was Maggie's turn to take Will's arm. "It will be all right, Will. I promise. It will be all right."

It was a good thing he couldn't see her crossed fingers.

Chapter 35

———∽———

Court House, Augusta, Maine, *1869 wood engraving from* Gleason's Pictorial. *Courthouse on corner, with elegantly dressed man on horseback, and family walking in road in front of building.* 4.5 x 5.5 inches. Price: $35.

Aunt Nettie's house was smaller than Maggie had assumed, and the crowd arriving from the cemetery filled it. Aunt Nettie gave Maggie a special hug as she entered. "You take good care of my boy," she whispered with a pat on Maggie's arm.

Will grinned at Maggie from the other side of the room where he was presiding over the "iced tea, lemonade, sherry, or soft drink" table and winked. Maggie steeled herself. The players were here. All she had to do was get some answers. It shouldn't be that hard. Just in case, she glanced over at Detective Strait, who was sipping iced tea as he chatted with Will. No one seemed to pay any attention to the detective's being there; everyone must know him well. Better this week than before.

The advantage of approaching people in a crowd

to discuss a difficult situation was that they wouldn't want too much attention to be drawn to themselves. And walking out would mean explaining themselves to everyone, or at least to the host. Of course, the disadvantage was that anyone could walk up and interrupt a delicate conversation.

Maggie felt like Amy, with a list. She took a deep breath and headed in the direction of Tom Colby, who had leaned his rifle up against the windows in back of the drinks table. He asked Will for beer and got a smiling shake of the head. This was Aunt Nettie's gathering, not Will's.

"Tom, could I talk with you for a moment?" Maggie herded him toward a corner not far from the table, but far enough so they wouldn't be overheard. "You did a wonderful job of organizing the burial, Tom. It was lovely."

"Fog burned off; that was nice. And we got a good group of mourners too, at pretty short notice." Tom looked around the room proudly. The buttons on his uniform shone.

There wasn't much time. No one would stay long sipping lemonade, or even eating the cookies on the coffee table. Sage and Sorrel were doing their best to ensure those plates would soon be empty. "Tom, several days ago Will and I went to Walter English's antiques mall. You were there."

"I go there once in a while. Walter sometimes finds Civil War pieces that I'd be interested in."

"You were showing him a rifle. A Sharps rifle."

Tom backed up a bit. "Maggie, now what do you know about rifles?"

"I know Homer's *A Sharp-shooter*. And I know there were half a dozen Sharps rifles hidden in the Douglas home. Now there are five."

Tom paled. "Why are you asking me?"

"Because you know their house; you live next door; and you're the only one who's been in and out of the house this summer who would recognize a Sharps rifle and know its value."

Will had edged his way over to the corner of the table and was listening to them both.

"Tom? Is Maggie right?"

Tom shrugged his shoulders in a grand gesture. "Will, you know me. I wouldn't take nothing. Maggie's right, and she's wrong. I did know about the rifles. And I took one to Walter, to see if he could verify it. But I didn't take it from the house. Shit, Will. 'Scuse me, Maggie, but I don't even know where it came from in the house." He looked down. "At first I was all excited. It being probably one of *the* Sharps and all. You would know, being antiques dealers and knowing about history. But I knew it wasn't mine. I would have put it back, surely I would have, if I'd known where it came from. It's at my house right now, on the top shelf of the closet in my bedroom. Put away so the girls wouldn't find it. None of today's bullets would fit in it, but I don't want Sorrel and Sage thinking they can play with firearms. I'm always careful with my guns."

"How'd you get it, Tom?" Will asked.

Tom shifted his weight from one foot to the other. "I don't like to be in this situation, you understand? I did a favor. I told her it wasn't a good idea, but she said she'd tell everyone if'n I didn't."

"Who'd tell? What?" Maggie could guess one, but she was lost on the other.

Tom glanced up, to make sure no one else was near. "I don't like to say ill of the dead."

"Crystal." Maggie had been almost sure, but now she knew. But what had Crystal threatened to tell?

"She said she'd found it in the house when she was helping Amy clean out. She said there were more too. She wanted to find out what they were worth, and she asked me. She needed the money, she said. She had plans. To go to New York. She knew no one would ask too many questions if I had an old rifle. I already had a few."

"So you took the rifle to Walter?"

"He told me it was probably worth more than Crystal ever dreamed." Tom stopped a minute. "Made me think, I have to say. A person having six of those beauties to sell could do a lot." He looked like a boy embarrassed at being caught sticking his tongue out at the teacher. "A person could even help his sister buy her own house so he could be left in peace again."

Maggie glanced over at Sage and Sorrel. They were arguing over whose cookie was bigger, and Shirley was threatening to take them both home. This instant.

"But of course I couldn't do that. Because I didn't know where the other rifles were. Only Crystal knew that. And I knew if I sold the gun and didn't give her the money, well, then, she'd tell."

"Tell what?" Would whatever Crystal had to tell have disappeared after her death? Then all Tom would have had to do was find the guns.

"Will, you'd understand! You were there!" Tom looked at Will, as though for help.

"I was where?" Will had moved around the table and stood so Tom's back was against the wall, and he and Maggie were blocking the rest of the company.

"You were around that summer Rachel got herself in the family way." Tom took a chug of his iced tea as though it were Jim Beam. "Well, she'd told me. That I was the daddy of that little baby."

Will's face flushed. "Rachel told you that when?"

"When she was maybe three months gone. She asked me for money to, you know, take care of the situation. She told me she'd never tell no one, and so far as I know she never did. Only I knew Crystal was my little girl. I wanted to do what I could to help her."

"Tom, how much money did you give Rachel, back then?"

"She needed five thousand dollars. I remember, because it was a lot of money, and I was still in school. Had to take a loan, and work a lot of overtime to get that money. Didn't want my folks to know." Tom hesitated. "Rachel told me she was going to have an abortion. But when she didn't, I daren't say a word, since I didn't want anyone to know. But all these years I've been looking out for that young lady.

And she was a beautiful thing, wasn't she?" Tom's eyes filled with tears.

Will ran his hand through his thick gray hair. "Tom, I need to tell you something. Something I've never told anyone." He looked at Maggie and then back at Tom. "Tom, Rachel told me the same thing."

"What?"

"She told me I was the father, and she needed five thousand dollars for an abortion. And I got her the money."

"Did she ever say anything else about it?"

"Never. I was real angry at the time when the baby was born, but she never said a word. I saw Crystal every summer, and Rachel seemed to be doing a good job of raising her. Never asked for any money or anything. I sent Crystal and Rachel nice Christmas gifts every year."

"You mean I wasn't that little girl's father?" Tom looked totally bewildered.

"I don't know if you were. I just know Rachel told me the same story."

Both Will and Tom looked across the room to where Rachel stood, sipping sherry, and receiving condolences.

"She was a good mother to Crystal."

"She was." Will hesitated. "But, Tom, I have a feeling Rachel told that story to someone else, too."

Maggie and Tom and Will all looked over at Giles Leary. Will said softly, "You see, Tom, Giles told me he thought he was Crystal's father. That's one reason he didn't want Brian spending time with her. Maybe he thought so for the same reason we did."

Maggie thought a moment. "That could explain where Rachel got the down payment for the house she bought. Remember you once wondered how she had managed to get that much money together when she was so young, and a single parent; that maybe her grandmother had left her some money?"

They were all quiet. Then Maggie shook her head. "Tom, I believe you didn't take the rifle. Crystal had the opportunity. But who would have killed her?"

"Not me!" Tom said. "I thought she was my own daughter. And she said she'd tell a secret if I didn't get her the money for the rifles. I figured Rachel had told her I was her father, and she was going to tell everyone. It's an old story, but I'm a teacher. I didn't want it getting around that I had done something like that when I was young. I'm supposed to be a role model. And Rachel was my second cousin."

"Mine too, Tom. Mine too." Will looked around the room. They were all silent.

Drew and Amy were talking with Aunt Nettie. "Will, Tom, would you find an excuse to talk with Drew? I need to talk with Amy privately." Maggie looked at both of them. "It's important. Please."

Will picked up an extra glass of iced tea and the two men went over to where Drew was sitting. In a few minutes they were deeply involved in a discussion of something. But whatever topic they'd chosen, perhaps the Civil War, didn't interest Amy. She headed for the refreshments table and a glass of sherry.

"Not exactly a lively party, Maggie." Amy raised her glass in salute. "But we won't have to stay much longer. We're just putting in an appearance."

Maggie moved a little closer and took Amy's arm. Amy's breath was heavy with sherry. The glass she had just poured was not her first. "Amy, you're a dear friend, but I know what you did. I think I know why. And you are going to have to turn yourself in to Detective Strait. It will be much better for you if you do. He's over in that corner. You can do it quietly and no one will even know."

Amy pushed Maggie away abruptly, moving back so suddenly she hit the table in back of her. Two glasses of iced tea fell over, and a small pool of brown liquid spread across the white, embroidered linen tablecloth and toward the floor. No one paid attention.

"What do you think you're talking about?" said Amy, her voice low.

"You killed Crystal Porter."

Amy suddenly broke into a raucous laugh that drew attention from everyone throughout the room. "You're out of your mind! How can you even imagine something like that? Me? You're crazy, Maggie. Me?"

Maggie moved closer again and spoke softly. "Amy. Turn yourself in. It will go much better if you do that now."

Amy slid away from Maggie and pushed the table again. The crystal glasses on the table glistened in the light from the window. A rainbow was on one of the curtains.

Amy's eyes flickered like those of a trapped animal. The room was full of people. Right now most of them were looking at her. She looked to the right, then to the left, as though seeking a way to escape. Then she pulled the table forward and moved in back of it, grabbing the rifle Tom had left there. Maggie reached across the table, but before she could reach Amy, the rifle was pointed directly at her.

No one in the room said a word.

Sage screamed. "That lady's going to shoot us!"

Detective Strait pulled his gun and pointed it at Amy. "Mrs. Douglas, put down that rifle."

Amy carefully moved the rifle and pointed it at Sage. "No. You drop your gun. Unless you all want to go to another burial very soon." Amy's voice was much too calm. "I said, drop that gun."

Shirley screamed, and Maggie, still facing Amy, heard Detective Strait's gun hit the floor.

"Amy, don't do anything foolish. Put down the rifle." Maggie voice was calm, although her mind was anything but.

"Why should I? What does it matter?" Amy waved the rifle around the room, pointing at one person after another. "They can't put me in jail for more than one lifetime, can they?"

"Amy, put down the rifle. It isn't worth it."

"She wasn't worth it. That lying schemer. I cried over that poor baby we buried today, but I won't cry over Crystal Porter. Whoever that baby was, he was too young to have betrayed anyone. Crystal was a liar and a cheat. She was ruining my life. She deserved to die."

"Amy!" Drew tried to get up and move toward her, but stumbled on his cast.

Amy pointed the rifle directly at him. "You and I agreed. We had it all figured out. But she changed her mind. She wouldn't go along. I did it to protect you, Drew. I wanted you to love me."

Maggie moved forward slightly, leaning against the table. With her right hand she reached down and picked up a glass of iced tea and threw the tea into Amy's face, while she threw her body against the table and pushed it—hard—toward Amy. The movement caught Amy off-balance, and she stumbled backward against the windows. As she did, Maggie moved around the table and grabbed the rifle. The two women struggled with it. Maggie vaguely heard movements behind her. The metal of the rifle was rough; her hands were scratched, she realized, and the rifle had hit the side of her face. Amy's strength was greater than she had expected. She hoped the people in back of her were getting out. Taking the girls away. She pushed hard, and Amy fell against the window. The rifle butt caught in the lace curtain and ripped it. The table moved farther away as Tom reached over them and put both hands on the rifle, while Will, the bigger of the two men, pushed Amy down. They all ended up in a tangle on the ground until, suddenly:

"Stop it! Everyone!"

The rifle was gone, Maggie realized. She and

Will were both on top of Amy on the ground, while spilled glasses of iced tea dripped down on them.

"Let her up. Slowly." It was Detective Strait. He had his gun. And he was holding a pair of handcuffs. Maggie and Will rose, pulling Amy with them. Without the rifle, which Tom held across the room, Amy stopped fighting. They moved her to a chair, where Nick Strait put the cuffs on. Maggie glanced around quickly. Good. The children had gone into the kitchen. With what they'd seen today they'd be having nightmares for a month.

"Mrs. Douglas, you're going to come with me, now. Quietly." Detective Strait read Amy her rights while Maggie stepped backward and felt Will's arms go around her. She leaned back slightly, grateful for the comforting gesture, as Detective Strait and Amy left the room.

As they reached the doorway, Nick Strait turned around. "An interesting party. Thank you for inviting me, Ms. Summer. I may have a few more questions for you, and for you, Mr. Douglas, later. First I'm going to find Mrs. Douglas a nice quiet place where she can think."

The door closed behind them.

Chapter 36

―⁂―

Thanksgiving Day—Hanging Up the Musket. *Winslow Homer wood engraving published in* Frank Leslie's Illustrated News Paper, *December 23, 1865. Man standing on chair, hanging Civil War–vintage rifle over fireplace. Rifle is labeled 1861 and is hanging beneath an earlier rifle, with a powder horn labeled 1776. 9.13 x 14.13 inches. Price: $260.*

The Learys lived only a few blocks away and left almost immediately after Detective Strait took Amy away. Brian looked pale. Shirley too wanted to remove her girls from the scene and promised French fries and ice cream on their way home, which seemed to lessen their trauma considerably. "Chocolate?" Sorrel asked as they left. "Can the ice cream be chocolate?" Rachel broke down and left with a woman Maggie didn't know.

Aunt Nettie sat on a high Queen Anne chair and surveyed her living room. Iced tea was still dripping slowly onto the floor. She had mopped up some of it, but had missed one spot. That tablecloth will have to be bleached, Maggie thought. And the curtains mended. Drew sat on a straight Hitchcock chair stenciled in gold and red. His injured foot stuck out into the room; his face was white with shock. Will and Maggie held hands and settled on an upholstered, blue-flowered couch that was so much lower than Aunt Nettie's seat that Maggie kept thinking she should stand up. Tom Colby paced from one side of the room to the other.

Aunt Nettie spoke first. "Would anyone else like a real drink? I think some Jack Daniel's would go down right well just now."

Tom and Drew joined her, Maggie poured herself some sherry, and Will found a beer in the refrigerator.

"All right, now would one of you explain just what went on here?" Aunt Nettie looked from one to the other. "I'm not daft. I understand Amy Douglas killed Crystal. But I don't have a clue as to why."

Maggie looked at Drew. "I'm so sorry, Drew. Did you have any idea?"

He shook his head. "I wondered. But, no, I didn't know. I kept hoping not." He looked at Maggie. "How did you know?"

"I wasn't positive. But the pieces fit. Amy told me how much you both wanted a child."

He nodded.

"And how you didn't want to adopt. You wanted a child biologically yours. Amy was afraid she couldn't have a child. She was afraid to tell you; she thought it might end your marriage."

Drew looked at Maggie incredulously. "It

wouldn't have ended our marriage! And I knew she might not be able to have children. Her doctor told me everything." Drew looked around the room. "I guess it doesn't make a difference anymore. Amy's stepfather raped her repeatedly when she was a teenager; she got pregnant. He arranged an abortion, but it was botched, and as a result she probably couldn't have children." Drew sighed. "She didn't tell me about the abortion, but her doctor thought I knew, and he referred to it once. I knew if she hadn't told me herself, she was embarrassed about it, so I never told her I knew. She had told me about the stepfather and the rapes, just after we were married."

"I didn't realize." Maggie shook her head slowly. "She told me about the abortion, but not about the stepfather. So that's why she stayed close to home in college?"

Drew nodded. "He would only pay for a college close to home so she would be—available. Her mother had no clue, and Amy was too afraid of hurting her to tell. And she didn't have the self-confidence to leave home and get a job or scholarship somewhere else."

"The poor girl," said Aunt Nettie. "That's a horrible thing to have to live through. But what had Amy's past to do with Crystal?"

Drew answered, "Amy knew I wanted a biological child. It was really important to me." He took a sip of the Jack Daniel's. "Not important enough to kill for, though. But without telling me, Amy worked out a deal with Crystal."

Maggie looked at him. "Crystal was going to have your child, wasn't she?"

"At first I thought it was crazy, but then it began to make more sense. Crystal agreed to get pregnant. To have my child. After the child was born she would relinquish parental rights to Amy and me and we would give her enough money to start a new life in New York, which is what she wanted."

The room was silent.

"It would be an open adoption; she could have come home and seen the child anytime she wanted to. And her son or daughter would have all the advantages Amy and I could provide."

"And Crystal did get pregnant."

"Yes."

"What went wrong?" asked Will.

"She changed her mind. She told me right after . . . you saw us together, Maggie. We didn't want you to know what we were doing, but you found out. What you didn't know was that Amy had arranged the whole thing. She wasn't embarrassed, except by the fact that you knew. But that afternoon Crystal told me she had changed her mind; she wanted to keep the baby." Drew took another deep drink of the liquor. "She also told me it might not be my baby, anyway. It might be Brian's."

Maggie nodded. She decided not to point out that there was no need for Drew to have kept sleeping with Crystal after he'd known she was pregnant. At this point, was it even important? So far this made sense. Horrible sense, but sense. "How did you feel?"

"I was shocked. I know that sounds stupid under the circumstances, but it never occurred to me Crystal might be sleeping with anyone else. She was cheating Amy and me out of the only child we might have who would be related to me. I was furious. I was disappointed. I didn't know what to do." Drew blanched a bit. "When Amy came home that afternoon, I told her, and then I got drunk. It seemed the only reasonable thing to do at the time."

Maggie nodded. "I remember. Amy said she had some work to do in her study, and when she was finished, she and I took a walk. And when we got home, you were a bit under the weather. That was the night Crystal didn't make it home."

"But then when did Amy do it?" Will asked.

"It must have been when I was in my room. Drew, you were drinking on the front porch, and Amy said she was going to her study." Maggie put it all together. "She went to tell Crystal she could go home. The Learys had already left for the day because they needed to pick up some supplies. So Amy and Crystal were alone."

"Amy was furious," added Drew. "I knew that. I was furious too. But I never thought of anything like murder! But Amy had planned the pregnancy and the adoption. She had talked Crystal into it. She had talked me into agreeing. She had already spoken with our lawyer in New York about the legalities regarding open adoption, and about our helping Crystal to make a start in the city."

Amy would have done that, Maggie thought. Amy wouldn't have wanted anything to get in the

way of her plans. It would have been illegal to pay
Crystal for the adoption, but, from what she'd seen
in the adoption books, Amy and Drew could have
paid for her pregnancy and birth expenses. No
doubt Amy's lawyer would have come up with
some way of getting Crystal started in New York,
perhaps arranging for an apartment, and a job. The
details didn't matter now.

Drew sat and looked at the wall. "I saw her leave
the house with Crystal. She wasn't yelling; she
wouldn't have wanted you to hear, Maggie, and you
were upstairs. But I knew she was really giving it to
Crystal. 'Betrayer, liar, whore.' I saw them walk
around the barn, back toward where Crystal's body
was found the next day."

"I wonder why they did that? Amy told me
Crystal usually walked through the other field to go
home."

"I can answer that," Tom spoke up from the corner. "Crystal was coming to see me. I had promised
to find out about the rifle, and tell her."

Drew frowned. "The rifle?"

Maggie looked over at Aunt Nettie, who also
looked confused. "We found five Civil War–era
rifles hidden in the floor of the attic. Will suspected
there had been six, but we didn't know for sure
until Tom told me. Crystal had found them and
taken one to Tom, asking him to get it appraised.
She wanted to sell the rifles."

"That must have been what she meant when she
told me she didn't need our checks; she had her
own way of making money." Drew looked around.

"Of course. She and Amy cleaned the attic. She found the loose board there."

"So you expected Crystal, Tom?"

"I did. I waited for her. But she didn't come. I even called Rachel, but by then Crystal was missing. I drove around looking for her that night. It never occurred to me to look in the back field."

"And you didn't tell anyone you'd expected to see her that day."

Tom shook his head. "I suppose now that I should have. But at the time I didn't think it was important. And I didn't want Crystal to get into trouble about the rifle."

"Or for you to get in trouble, Tom Colby. You were helping that girl steal rifles!" Aunt Nettie shook her finger at him.

Tom didn't answer. But he shrugged acceptance. "I made a mistake. A bad mistake."

Will picked up the thread. "So most likely Amy followed Crystal out into the field. They were still talking. Amy was furious. And she must have picked up a rock and hit Crystal."

"And then she came back to her study, where I found her forty minutes later." Maggie shook her head, remembering how calm Amy had been. "She had changed the bandage on her arm. I remember thinking the blood had seeped through. She must have stressed it when she knocked Crystal down. So she came back and cleaned herself up, but the wound from the window a few days before had opened. Or," Maggie said suddenly, "it might have been Crystal's blood."

Drew pulled himself up from the chair. "Why did we ever come to this place? We weren't wanted here. All those stories about ghosts, and the baby crying, and the fire, and my accident, and now Crystal is dead, and Amy's in jail. And there will be no child, and I have no wife, and . . ." Drew sat down suddenly and burst into wracking sobs.

"That's right. What was all that with the ghosts and the baby crying? And the telephone calls. And . . ." Maggie looked around the room.

"All right, all right! That was Shirley. And me." Tom came and sat down with the rest of them. "Shirley was real angry when the house was sold. She thought it should have been hers. And, I'll admit, I had hoped she'd get the house too. I missed the peace of living alone. Shirley is my sister, but those kids of hers are a real handful. Anyway, she thought we could scare those city folks right back to the city, and that maybe then they'd sell the house for about what they'd paid for it. More than we could really afford, but we might be able to swing it, if Shirley could get a settlement from her ex-husband. I figured it wouldn't do no harm to try. There had always been stories about a woman and a baby at that house. So I went and made a tape recording of Sue Smithson's baby crying, down the road, and put it on a timing device. If the batteries are holding up, it'll still be playing two or three times a week. The recorder is hanging down in the chimney flue near the master bedroom fireplace. Brian thought it was a fun game; he helped me rig it up." Tom hesitated a moment. "Crystal knew about it too. She used to talk about what a great job we were doing, scaring Mrs. Douglas. Course, I guess by then she knew how important babies were to the Douglases."

"And the phone calls?" Maggie leaned toward Tom.

"Shirley did that part. She isn't a good sleeper. She thought that would drive them crazy."

"The ghost?"

"Don't know nothing about any ghost. Seems to me Amy probably dreamed that one up herself."

With a baby crying in the walls and strange phone calls, she might have, Maggie agreed to herself.

Will now asked, "And the fire?"

Tom looked sheepish. "That was me too. I didn't intend for it to burn down the house, or hurt anyone. I just wanted to scare them."

Drew looked up at him incredulously.

"That was before I got to know you, Drew. I wouldn't do it now."

"You dropped the fire down the ell flue?"

"Right! It was easy to walk in through the barn during the day and leave the oven open there." He looked at Aunt Nettie, as though she would understand. "The Douglases didn't spend much time in that part of the house."

"And I suppose you cut my brake line too? As something else that would be amusing?" Drew pushed his leg toward Tom as if to demonstrate the damage.

"Nope. Didn't do that. You might have gotten

hurt! Shirley and me was trying to scare you folks a little. Not hurt anyone."

The room was silent.

"I think," said Maggie, "I think Amy cut the brake line. Maybe we'll find out for sure sometime in the future. But she knew something about auto mechanics. I think she cut the line to make it look as though her family was being targeted, maybe by the same person who'd killed Crystal. To take the spotlight off her and Drew."

"But she might have killed me!"

Maggie shook her head. "She knew most of your errands were to Waymouth, and that your brakes would give out at that corner. You wouldn't have been going fast enough to kill yourself. Although you did, of course, mess your leg up pretty well."

Will reached over and took Maggie's hand again. "You figured it all out. And you were brave enough to grab that rifle from Amy. I thought for sure you were going to be shot!"

"She wouldn't have been," said Tom.

"I knew that," agreed Maggie. "But I don't think Amy knew."

"Knew what, Maggie?" Aunt Nettie shook her head. "I'm trying very hard to follow along and understand all these crazy things, but Amy looked dangerous. Why wouldn't she have shot anyone?"

"Because she had Tom's rifle. When we were looking up and asking about rifles the other day, I thought back over what I knew about Civil War–era weapons. And I went to see Walter English this morning, to confirm my suspicion that it had been

Tom who had taken the rifle in for an appraisal. He mentioned that one of the reasons the Sharps rifles were especially valuable during the Civil War was because they could fire more cartridges than other rifles without reloading. I thought of that when Tom fired a salute at the cemetery. I assumed that, for safety's sake, he hadn't reloaded. There was no reason for him to do so. So I took a chance. I assumed the rifle wouldn't have fired."

Aunt Nettie shook her head. "Will, your new friend seems to know all too much about everything." She turned to Maggie. "And I suppose you know who that poor baby was that we buried this afternoon?"

"No. I have no idea about that baby," said Maggie. "But at least he or she is resting in peace with the rest of the family now."

She raised a glass to the child, and the rest of the group joined her.

"To peace," said Aunt Nettie. "The good Lord knows, this family could use some."

Chapter 37

—❦—

Moll Pitcher at Monmouth, *1860 wood
engraving used as illustration for history book.
Molly Pitcher, 1744–1832, born Mary Ludwig,
was the wife of Revolutionary War soldier John
Hays and carried water to her husband and
other soldiers during the Battle of Monmouth,
where legend says that after her husband was
shot, she manned his cannon, earning her the
nickname "Molly Pitcher." Engraving shows
her dying husband, the bucket she has cast
aside, and Moll loading the cannon. Signed
W. H. Van Ingen, possibly the father of noted
nineteenth-century mural painter William
Brantley Van Ingen, who was known for his
historical murals painted in government build-
ings. Foxed. 5 x 6.5 inches. Price: $35.*

"When will you go back to Jersey, Maggie?" Will
asked. The sunset was a brilliant design of purples
and reds as they shared a chaise on the Douglas
porch and sipped Chablis. Drew was inside, tele-
phoning local lawyers Aunt Nettie had suggested.
Amy was at the Lincoln County Jail.

"I'll stay another day or so and make sure there is nothing I know that the police don't. I don't think there should be. But then I have to head back and get my schedules and class list set for the fall semester. I'm still a professor. And you're leaving?"

"In two days. What do you think Drew will do?"

"He said he'll stay here, at least for now, to help Amy. He really does love her, Will. Maybe he'll look for a job teaching. He talked about that before all this happened."

"Sometimes talking about the past makes the present easier to understand."

"It might," said Maggie. "The past is always a good place to start."

She put down her glass and cuddled against Will's shoulder. A red sunset meant a clear day ahead. She hoped their tomorrows would bring clarity and answers to Amy and Drew.

"When am I going to see you again, Maggie Summer?" Will said softly. "My life always seems more exciting when we're together."

"The early part of the fall semester is always hectic. But there are a lot of antiques shows in New Jersey then. I'll bet a few of them could find a booth for a dealer in early-fireplace equipment." Maggie looked up at him.

Their kiss, like the sunset, promised a bright tomorrow.

The following document was among papers donated to the Waymouth Library archives by Mr. and Mrs. Andrew Douglas. The papers were found in the Douglas home, which was originally owned by the Brewer family. There is no date on this document, and no attribution.

Transcription by Ms. Rachel Porter, Waymouth Librarian.

As a child there was only one place on this island I was forbidden to go, and therefore that place was where I most longed to be. About an hour's walk through the pines was Jewett's Cove. After Widow Jewett's husband was claimed by the sea, she was left only a house and barn. She was a big woman, in body and in spirit. When she determined to turn her house and barn into a seaman's inn no one questioned her ability to run a tight house. Widow Jewett could raise a barrel of cider to her mouth and drink without spilling a drop. She was known to take a fist to any man who'd had too much rum and decided to make something of it. A man might drink too much at Widow Jewett's, but he didn't make trouble.

Most important to me, she listened to my dreams. And she helped me find ways to stay in this house, even after Father's ship was lost at sea, my sisters married, and Mother was lost to nightmares. She taught me to bake bread, and to grow vegeta-

bles, and to care for the chickens and the cows, even in their sicknesses. And she bought what other supplies Mother and I had need of. After Mother's death, Aunt Tempe tried to convince me it was not proper for a young woman to stay alone; that I should join her family in Belfast. But I had no desire to care for her children—seven then, and more coming—and I stayed. A woman cannot own property, so this house was held by her husband. But no one in Belfast had need of it, and times were not prosperous; one more house on an island was not thought of value. There was no one to care what I did, so I suited myself, and remained where I had always been.

And one summer a mariner staying to Widow Jewett's took my fancy, and he mine, and there was no one on the island to see or care what was done. The man left, as Widow Jewett had said he would, since men are restless as the tides, and come and go as often. But he did not leave me alone.

Who was to know, alone in the winter cold of an island? Who was to know what shape my body or my mind took?

But when spring came, and my time with it, I knew a child would not be safe with me. A child without a father would be worse off than if he had never been. And so I made my choice, and Widow Jewett helped me do what had to be done.

And ever since I have lived here with my baby who would never be a child.

But although the child did not age, I have. Now Aunt Tempe's oldest boy is marrying and has claimed this house as his own. He will move the house to the mainland of Madoc when the river freezes. I will not go with it. My life has not been one shared with others, and this is not the time to begin doing so.

But my child has known no other home than this one, and he shall stay here. He shall be safe. I will find a way. And then I fear I will walk on ice too thin to bear weight. A simple mistake, made by a simple old woman.

And it will be over. I will not be remembered, and my child was never known. But as long as this house shall stand, we will be a part of it.

Afterword

————✦————

During the 1950s my parents and grandparents bought a run-down Colonial home in a riverside community on the midcoast of Maine. We were the first to own the house outside the family that had built it in 1774, and then, four generations later, had moved it from Westport Island onto the mainland, where the ell and the barn were added. When I was a child, I helped my mother and grandmother tear down the plaster wall in the old kitchen to reveal the original fireplace, where we found its crane still intact. You can see the fireplace on my website, *www.leawait.com*.

The house is locally known as The Marie Antoinette House, because of a legend that Stephen Clough, its second owner, masterminded a plot to rescue Queen Marie Antoinette during the French Revolution and bring her to live in Maine. When the plot was discovered, Clough left France quickly, bringing with him a shipload of exquisite French clothing and furniture. Clough did have business connections with members of the French court, and he was in

France when Marie Antoinette was executed. Was he ever really involved in a plot to free Marie Antoinette? No one will ever know for sure. But he was, no doubt, trying to help some fleeing French aristocrats. Clough named his youngest daughter Hannah Antoinette, and ever since there has been an Antoinette in each generation of their family.

Today I live and write in that house, and its history has inspired not only this book, but several of my historical novels for children. (Stephen Clough's daughter Sally is a character in *Stopping to Home*.) So far as I know, no one living here has ever seen a ghost, or heard a baby crying in the night, or found a skeleton in the chimney or rifles in the attic. . . . But sometimes, especially when the river winds blow down the chimney on dark winter days, the howling sound is almost a human cry.

And in the early nineteenth century Widow Jewett did run an inn for mariners on nearby Westport Island.

Lea Wait

Interested in learning more about the antique prints in Maggie Summer's business?

The following books and periodicals will give you additional information.

American Historical Print Collectors Society (publication: *Imprint*). Post Office Box 201, Fairfield, Connecticut 06430

Beam, Philip C. *Winslow Homer's Magazine Engravings*. Harper & Row Publishers, New York, 1979

Blum, Ann Shelby. *Picturing Nature: American Nineteenth-Century Zoological Illustration*. Princeton University Press, Princeton, New Jersey, 1993

Blunt, Wilfrid, and William T. Stearn. *The Art of Botanical Illustration*. Antique Collectors' Club in association with The Royal Botanic Gardens, Kew, England, 1994

Book Source Monthly. 2007 Syossett Drive, Cazenovia, New York 13035

Cikovsky, Nicolai Jr., and Franklin Kelly. *Winslow Homer*. National Gallery of Art, Washington, D.C., and Yale University Press, New Haven and London, 1995

Hamilton, James. *Arthur Rackham: A Life With Illustration*. Pavilion Books Limited, London, 1990

Harthan, John. *The History of the Illustrated Book: The Western Tradition*. Thames and Hudson, Ltd., London, 1981

Hults, Linda C. *The Print in the Western World: An Introductory History*. University of Wisconsin Press, Madison, 1996

Journal of the Print World, Inc. Post Office Box 978, Meredith, New Hampshire 03253

The Magazine Antiques. Brant Publications, Inc., 575 Broadway, New York, New York 10012

Maine Antique Digest. Post Office Box 1429, Waldoboro, Maine 04572

Meyer, Susan E. *A Treasury of the Great Children's Book Illustrators*. Harry N. Abrams, Inc., Publishers, New York, 1983

St. Hill, Thomas Nast. (Introduction to) *Thomas Nast's Christmas Drawings*. Dover Publications, Inc., New York, 1978

SCRIBNER
PROUDLY PRESENTS

SHADOWS ON THE IVY

LEA WAIT

Available in hardcover August 2004

Turn the page for a preview of
Shadows on the Ivy. . . .

Chapter 1

The Banquet Where the Really Grand Company Were Assembled in the Elfin Hall. Lithograph by Arthur Rackham (1867–1939) from Hans Christian Anderson's Fairy Tales, 1912. Rackham was a major Edwardian illustrator who specialized in magical, mystical, and legendary themes. His work influenced the surrealists. This print is of a large room crowded with elves, animal-people, trolls, fairy princesses, and other imaginary creatures who are dining on frogs and snails and sipping from cups overflowing with frothing beverages. 9.75 x 7.75 inches. Price: $70.

Dorothy and Oliver Whitcomb's home was elegant, their food delicious, and their bar open, but Maggie Summer wanted to be at home sorting prints for next weekend's Morristown Antiques Show. Her roles as an antique print dealer and a college professor sometimes complemented each other, and sometimes conflicted. Today they conflicted.

She shifted her weight from one foot to another, cursing her decision to wear the sexy crimson silk heels that had tempted her at the Short Hills Mall last evening. Women alone on Saturday night should not be allowed to go shopping! Last night the shoes had made her feel young and alluring. Today they just hurt. An hour ago a small blister had appeared on her left little toe.

Her eyes wandered from four of John Gould's prints of hummingbirds that were hanging near the windows to the six hand-colored steel engravings of Burritt's 1835 view of the sky at different seasons that hung over the large black marble fireplace. The Whitcombs were devoted customers of Maggie's antique print business, Shadows. They were also Somerset College trustees and major donors. When they issued an invitation, she accepted.

The Whitcombs had spent almost as much on framing as they had on the prints, but the result was worth it. The Burritts fit especially well in this room. The delicate figures drawn between the constellations blended perfectly into a library furnished with comfortable leather chairs and couches. Knowledge of the past combined with desire to know the future. Maggie walked closer, admiring the familiar star-defined astrological patterns. As always when she looked at the stars she looked for her sign, Gemini. Two figures; two destinies.

Did the stars represent her two professions? Or her two emotional selves . . . the self-contained, intelligent, respected woman most people saw . . . or the frustrated, conflicted self she hid beneath the surface? Were either of them the sexy lady in red heels?

Gemini was green in this edition of Burritts. Green for jealousy? Jealousy of those for whom the patterns of life seemed to fall into place so easily. Career . . . marriage . . . children. . . . The white wine was taking her mind down paths she didn't want to follow. At least not right now.

Maggie turned her thoughts to business. She had another edition of these Burritt engravings in her inventory at home. Should she pay to have them matted and framed? They'd be much more striking if they were framed, but she'd have to charge considerably more for them. How much more would people pay so they could take artwork home from an antiques show and immediately hang it on their living room wall? She should experiment with the Burritts. She could use some good sales. If customers wanted frames, frames she would give them. She made a mental note to consult Brad and Steve, her local framers.

Her next beverage would be Diet Pepsi—with caffeine. And maybe she could scavenge a Tylenol from someone. She sighed, looking around the room again. If only she'd resisted wearing the red heels.

Across the room, Dorothy Whitcomb was talking to freshman Sarah Anderson, backing her up against a bookcase filled with what appeared to be nineteenth-century first editions. They were probably just decorator leather bindings purchased by the yard, but in this setting they worked almost as well as the real thing. Neither Dorothy nor Oliver were, to Maggie's knowledge, book lovers. Certainly they weren't antiquarian book collectors. But major donors to Somerset College should have an elegant library. It was part of the unwritten job description. And no doubt why the Whitcombs chose to host this reception in their library rather than in their equally posh living room.

Sarah's shoulder-length red hair was bouncing as she nodded at Dorothy politely.

Twenty-three-year-old Sarah was pretty, but not too patient. She wouldn't listen forever. She had clearly dressed up for this reception. For Sarah, gray slacks and an almost-matching turtleneck was about as elegant as her wardrobe got. Dorothy never seemed to consider that the scholarship students she invited to her "informal get-togethers" (read: "cocktail parties") might find dressing for these occasions a financial challenge. Maggie sighed. She should rescue Sarah. Would her feet hold up?

Paul Turk provided a welcome interruption to Maggie's gloomy thoughts. "Help! I know the Whitcombs, and some of the students, but I'm getting weary of smiling."

Maggie lightly touched Paul's arm in friendly understanding. His cologne was an attractive spicy scent, with traces of musk. Not the usual aftershave he wore on campus. Very nice. She moved out of range of the scent. Her life was complicated enough just now.

Paul was the newest member of the American Studies faculty. A corporate dropout and former Wall Street associate of Oliver Whitcomb's, he'd had the inside track for a teaching opening this fall when he'd decided to capitalize on his masters in American history and exchange his windowed office at an investment firm for a small cubicle at Somerset College. Slender, and taller than Maggie at perhaps five feet ten inches, Paul had started to let his brown hair go a bit shaggy, and the look was good for him, even if it was obvious that he was consciously transforming himself into his vision of what a history professor *should* look like. She suspected the female students she'd seen loitering outside his office were suitably impressed.

Paul's office was next to hers, and she often helped him with new-kid-on-the-block issues. "It isn't the smiling during these parties that's so challenging," she said, "it's knowing you have to smile."

He raised his eyebrows and nodded in agreement. "As always, the voice of experience. On your way to the bar?"

"Turning in my white wine for a diet soda."

"And here I was going to pour you one of my perfect Grey Goose martinis."

"Not tonight, thank you," said Maggie, as they reached the table of drinks. "But you can do the Diet Pepsi honors. Or maybe I'll just have a Virgin Mary."

"Your choice. Everything's here. I helped Oliver set all this up earlier."

"I'll stick with the Diet Pepsi," Maggie decided. "With caffeine."

Paul reached past empty bottles of vodka and scotch for the last bottle of Diet Pepsi on the do-it-yourself bar. "Looks as though our fellow guests have been joining us in taking full advantage of the libations." He moved several empties to an overflowing carton beneath the table and replaced them with full bottles.

They moved aside to make room for their host, a big white-haired man of perhaps sixty whose navy suit had been made to order for his large build. The tailor had succeeded. Oliver looked every bit the wealthy suburban gentleman.

"Enjoying yourself, Paul?" said Oliver. "I'm afraid the company here is a bit tamer than what you're used to in New York," he added, giving Paul a knowing cuff on the arm. He opened the bottles Paul had pulled out, and refilled pitchers labeled "orange juice" and "Bloody Mary mix."

Paul added to the ice bucket from the chest on the floor next to the table.

"I wish we'd hired someone else to set the drinks up, but Dorothy thought the students would find a bartender ostentatious." Oliver shrugged. "The caterer could have supplied us with someone."

Paul grinned at him. "How could anyone possibly think you and Dorothy were ostentatious?"

"Hard to imagine, isn't it?" answered Oliver with a bit of a twinkle, looking around the mahogany bookcase–lined room that was almost as big as the basketball court in the new gymnasium he had bank-rolled at the college. "Dorothy does like to act the grande dame. I'd be just as happy on a smaller stage. But, hell—'if you've got it'—and all that. In any case, have fun. You, too, Maggie." He nodded at her. "I've got to get back to playing host."

Oliver headed across the room toward the college president, Max Hagfield, but was intercepted by a group of students Maggie didn't recognize.

"Those students work out at the gym," Paul answered her unspoken question as they watched. "Oliver will no doubt now expound on the merits of the weight machines he's ordered for the gymnasium." Paul raised his martini to Maggie's cola.

"The WHITCOMB Gymnasium," she corrected, as they clinked glasses and moved away from the bar. Campus gossip reported that Oliver donated the gym on the condition that he, as a member of the Board of Trustees, could use it at any time, and he'd made sure it contained the equipment he'd preferred at New York's Downtown Athletic Club. The gym had been completed just in time for his retirement. Max Hagfield had eagerly accepted the gymnasium, the weight machines, and any conditions attached to them. "Did Oliver work out much in New York?" Maggie asked. His large figure didn't appear to have been honed during long workout hours.

"Pretty regularly," Paul said. "But talk to me about the scholarship students who are here tonight. Are they all part of Dorothy's pet project to save the world?"

Oliver Whitcomb had donated the gym; his wife's inspiration had been to create a special dormitory for single mothers and their children. No doubt seeing a possibility for great publicity and improved community relations, Max had agreed. Dorothy had spent the past year purchasing a large Victorian house across the street from the main entrance to the college, having it brought up to dormitory code, and, of course, redecorating it. Whitcomb House was now home to six single parents, each with enough living space for themselves and one child. Max Hagfield had required only that the new dormitory be safe, handicapped accessible, and that the single parents it housed include at least one single father. Somerset College must not discriminate against any subset of students. Max's concern for students was exceeded only by his concern for the college's reputation. And his own.

Maggie nodded at Max, who had left his chair, refilled his Cognac snifter at the bar, and was now heading toward a group of students by the fireplace.

Max had long since given up the possibility of a berth at a more prestigious university. Instead, he'd tried to elevate the stature of presidency of the community college so he now saw little difference between himself and his counterpart at Princeton University, a was his county. Somerset College was his college. The money Oliver and Dorothy Whitcomb donated enhanced the institution; it therefore enhanced Max Hagfield. It was all one and the same.

The students he was now talking with towered over Max. He was shorter than Maggie, and clearly a man who spent more time with his Cognac and his tanks of tropical fish than he did in Oliver's new gym.

Max's home was lined with fish tanks, and the small pond in his backyard contained koi and goldfish. His problems with flukes, organic debris, and neighborhood cats were all too familiar to Maggie. There was a small pond in her own yard, and before her husband, Michael, died last year, he and Max would often temporarily escape parties such as this one to smoke and discuss the challenges of fish maintenance in home ponds. Michael's fish had become trophy catches for seven-year-old neighborhood anglers shortly before his death. Maggie hadn't bothered to replace them.

"All the Whitcomb House students are here," she said to Paul. "They're ambitious young people, and they're taking real advantage of this opportunity to attend college. I doubt any of them would be in school without Dorothy's help." One of Dorothy's requests was for one faculty member to be assigned to all six of the young families. To her delight, Maggie was given that job, so she knew them all well.

On the opposite side of the room, Kendall Park, Whitcomb House's token father, was draining a glass of beer and chatting earnestly with another student. If Somerset College had fielded a football team, Kendall, heavily muscled and well over six feet tall, could have played fullback. But Kendall filled most of his hours studying and caring for thirteen-month-old Josette. When Josette's mother left a note last spring saying California beckoned, she had also left their baby. Twenty-year-old Kendall became a surprised, but devoted, single dad. Defying all stereotypes about male and female parenting skills, Kendall was among the most concerned and nurturing of the Whitcomb House parents.

Maria Ramirez and Heather Farelli were standing by the antipasto table; Tiffany Douglass, her streaked blonde hair cascading over one shoulder and wearing a long patterned skirt and a red blouse cut a smidge—or perhaps two smidges—too low, was talking with a biology professor. Kayla Martin had on a short orange knit dress that showed off her legs, and was filling her glass with red wine. Sarah Anderson was still talking with Dorothy Whitcomb. Or at least Dorothy Whitcomb was still talking to Sarah.

"Dorothy sees herself as their savior," Paul said.

"And she may be. But she gets too proprietary with them. Like inviting them to all of these receptions, and even hiring a babysitter for Whitcomb House so they don't have an excuse not to come." Dorothy was supporting the students; they may have owed her, but she didn't own them. Sometimes Maggie wondered if Dorothy understood the difference.

"Dorothy wouldn't tolerate excuses, would she?" Paul said.

"Do you know her well?"

"Not as well as I know Oliver. But she's been very hospitable since I moved to New Jersey. I didn't know his first wife at all."

"First wife? When he moved here, and started donating to Somerset College, Dorothy was his wife."

"Oliver and Dorothy were newlyweds when I first

went to work for Oliver's firm. They've only been married six or seven years."

"I remember hearing that he has adult children."

"A boy and a girl, from his first marriage. They're in their late twenties and live on the West Coast. They grew up over in Bernardsville, where Oliver used to live. He sold their old house and bought this one for Dorothy. 'A new house for a new marriage' is how he put it."

Maggie and Paul both looked at Dorothy, whose gold turtleneck and form-fitting black silk slacks matched the drama of her short blonde-tinted red (or was it red-tinted blonde?) hair. She was still holding Sarah Anderson in conversation.

"How much younger is Dorothy than Oliver?" Maggie was curious, and Paul didn't seem to mind sharing what he knew about them.

"He retired at sixty; I think she's in her midforties."

"Really? I thought she might be older," said Maggie. "She doesn't look it, but she has a sort of attitude that says . . ."

"She's pretentious as hell, you mean," Paul said, grinning. "Absolutely. If she knew that attitude would make people assume she was older she'd drop it as fast as she'd drop a manicurist who smudged her nails. But I suspect no one's ever had the guts to tell her."

"And I'm certainly not going to be the one," said Maggie. "But I do think I'm going to rescue poor Sarah. Dorothy's been talking at her for long enough."

"If you're going to play Good Samaritan, I'll return to the herd. I know a couple of students over by the window. I'll go and act professorial."

"Sounds like a plan." Maggie glanced toward

Geoff Boyle and Linc James, two other professors, and headed for Sarah and Dorothy. She concentrated on not limping. The blister must be getting worse. And she really shouldn't stay much longer; she had to organize prints before her morning lecture, and she should pack her van. Not to mention the joy of replacing these blasted shoes with a pair of cozy fleece slippers.

"Have you ever taken Aura to a children's theater performance?" Dorothy's hair was blocking Maggie's view of Sarah's reaction. "Perhaps we could arrange for tickets for all of you some weekend."

"That's a lovely idea, Dorothy," Maggie interrupted. "As long as it isn't near exam time! Maybe after the holidays. Sarah, have you tried the roast beef? It's delicious. Dorothy, your caterer has done wonders with the horseradish sauce."

Sarah slipped away with an appreciative nod at Maggie.

"We do have a wonderful caterer, don't we?" agreed Dorothy. "And nothing too fancy. We wanted the young people to feel right at home. I'm so glad everyone from Whitcomb House could come, and some of the students Oliver has met at the gym, too." She gestured at a group near the French doors that opened onto the patio in warmer weather. "And, of course, some of the faculty. Students mixing with faculty *is* part of the college experience, don't you think?"

"I enjoy getting to know my students," Maggie said. "It helps me plan classes so the material I cover best meets their needs."

"That, too, of course," said Dorothy. She held a glass of sparkling water, and her pale pink nails—not a smudge in sight—were reflected in the crystal.

"Young minds meeting"—she glanced at Maggie—"more mature ones. Culture being passed from one generation to another. That's what this is all about, isn't it?"

Most students at the community college were living at home and working part time. Many supported families. A cocktail party at Somerset County Community College was not a humanities seminar at Yale. Maggie glanced around the room. Few students were conversing with professors; most were taking full advantage of the free food and open bar, and talking with each other.

"I think perhaps a beautician . . ." Dorothy was saying.

Maggie focused in on the red hair and the pink nails again. "Oh?" she said noncommittally. What had Dorothy said?

"A beautician, and then perhaps an interior decorator, would make marvelous guests for those Monday night seminars you organize for the house, don't you think?"

Maggie spent every Monday evening at Whitcomb House, bringing with her an expert in an area she hoped the students would find helpful—childhood nutrition; legal issues related to single parents; financial planning; time management. The sessions were usually full and lively, since they always included at least some of the six children whose existence qualified their parents for residence at the house.

But a beautician and an interior decorator? Just what six struggling young parents who were exhausted from childcare and studying would need. "Maybe later in the year," Maggie compromised. "The women might enjoy having makeovers. Especially if we found someone who could donate makeup for them."

Tiffany Douglass was the only one with any expertise in that area, Maggie realized. Tiff always looked ready for a photo session. Maria, Heather, Kayla, and Sarah had more . . . natural . . . styles. Unless you counted Maria's seven earrings and nose ring or the vine tattoo on Heather's right leg that climbed past all parts of her visible to the general public.

"Oh, I'm sure it could be arranged that the girls get some free makeup," Dorothy said.

Thank goodness she'd found something of value in Dorothy's suggestion, Maggie thought. She'd discouraged Dorothy's last two brainstorms—a catered Halloween party and sterling silver flatware—and Dorothy had been hurt.

"And don't you think Santa should visit for Christmas?"

Maggie sighed inwardly. The Whitcomb House students felt indebted enough to Dorothy for room and board and tuition; they didn't need reminding that they had little money for Christmas gifts. Especially when Dorothy visited at least once a week, leaving presents each time she came. It was nice for the kids, but hurtful for the parents who couldn't provide toys themselves. "I'll talk to everyone and see what their Christmas plans are. Some may want to stay at the house; others have family they'll visit."

"Poor Sarah. She has no one. Oliver and I were thinking of inviting her and Aura to spend the holidays with us." Dorothy and Maggie watched as Sarah poured herself a glass from a pitcher labeled "Bloody Mary mix." She didn't add vodka.

"I'll talk to her," said Maggie. "But don't make any plans until I do."

"Of course not." Dorothy squeezed Maggie's arm. "I'm sure you'll find a good way to introduce the idea to her. So she won't feel we're being patronizing."

A trace of insight? Maggie wondered, as Dorothy headed for the bar to refill her sparkling water.

So far as Maggie knew, Dorothy didn't have any children, and clearly the young Whitcomb House students and their families were filling that role for her. They are for me, too, Maggie admitted to herself. She enjoyed the kids at Whitcomb House, from the youngest, Kendall's Josette and Maria's eighteen-month-old Tony, to the oldest, Mikey Farelli, who at six would be too old next year for his mother to qualify for residence at the house.

Sarah's daughter, Aura, and Kayla's daughter, Katie, were favorites. Both four years old, they quickly became a team: masters of intrigue and disguise; experts at making costumes out of anything they found, from couch pillows to napkins. Last Monday Aura and Katie were princesses, dressed in their mothers' half-slips and balancing Beanie babies they liberated from Mikey Farelli's collection on their heads as if they were crowns. Aura's pale red-gold curls and Katie's black ones bounced as the girls giggled and pranced in front of Whitcomb House's most recent guest, a Montessori teacher there to give the young parents advice about early childhood education.

Wonderful kids. And their parents were learning parenting skills from each other as well as from the college. Only Tiffany's Tyler, who was two, seemed less cared for than the rest. There was always someone to clean him up and head him in the right direction, but that person wasn't always Tiffany. Tiffany had missed more of the Monday seminars than anyone else, too. Where did she spend her evenings? Based on her American Studies grades, not at the library. Maggie sighed. Tiffany had skipped her Myths in American Culture class again last Friday. Maybe Tiff was doing better in her other classes; she should find out, and then have a serious talk with her. Soon. Scholarship students had to keep up their grades.

As Maggie watched, Sarah joined Tiffany at one of the bookcases. Sarah looked unsteady. Maybe her earlier drinks had been stronger than Bloody Mary mix. Tiffany guided Sarah to a chair.

It wouldn't be good for the Whitcombs to see one of "their" girls drunk. Maggie crossed the room quickly.

"Sarah, are you all right?" Maggie bent down next to her.

"No. It's not June. Don't let Simon know." Sarah looked at her strangely. "But I smell roses." Her body listed toward the side of the chair. "I think I'm going to puke."

"Tiffany, take her arm." Together they helped Sarah stand.

"My head hurts, too. Bad."

Maggie quickly smelled Sarah's breath. No alcohol. But she did smell as though she'd been smoking. Funny; she'd never seen Sarah smoke. "Let's get her out of here." Maggie headed Sarah and Tiffany toward the door.

"Shouldn't we say good-bye to the Whitcombs?" Tiffany said. "I'll go tell them." She dropped Sarah's arm and headed for Oliver.

Maggie just managed to keep Sarah upright. She was becoming weaker, and a puddle of drool was dripping onto the front of her soft gray turtleneck. Please, don't let her throw up on the Aubusson carpet, Maggie thought, just before Sarah's legs gave way and she collapsed onto the floor. Within seconds her limp body was surrounded by curious and well-meaning guests. "Give her some space!" Maggie commanded firmly. She knelt and took Sarah's wrist. The pulse was too rapid to count. Dangerously rapid.

"What's the matter with Sarah? Is she drunk? What can we do?" Dorothy looked aghast. "She seemed fine . . ."

"Call 911," interrupted Maggie. "Now."